IRON SKY

BOOK

CALL OF THE PHOENIX

ALEX WOOLF

SCRIBO

A division of Book House

First published in Great Britain by Scribo MMXV
Scribo, a division of Book House, an imprint of
The Salariya Book Company
25 Marlborough Place, Brighton, BN1 1UB
www.salariya.com

ISBN 978-1-910184-87-5

The right of Alex Woolf to be identified as the author of this work has been asserted
in accordance with sections 77 and 78 of the Copyright, Designs
and Patents Act, 1988.

Book Design by David Salariya

© The Salariya Book Company
MMXV

Printed and bound in India

The text for this book is set in Cochin
The display type is GRK1 Ivy No. 2

www.scribobooks.com

Cover illustration: Matthew Laznicka
Map: Carolyn Franklin

Scan to see the Youtube video

IRON SKY

BOOK 2

CALL OF THE PHOENIX

ALEX WOOLF

SCRIBO
A division of Book House

Reader reviews of Iron Sky 1: *Dread Eagle*

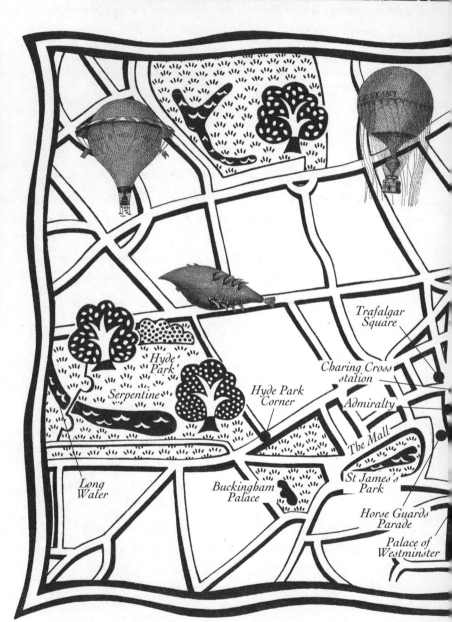

Trafalgar
Square

Charing Cross
station

Hyde
Park

Serpentine

Hyde Park
Corner

Admiralty

The Mall

St James's
Park

Long
Water

Buckingham
Palace

Horse Guards
Parade

Palace of
Westminster

LONDON

Tower of London

Thames St

River Thames

Strand
Bridge

Billingsgate Market

Tower
Bridge

From you, as from burning chips of resin,
Fiery fragments circle far and near:
Ablaze, you don't know if you are to be free,
Or if all that is yours will disappear.
Will only ashes and confusion remain,
Leading into the abyss? — or will there be
In the depths of the ash a star-like diamond,
The dawning of eternal victory!

Cyprian Norwid (1821–1883)

PART I

19 JULY 1845

CHAPTER ONE

THE
EQUESTRIANS

The sun sat like a smouldering pearl in the yellow haze above Paris. Grand edifices shimmered, ghostlike, in the morning mist, and thick white plumes blossomed from the smokestacks all across the city. It seemed to young Jacques, as he gazed upon this scene from the hill of Montmartre, like the start of any other day. There was the usual sulphurous reek from the gypsum mines, the cry of street hawkers and braying tunes from the organ grinder, the distant roar of steam carriages and the clip-clop of hoofbeats on cobblestones – it all felt so normal. Yet this was no ordinary day. Jacques could sense big changes coming – for himself, and for his country.

He checked the chronometer on his wrist. Time to get going or he'd be late for his meeting, and the boss was a stickler for punctuality. He began threading his way down the hill, past the pastry stands and cafés, their fresh-baked aromas briefly masking less pleasant smells. Portrait artists lined the kerb with their easels, and impromptu galleries hung on the railings behind them. One yelled to Jacques that he had a lovely profile. Jacques kept his head down, hands dug deep in his trouser pockets. On no account must he be noticed in this neighbourhood. The boss had been very firm on that point.

Still, he couldn't help glancing up from time to time, when he sensed a young woman passing close, or caught the scent of perfume. Hurriedly, he would scan her face, hoping against hope that she might be the sister he missed so badly. Of course, she never was.

Jacques turned a corner into one of the *petits boulevards* off the Rue des Saules, and entered a café. A few men sat at tables drinking coffee and playing chess. The murmur of their conversation was like the lazy drone of flies. A ceiling fan turned slowly overhead, squeaking on a badly oiled chain drive. Jacques spotted a bow-tied, jacketed waiter with a small moustache. The man approached.

'Please take a seat, monsieur. I will be with you shortly.'

'Do you have a stable for my iron horse?' said Jacques. He spoke the words slowly and carefully

– words he'd picked up on a secret aetherwave frequency the night before.

The waiter nodded and beckoned him to follow. He led him through an archway at the back of the café, along a gloomy corridor, to a door. The waiter gave three sharp knocks before pausing and knocking once more. The door opened. Jacques' boss stood there – the man he'd worked for since the age of twelve, the man he hated almost as much as he feared: Marshal François Guizot, head of Napoleon's secret police.

'You're late!' growled Marshal Guizot, grabbing Jacques by the lapel and pulling him into the room. Guizot was several inches shorter than Jacques, but powerfully built through the neck and shoulders. He had receding black hair that clung to his narrow skull like slimy pondweed. Warily, Jacques noted the iron-grey glare and the thin lips, pressed tightly together as if about to spit poison.

'I'm sorry,' muttered Jacques.

'When I say nine o'clock, I mean nine o'clock,' hissed Guizot. 'Next time, I'll chop off a finger for every minute you're late. Now, find somewhere to sit.'

There was a smell of old grease from the grimy ceiling lantern – the only illumination in the dingy, windowless room. Four other men were gathered there, seated on stools or on the floor, leaning back against the cracked brown walls. They were young, like Jacques – still in their teenage years. Though he could barely see their faces, Jacques knew them all.

The sight of them gathered here made him shudder, for it could mean only one thing: the next few days were going to be very dangerous indeed!

Jacques scrambled into a corner and tried to get his breathing under control.

'Do you know why you are here?' Guizot asked them all. He stood in the middle of the room, directly under the lamp, so everyone could see his face.

'If you've brought the Equestrians together again, it must be for another crazy, suicidal mission,' muttered Henri Bilot, the biggest of the young men.

Guizot turned on Henri and looked about to strike him for his impertinence. But then he calmed himself and even allowed a small smile to creep onto his lips. 'Crazy… suicidal… *bien sûr*! And is this not what your country expects of you? Is this not what your emperor expects? You have always known the situation. It is the life of an Equestrian.'

Jacques had been recruited to the top-secret Equestrians a couple of years earlier, and so far they had performed three missions, each of which had very nearly cost them their lives. The scar on Jacques' right cheek was his memento from their last operation: to destroy a fort on the south coast of Britain. The only time they ever saw each other was during these missions. For security reasons, Guizot had forbidden any other contact between the five young men.

'You have no prospect of growing old, Henri Bilot, it is true,' said Guizot. 'But then neither do the troopers in the *Volcans* and the *Tirailleurs*, who night after night fly bombing missions over British cities. Twenty missions is the average number they complete before they're killed. Some don't even make it to ten. And they enjoy none of the glamour of you Equestrians... Grumble one more time, young man, and you'll be joining the crew of the bombing fleet, *aviateur de deuxième classe*!'

Guizot stared at each of them in turn, catching them like rabbits in the steel traps of his eyes. 'What I am about to tell you', he said, 'is information of the utmost sensitivity, which, if it gets into the wrong hands, could threaten the very survival of our beloved Empire. I am sure I don't need to explain what that means. But in case you need a reminder, it means that if I hear that one of you has so much as whispered a word of what I'm about to say to *anyone* outside this room, then not only will I kill you, but I will kill the person you spoke to, and then I will kill your family. Slowly. And with as much pain as I can find ways to inflict. Is that clear?'

There was a pause, then a flurry of nods.

Satisfied, Guizot flicked open the top of his cane and pushed a button. With a grinding of gears, a white screen descended across one of the walls. The marshal reached up and adjusted a small disc near the base of the lantern, lowering the wick and casting the room into deep shadow.

An engine whirred and, from somewhere near the back of the room, a beam of much sharper light cut through the murk and illuminated the screen. Five daguerreotypes of faces appeared there – two at the top of the screen and three underneath. All five were women, all of them young.

Instinctively, Jacques scanned each of them in the hope of recognising his missing sister. He was disappointed.

There was a snicker from somewhere behind Jacques – Henri, he guessed. It was followed by the whistle of a stick passing swiftly through the air, and then a scream of pain.

Guizot had struck. Henri had been a fool to goad him a second time.

'Pretty these women may be, Henri Bilot,' said Guizot to the whimpering boy. 'They're also highly dangerous. In fact they're the most dangerous enemies we face at this moment. So look on them not with desire – but with hate! Take note of their faces. Take note of their names.'

Beneath each head-and-shoulders portrait, a name was printed. Jacques read them to himself: Major Emmeline Stuart, Diana Temple, Cassiopeia Ray, Beatrice Darlow, Lady Arabella West. The names meant nothing to him; neither did the faces. One of them, though – the West girl – intrigued him. There was something about her bright, direct gaze – strength combined with innocence...

'They're a team of British spies,' said Guizot. 'Code name: the Sky Sisters. They perform secret missions, much as you do. And they fly aerial steam carriages. Last month they came very close to discovering the secret of the Aetheric Shield...'

The Aetheric Shield – an invisible force field that could repel any attack! Guizot had told them about that before. It seemed an almost mythical thing to Jacques – like something given by a god to a hero in a Greek legend. Sometimes it was hard to believe it actually existed.

'I have no doubt', said Guizot, 'that they will be active again tonight, trying their best to foil the invasion, which, by the way, will begin at midnight – seventy-two hours earlier than planned. They will come to Granville, where our fleet is gathered, and will try to destroy the Aetheric Shield Generator, possibly even the great airship *Titan* herself. Your mission, boys, is to hunt them down and kill them before they get the chance.'

CHAPTER TWO

THE FLIGHT

omanche Prince, the small, red aerial steam carriage, slipped serenely through the night sky, making scarcely a sound save for the gentle burble of its boiler and the thrum of its propeller. Lady Arabella West, seated at the controls, peered out of the cockpit window at the bright wash of stars glittering through a wisp of cloud, and they appeared to her in that instant like sequins on a gauzy, silken dress. In other circumstances, all this might have been so very agreeable – just her and her *Prince* alone in this glorious, celestial world. But tonight she was on a mission, and fears of the dangers ahead were doing their best to spoil the moment.

Operation Enyo, it had been dubbed. Enyo – Greek goddess of war and destruction. How appropriate!

Arabella and her fellow Sky Sisters were heading for the French port of Granville like a flock of warrior-goddesses, preparing to rain war and destruction from above.

Well, not quite! If they tried to overfly the port they'd be spotted in minutes by the wandering search beams, then picked off at leisure by giant gun batteries. No, their attack would have to be subtler than that. They would make their final approach by sea, and pray that stealth and secrecy would work where brazen aggression had failed... For, just twenty-four hours earlier, a task force of British warcraft had been wiped out, and the bodies of hundreds of her compatriots now littered the sea off the Cherbourg Peninsula.

So it had come to this: the nation was counting on the Sky Sisters to succeed where the task force had failed. They had to destroy the Aetheric Shield Generator, or ASG – the device that would cloak the French flagship *Titan* in invisible armour, rendering it impervious to attack. Intelligence reports had confirmed that the invasion would be launched in three days' time, and the science boffins had worked out that this was the time needed to power up a *Titan*-sized aetheric shield. Therefore it was imperative that they destroy the ASG *tonight*, before the shield could be put in place. Operation Enyo was Britain's last hope. If the Sky Sisters failed, then nothing could prevent the defeat and conquest of their country.

To take her mind off the sick feeling in her stomach,

Arabella checked her controls for the umpteenth time. The dials, dimly visible in the yellow glow of her carbide lamp, were reassuring: she had an altitude of 2,000 feet, on a heading of 210 degrees; speed: 100 knots; slight easterly wind – no need to correct for drift…

Somewhere else in the sky, making their own independent journeys to the rendezvous point, were the other Sky Sisters: Emmeline, Diana, Cassie and Beatrice. It had been sensible to travel this way, rather than as a squadron – individual air carriages were always harder for enemy ANODE* systems to detect. Yet it did make one feel rather alone. For night flying was lonely – every honest aviator would admit that. The world disappeared from you in a way it never quite did on the ground – even in the bleakest, loneliest spot on Earth, you still felt connected somehow, held fast by the planet's maternal, gravitational embrace. Not so up here. It was just you on your own, surrounded by three dimensions of darkness. Arabella loved it – yet she also feared it.

Her aethercell crackled and a low female voice filled her headphones: 'Arabella, it's Emmeline.'

Arabella was surprised. They had been ordered to maintain aethercell silence throughout the flight, in case any French spies were listening in. Emmeline was the founder and leader of the Sky Sisters. She was also Arabella's aunt, though only three years older than her.

* *AetherNet Object Detection Echo.*

'Auntie!' blurted Arabella, momentarily forgetting protocol – she was supposed to address her as 'ma'am' or 'Major Stuart' when on duty.

'Switch to 109.2 megaholtz, so we can talk,' Emmeline instructed.

Arabella twisted the dial on her aethercell to the stated frequency, then waited through a cloud of static until her aunt's voice returned.

'Arabella, can you hear me?'

'Yes, ma'am. You're coming through a little faint, but perfectly audible.'

'We need to talk,' said Emmeline.

'Are we secure?' asked Arabella.

'Reasonably,' said Emmeline. 'For a few minutes, at least.'

'What did you wish to talk about?'

'Something I couldn't mention in front of the others…'

Arabella waited for her to go on.

'As you know, someone warned the French about Operation Zeus,' said Emmeline. Operation Zeus was the code name for last night's calamitous attack on the French fleet at Granville. 'We were expected,' continued Emmeline. 'That's why it all went so badly wrong. Yet the only people who knew about the attack, apart from the officers aboard the warcraft taking part, were the Prime Minister, the Minister of War, our boss Sir George Jarrett, and the Sky Sisters. Now, I hardly think the heads of government and the security services would betray our country. Nor do I believe the officers involved in the attack would have warned the French of their coming, as that would have been tantamount to suicide. So I'm afraid that only leaves you, me and the other Sisters.'

Arabella felt a deep and painful shudder inside, as if she'd just swallowed a sharp piece of ice. 'Do you think it was *me*?' she asked, her voice sounding thick in her ears.

'No, Arabella. No, I don't. I trust you. We're family, after all... I know you would never betray your country. But I can't say the same for the others: Cassie, Diana and Beatrice. I want to trust them, but I simply don't know them as well as I know you...' There came another wash of static, and Arabella thought for a moment that they'd lost contact. Then Emmeline's voice came through once more: 'I want you to monitor them for me, Arabella – while we're on the mission. I want you to keep an eye on them. Then, when this is over – assuming we survive – we can have another chat.'

Through her cockpit window, Arabella could see the lights of Cherbourg – they were approaching the northern coast of France. She banked west, determined to keep well out of sight of any spotters stationed there.

'We're getting close now,' said Emmeline. 'I'll see you on the landing strip. Remember: keep this strictly between us.'

'I understand, ma'am. See you shortly.'

Arabella guided *Comanche Prince* in a wide arc around the northwestern coast of the Cherbourg Peninsula, passing over the isles of Alderney and then Jersey. Emmeline's words echoed in her head, as she navigated southwards along the peninsula's western coastline. *I want you to monitor them for me, Arabella… I want you to keep an eye on them.*

Spy on the Sisters? It seemed absurd! They were almost like family – especially Cassie, whom she had grown very close to. The mission, which already filled her with foreboding, was now taking on even more sinister tones in her mind.

Soon she was flying over the Isles of Chausey, a group of tiny rocks and islets just eleven miles out from Granville. Chausey had been a French possession until the islands were quietly seized a few weeks ago by a small British force. The landing party had interned the thirty or so islanders, mainly fishing folk, then turned the islands into a base to spy on Granville – a development that the French had yet to wake up to.

Arabella made for Grande-Île. At almost a mile long and a third of a mile wide, it was the largest of the isles, yet still quite hard to spot amid the dark swell of the sea. At last she saw the landing strip, marked out for the Sisters with parallel rows of flaming gas jets. It was very short and somewhat hemmed in by trees to the south and a sandy beach to the north, so she opted for a steeper-than-normal approach. Coming in at fifty knots, touchdown was a little bumpy, but not too bad.

Hastily Arabella reversed the engine, bringing her craft to an almost immediate stop just a hundred or so feet from where she'd landed.

Pulling back her canopy, she took a moment to breathe in the salty sea air, then she climbed out onto the lower wing and jumped lightly to the turf. Arabella took off her flying goggles, removed her leather flying hat and shook out her long, chestnut hair. Glancing towards the beach, she spotted a young man in Royal Navy uniform running over the dunes towards her, holding down his beret against the breeze.

'Corporal Tim Powers at your service, ma'am,' saluted the young man breathlessly when he reached her. 'Welcome to Grande-Île. I'm your liaison officer and helmsman. Please let me know if there's anything I can do…'

'Well, you might start by helping me with this,' she said, opening the cargo hold in the side of the fuselage and indicating a brass-studded leather trunk that lay inside.

'Certainly, ma'am. May I ask what you've got in there?'

'Something most important, Corporal, so please be gentle with it.'

Together they hauled the trunk out of the hold and placed it on the ground. When Arabella opened it, the corporal stared, quite lost for words, at the object inside. It was a small metal man, about three feet in height, dressed, as if for an evening on the town, in a miniature frock coat, cravat, breeches and top hat. Arabella pulled the automaton out of its trunk and set it carefully on its feet. She pressed the ignition switch in its back and a gas-burning engine spluttered to life. The formerly lifeless eyes glowed yellow and a small cloud of steam puffed from a little pipe in the top of the metal man's hat.

'Hello, Miles,' Arabella greeted him warmly.

'Good evening, my lady,' responded the automaton, tilting his head upwards to address her. 'I trust we have landed safely in Chausey.'

'Indeed, we have. May I introduce Corporal Powers.'

Miles gave a little bow, causing his joints to squeak. 'A pleasure to meet you, Corporal.'

The corporal looked from Miles to Arabella in confusion. 'Is it… alive?'

Arabella frowned. 'You know, I've never really thought about that one. Are you alive, Miles?'

The yellow eye-lights dimmed and Miles emitted some muffled clanking sounds as he processed this question. 'I cannot answer that, my lady,' he said eventually, 'since I have no idea what "alive" is like. If I *am* alive, then is my "alive" different from yours? Who can say? And should we even be wasting time with such philosophical speculations? We are not French, after all! What matters is not whether I am "alive", but how I can help. And to that end, Corporal Powers may be assured to know that I come equipped with the very latest analytical engine for a brain, which means that, alive or otherwise, I can think more logically than any human.'

'He's the Logical Englishman,' said Arabella proudly.

From behind them came the drone, bump and screech of an air carriage landing.

Squinting past the gas-jet flares, Arabella spied a small yellow Motorbird taxiing towards them. It was Diana, in her *Amazon Queen*. They watched her climb out. Diana looked immaculate, as usual, in her tailored flying jacket, silk scarf and leather trousers. There was an effortless charm in her hooded eyes and half-smile – but also a certain arrogance. *Could she be the traitor?* Arabella wondered.

Corporal Powers, startled by Diana's dark beauty, didn't know where to put his eyes, so he trained them on her shiny black boots. 'Welcome to Grande-Île,' he blushed. 'Once you're all here, I'll brew us up some tea.'

'Oh, how jolly,' said Diana, removing her gloves with a dainty snap of the wrist. 'I could murder a cuppa.'

CHAPTER THREE

THE IRON HORSE

J acques should not have been surprised – he had known the invasion was coming. Yet to be told like this, in passing, so matter-of-factly, was still a hammer-blow. Napoleon was leading the world into disaster – more death, more suffering, on an incalculable scale.

'We cannot afford to delay any longer,' said Guizot. 'Not after the British attempt to attack our fleet at Granville last night.'

Jacques had seen the headlines on that morning's news-sheets. *Victoire à Granville!* they'd read – the whole of the front page filled with the story of a 'disgraceful and unprovoked' British surprise attack on the Channel port, and how it had been repelled by 'doughty' French defenders. This was the ultimate provocation, they'd thundered. France could not let this outrage go unpunished!

Jacques hadn't been fooled. He knew Napoleon Bonaparte had been assembling an invasion fleet and that was the reason for the 'unprovoked' British attack. For weeks the skies above the city had bulged with heavy, ironclad airships, their gondolas spiky with guns – all heading west towards Granville. Napoleon was throwing everything he had into one final strike against the old foe.

Napoleon's propaganda machine, with its endless stream of anti-British vitriol, had been running at fever pitch these past weeks, trying to re-energise a war-weary people for yet another military adventure. Once, the magic of the emperor's name might have been enough. In years gone by there would have been cheering crowds down the Champs-Élysées. The Tricolour would have hung from every window. But Jacques had seen none of that this time. People were tired of war. Napoleon had given them an empire, but none of the riches that should have flowed from that. For years they had suffered food shortages and wretched conditions in the hope that better times lay ahead. Jacques had suffered more than most – he'd lost both his parents, killed by this war. And now his sister had gone missing.

But what did Napoleon care about that, or about any of the hurt he'd caused? The empire was, in the end, his personal vanity project. It had always been about him and him alone. The people were there merely to serve in his armies and sing praises to his name.

Well, not any more.

Jacques wondered vaguely if there was anything he could do at this late stage to stop the invasion. Would killing Guizot help? Probably not.

The Sky Sisters will be there in Granville tonight, Guizot had said. *They will try to destroy the Aetheric Shield Generator, and possibly* Titan *herself.*

What if Jacques sabotaged the mission – let these Sky Sisters destroy Napoleon's dream? Now that was something he might be able to do…

'How do you know the Sky Sisters will be there?' asked Isaac Dreyfus, a tall, curly-haired boy, expert in lassoing and explosives.

'Trust me, they will be,' said Guizot. 'The British are well aware that the invasion is imminent. And after the failure of their operation last night, they will have no time to raise another big strike force. They'll be forced to use the best attack team they have at their disposal, which is these women. All this has been confirmed to us by our top agent in London – who just happens to be one of the Sky Sisters.'

This raised a few grunts of astonishment.

'You mean one of those girls there?' asked Isaac. 'One of the girls we're supposed to be killing?'

'Precisely,' said Guizot.

Jacques stared once more at the five faces, wondering which one might be the double agent. For some reason he found himself hoping it wasn't Lady Arabella.

'Which one is it?' asked Gérard Mesnier, a skilled marksman whose sharp face and long, supple body had always reminded Jacques of a weasel.

Guizot's finger hovered near the screen for a moment, as if about to point to one of the women. Then his hand dropped. 'I'm not going to tell you,' he said. 'It has no relevance to your mission, and such knowledge might sow doubt or hesitation in your minds. I want you to be clear: all these women must die.'

'Including the double agent?' frowned Isaac.

Guizot nodded, his smile as cold as the winter sea. 'She's fulfilled her purpose. We have no further need of her.'

In the basement of the café in Montmartre was a makeshift stable. But instead of smells of straw and manure, the prevailing odours were grease, metal polish and coal dust. Five mighty horses stood there in the gloom, still and silent as statues – every muscle beautifully defined in their gleaming iron bodies.

One by one, the Equestrians mounted their horses, laughing as they donned their tricorn hats, fitted their domino masks and kicked back their heels, striking the levers that brought their beasts to steaming life. With slow clanks and hisses, pistons began to pump and inner cogs began to turn, awakening the iron limbs to graceful movement. One by one, out of the shadows of the basement they trotted, up the ramp and into the quiet streets of Montmartre.

Jacques was the last to climb astride his horse, *Pégase*. He always felt a strange peace in the saddle. Looking down from this lofty position, the world seemed a lot more controllable, and a great deal less intimidating. He and *Pégase* had been partners since he was twelve, and he could ride her better than anyone had ever ridden an iron horse. He could gallop her faster than a steam train, coax her over ten-foot walls and turn her 180 degrees on one hoof. He knew her down to the last spring and sprocket, could strip her and rebuild her in a day. And he knew every quirk and peculiarity of her character. For even mechanical horses had characters – all the Equestrians would agree on that.

He was about to follow the others up the ramp when he was stayed by Guizot's voice, calling him to wait. Jacques' neck hairs prickled with alarm. Why had the marshal followed him down here? Had he somehow read his earlier treasonous thoughts? Jacques tried to keep his expression innocent as he turned *Pégase* about and trotted over to where Guizot was standing.

'I have received news of your sister,' said Guizot.

Jacques' mouth fell open in shock. 'You've found her?' he cried, completely forgetting in that moment who he was addressing.

'Not quite,' smiled Guizot. 'But my sources inform me that she is alive and well.'

Elation flooded Jacques. For the first time in his life, he actually felt warmth for his boss. 'Thank you, sir. Thank you so much!'

'As you must know,' said Guizot, 'she was travelling with your aunt aboard the aircruiser *La Fayette…*' When he saw Jacques' blank look, the marshal hesitated. 'But surely you knew that?'

Jacques looked down at the pommel of his saddle, suddenly ashamed. 'We had a fight, sir,' he confessed. 'She took off. I didn't know where she was going. I didn't realise she was on *La Fayette*.'

Marie had always been a bit crazy – ever since the sadistic Englishman, Allenson, had murdered their parents right in front of her. Jacques hadn't been there at the time – perhaps if he had been, he'd have been driven crazy, too. The incident had turned her rabidly anti-English, whereas Jacques was simply anti-war. That difference had led to some explosive arguments…

'Well,' said Guizot, 'as it turns out, *La Fayette* was captured by sky pirates. And yesterday, the pirates' floating city, Taranis, was seized by the British, who took all the surviving prisoners back with them. There was no mention of your aunt, I'm sorry to say. But I have it on good authority that your sister, Marie

Daguerre, was on the list of survivors and is now in British custody.'

Jacques' hopes sagged. 'So the British have her.'

'Not for long,' said Guizot brightly. 'If the invasion goes according to plan, your sister, along with every other French prisoner currently held in British jails, will soon be free to come home.'

'But the British will probably kill her before that happens,' muttered Jacques morosely. Then he looked up. 'Sir, I'd like to volunteer to be part of the mission to rescue the French prisoners.'

Guizot laughed through his thin yellow teeth. It was an unnerving sight. 'It's a possibility,' he said. 'If you do a good job in Granville tonight, we can talk about that. But if you fail to stop the Sky Sisters, who knows what disasters might ensue? It could scupper the invasion, and if that happens you will certainly never see your sister again.'

CHAPTER FOUR

THE
STRANGE
CRAFT

One by one the other Sky Sisters arrived – first Emmeline in *Duchess*, her purple Skyhawk; then Cassie in the green Steam Glider *Sultan of Mandara*; and finally Beatrice in a brown Turboswift – a replacement for her regular craft, currently undergoing repairs after a recent crash.

Corporal Powers led the Sisters over some dunes and down the beach towards a narrow wooden jetty. Miles trailed behind them with clanking, jerky strides. Moored to the jetty was one of the strangest craft Arabella had ever seen. In some ways it resembled a predatory crocodile, lurking in the shallows, waiting for its prey to stray too close. Although much of its long, tapering body was submerged beneath the water, a couple of raised portholes, like eyes, broke the surface, and in front of these a narrow snout sloped gently down beneath the waves. Instead of scales the craft was covered in riveted brass plates that gleamed ominously in the moonlight. Bone-like iron ridges along its spine added to the impression of a monstrous aquatic reptile.

'Come aboard, ladies,' coaxed Corporal Powers, opening up a circular hatchway positioned behind the 'eyes'. 'She's called *Kraken*. She won't bite.'

A short ladder took them down into the craft. Arabella helped Miles in, handing him down to Cassie. The interior had an industrial smell of oil and steam, reminding Arabella of the workshop where she took *Comanche Prince* for repairs and maintenance. The grey walls were lined with a complex arrangement of pipes, as well as pressure valves and dials and bright red wheels. Heavy, circular steel frames, spaced at regular intervals along *Kraken*'s length, gave structural support to the hull. Though generously proportioned at the centre, the craft became progressively narrower fore and aft. The entire bottom half of *Kraken*'s front end was taken up by a large, curving, mullioned window, roughly where the crocodile's mouth would be. Through this window Arabella glimpsed a patch of moonlit sandy seabed. Next to where they stood, in the relatively spacious middle section of the craft, was a sunken circular pit, lined with handsomely upholstered red-leather seating. This ring-shaped bench encircled a low, round table.

Corporal Powers got on with tea-making duties in the galley area towards the stern, as the Sisters gathered themselves around the table. Emmeline spread a detailed map of Granville across its surface and began taking them through the stages of the plan.

Arabella sat next to Cassie – big, blonde, and strong as a lioness. Arabella normally felt such strength and reassurance from her friend's presence. But not tonight – not when all she could think about was that Cassie might be a traitor. 'It'll be all right, Bella,' Cassie whispered. Arabella smiled back stiffly, hoping her reserve would be taken for nervousness.

Beatrice, always the most unobtrusive of the group, was seated on Arabella's other side, listening to Emmeline and saying nothing, while Diana was leaning back in her seat and engaging in murmured conversation with Corporal Powers behind her.

'Diana, do pay attention,' Emmeline said.

'We've already heard the plan twice, ma'am,' pouted Diana.

'Well, now you'll listen to it again!'

Petulantly, Diana returned her attention to the map.

Having handed the Sisters their steaming mugs of tea, Corporal Powers briefly disappeared up the ladder to cast off the mooring rope. Then he seated himself at the helm, before the big mullioned window, and fired up *Kraken*'s steam engines. There was a low, grinding, bubbling sound, a hissing of pistons, and the submersible eased away from the jetty and out into the open sea. Arabella found herself mesmerised by the curtains of shimmering moonlight that wafted through the dark blue waters as they nosed their way forward. Occasionally she'd spot the silver flicker of a fish. They sank deeper and the view began shading towards black, until Corporal Powers pressed a button on a teak panel above his head and an external gas-lamp came on, sending a beam of green, ethereal light into the depths.

Emmeline slid out a trunk from beneath the table and handed out black tops and trousers to the Sisters. 'Put these on,' she instructed, before turning to Corporal Powers: 'I expect you to keep your eyes front for the next few minutes, corporal.'

'Certainly, ma'am.'

As the Sisters got changed, Emmeline reminded them that they would need to move with speed and silence once they landed.

'I'm afraid you're going to have to stay here and keep Corporal Powers company,' Arabella said to Miles. 'You're simply too slow and clanky for a mission like this.'

Miles looked up at her, his eye-lamps dimming. She began to worry that she might have hurt his feelings, until she reminded herself that logical machines didn't have any feelings to hurt.

'Nonsense, we need Miles tonight,' said Emmeline. From the bottom of the trunk she pulled out a pair of heavy steel objects. Each one was about eight inches long by two inches wide and consisted of four small sprocket-wheels placed alongside each other. The wheels were enclosed by a chain of thin steel plates that fitted into the grooves in the sprockets.

'What are they?' asked Arabella.

'Caterpillar tracks,' replied Emmeline, 'to give your automaton speed and stealth.' She knelt down and began fitting them to Miles, securing them to the outside of his feet with the help of a spanner and a few bolts.

'There we are!' she said at last, leaning back on her heels. 'Now, why don't you try them out?'

They cleared some space for him, and Miles began to roll smoothly forward on his new treads. Suddenly he accelerated, and *whoosh!* – he flew towards the galley in the stern. *Bang!* – he collided with the gas stove and fell backwards. The collision sent a pan flying and boiling water cascaded onto his frock coat and trousers.

This made Diana laugh raucously. Arabella ran to him and gently lifted the steaming metal man to his feet.

'Less speed, more stealth, perhaps?' suggested Emmeline.

'Miles, are you all right?' Arabella asked.

'Perfectly, my lady,' he assured her after a few rapid puffs from his hat-funnel. 'Perhaps I was a little overzealous just now in my application of thrust to this new footwear of mine. I was not expecting quite so much torque in the drive wheels.'

'I don't want you to rust,' said Arabella, grabbing a tea towel and dabbing the hot damp patch on his coat.

'Please don't exert yourself on my account, my lady,' said Miles. 'This garment is made of extremely hard-wearing, water-resistant fabric.'

'Well, if you're sure…'

'Oh, look! An octopus!' came Cassie's voice from above their heads.

Arabella looked up. There was no sign of Cassie, but she did spot the entrance to an upper deck, accessible from the ladder, that had eluded her notice until now. After satisfying herself that Miles really was fine, Arabella ascended the ladder to join her friend.

The 'upper deck' was no more than a sleeping area, wide enough to contain six berths and not much else. Yet its two side walls boasted spectacular observation windows – the 'eyes' of the crocodile. Cassie was standing at one of these and Arabella joined her there. Together they stared at a huge, many-tentacled thing with a bulging sack for a head and deep black eyes, caught in the glare of one of *Kraken*'s gas lamps. The creature appeared intrigued by *Kraken* and was keeping pace with it by clambering along the sea bed. Its flesh undulated and rippled and its tentacles twirled like frolicking snakes, showing hundreds of pale suckers on the underside.

'I've seen paintings of them in books, but it's nothing like actually seeing one in motion,' whispered Cassie.

'I completely agree,' said an awestruck Arabella.

Suddenly, the window darkened as an enormous, five-foot-long fish moved in close to the glass.

The women took a step backwards in fright. The monster had a huge face, bulging eyes and thick lips.

'What is it?' cried Cassie.

'I have no idea,' said Arabella. 'But it looks a little like… like Napoleon Bonaparte, don't you think?'

They looked at each other, and smiles soon cracked the corners of their mouths. Within seconds they were laughing uproariously. They fell back onto one of the berths, helpless with mirth. Even in the midst of it, Arabella wasn't exactly sure why they were laughing so hard. Perhaps it was just their way of coping with the fear of what was to come. She looked into Cassie's creased-up face, the tears running down her cheeks, and suddenly felt an urgent need to be reassured that her friend was genuine.

'Cassie?' she said, once their laughter had finally petered out.

'Yes?'

'You do… love your country… don't you?'

Cassie's amused smile turned to a frown. 'Why of course I do, Bella. What an odd question.'

'I'm sorry,' said Arabella, blushing. 'Please forget I asked.'

Then all she wanted was to see Cassie smile again.

She beamed at her. 'It really did look like Boney, though, didn't it?'

Cassie nodded, but her expression didn't change.

Oh no, I've offended her, fretted Arabella.

Just then, Beatrice poked her head into the little cabin. 'You're wanted downstairs,' she said. 'We're approaching Granville.'

CHAPTER FIVE

THE RAID

Everything went dark outside as Corporal Powers doused the gas lights and *Kraken* rose to the surface. Emmeline handed out the aetherwave transmitters. These miniature devices, no bigger than a pearl, were to be pinned to the inside of their clothing. They would transmit a beeping sound every three minutes on a secret frequency, so that the locations of the Sisters could be monitored back in London.

Beatrice's role was to break them into the harbour, Diana's to lead them to the Aetheric Shield Generator, and Arabella's to lay the explosive charge that would destroy it. Miles was there to provide surveillance, and Emmeline and Cassie were responsible for security.

Emmeline handed out black canvas utility belts to everyone, containing useful tools and survival aids. She gave a carbide lamp to Diana and explosives to Arabella: fourteen sticks of dynamite with a five-minute fuse – enough time, hopefully, to get to a safe distance. 'If anything goes wrong, we'll have to improvise,' said Emmeline. 'All that really matters is that we destroy the ASG. We cannot leave here without doing that. Understood?'

They all did – perfectly! Emmeline was telling them in her polite way that their lives were expendable. If they were destroyed along with the ASG, then so be it.

Arabella no longer felt scared. She could feel the weight of the dynamite in her backpack and she knew what she had to do. Her mind was entirely focused on the mission.

There came a shuddering, scraping sound from below. '*Kraken* has tracks,' explained Corporal Powers, 'much like Miles's new shoes, but a lot bigger. It means she's amphibious. We're moving ashore now.' The window in front of him was showing frothy white surf and sandy beach. 'There are some rocks ahead that'll give us cover. I'll park up there and let you ladies out.'

When *Kraken* had come to a halt, the Sisters climbed out, one at a time, sliding down the gleaming wet surface of the craft to drop lightly on the sand. After Arabella had helped Miles out, she looked up at the craft they had just travelled in. Glittering wetly in the moonlight, *Kraken* looked like a huge, prehistoric predator with a brutal snout and a long, copper-coloured body.

They were in the shadow of a rocky headland. Ahead lay four hundred yards of grey, sandy beach, and beyond that – Granville. Search beams fanned the night above the harbour. They illuminated the billowing undersides of giant transport vessels – *Champlains* and *Cartiers* – lashed to iron-strutted mooring towers by long, trailing ropes. Beneath these, huge steamships lined the quayside, wreathed in clouds of black funnel smoke. Behind the docks rose warehouses, factories and town buildings: a confusing mix of soaring gothic edifices and grimy, tin-roofed sheds.

The Sisters spread out and began running along the beach, keeping low to the ground. Arabella thought she might have to curb her pace for the sake of her mechanical friend, but not so. On his powerful yet surprisingly quiet caterpillar tracks, Miles zoomed along, and she had to sprint just to keep up with him.

The moon was not their friend tonight. It shone bright enough to make shadows of their speeding figures on the soft, wrinkled surface of the sand. Luckily for them, no one was watching the beach. The entire focus of harbour security was on the sky – if an attack came, the French expected it from there.

When they drew close to the path that led to the harbour, they took cover behind one of the sailing boats that had been dragged up onto the beach.

Peering over the gunwale, they saw, at the far end of the path, a couple of armed men guarding the harbour entrance – a heavily padlocked gate topped with razor wire. Emmeline nodded at Cassie and the two of them moved out from behind the boat. They began to clamber along the rocks that were piled haphazardly to either side of the path – Emmeline to the left and Cassie to the right.

Arabella, crouching behind the boat, soon lost sight of them in the gloom. For a while nothing happened. Then, with startling suddenness, both women flew out from their high perches like a pair of bats. They dropped onto the guards, forcing them to the ground.

Taking this as her signal, Beatrice leapt to her feet and raced up the path. While the guards were still dazed, Cassie and Emmeline performed the sleeper hold, flinging an arm around their victims' necks and squeezing. The guards didn't make a sound, and within seconds they were unconscious. Beatrice removed a set of keys from one of the guards' belts and set to work opening the padlock.

Diana, Arabella and Miles then scooted up to join them. By the time they got there, the gate was open. They were in! So far, the plan was working perfectly. Now Diana took pole position, leading them through the deep purple shadows thrown by a row of giant warehouse buildings.

To their left, the dockside, lit by the yellow glow of gas mantles, was an ants' nest of activity, with workers pushing trolleys back and forth, fetching and carrying. Cargo was being carried from the ships and warehouses and loaded into huge iron cages at the base of the airship mooring towers. When these were full, concertina-like gates were rattled shut and, with a great clanking and steaming, the cages began crawling up the towers to be loaded aboard the gondolas of the waiting transporters. At this hour, such bustle could mean only one thing: the invasion was imminent. In the back of Arabella's mind, a vague anxiety formed: intelligence reports had said the invasion would take place in three days, so why were they loading up the air transports *now*?

But she and the others had more immediate concerns: in such a busy setting, they could be spotted at any second. Their only hope lay in speed and silence. Arabella imagined herself as a fleeting shadow – people might glimpse her, but by the time they turned to look, she'd be gone. They sped along a stony path, skidding around a corner and down a narrow alley between tall buildings, then round a bend and over a bridge above a dark canal overhung by factory outlet pipes dripping their sludge into foul-smelling waters. Arabella was soon lost in the maze of harbour streets, but Diana had memorised the plans. Her brain was like a map. Again the thought distracted Arabella: Could Diana be trusted? Where exactly was she leading them?

Above them, airships the size of clouds swayed – soft-bodied, yet deadly. Arabella recognised them as *Ballons* and *Finisterres* – surveillance craft. They projected their roving search beams onto the ground, and the Sisters and Miles were forced to dart beneath a colonnaded terrace to escape them.

Then came the sound they had all dreaded: *'Arrêtez!'* – 'Halt!'

CHAPTER SIX

THE FLAGSHIP

The barked order came from their rear, echoing around the stone passageway they were running along. Arabella was tempted to increase her pace and try to escape. But Diana and Emmeline, ahead of her, immediately stopped and turned. Diana flashed a charming smile as she approached the grizzled-cheeked, gun-toting guard who had stepped out of the building to their right.

'Who are you?' demanded the guard. 'What is your business here?'

Though a touch pink-cheeked, Diana scarcely seemed out of breath – or words. 'Monsieur,' she said in her perfect French, 'we are from the Bureau of Internal Security. Marshal Guizot sent us here to investigate a possible infiltration by British spies. We are currently engaged in chasing down an intruder. You must allow us to proceed, or he will get away.'

The guard wrinkled his nose suspiciously. He jabbed the air with his gun. 'I've not been notified of any of this. Show me your papers.'

'Monsieur, with all due respect, I could ask the same of you,' said Diana, her tone growing noticeably chillier. 'But we do not have time for such bureaucratic niceties. We need to get after our suspect. If you detain us any further, I shall be forced to report you to the Marshal. I dread to think what will become of your career once he learns that you obstructed a security operation that he personally authorised.'

There was the briefest flicker of hesitation in the guard's eyes – had she scared him? Then his hands took a firmer grip on his weapon and he came closer.

A voice sounded from within the building. *Tout va bien, Jean?'*

Arabella felt a bristling of tension at the back of her neck. If another guard arrived now, the situation could quickly spiral out of control. Cassie, she noticed, had slipped out of sight, into the shadows to the guard's left.

'I'm dealing with it,' the guard called out to his colleague as he came nose to nose with Diana. 'Mademoiselle, if there is an intruder, we should sound the alarm, no? My men could help you in your search.' His smile suggested that he smelled a rat.

'That is most kind of you, monsieur,' said Diana, maintaining her composure, 'but if you sound the alarm, the suspect will undoubtedly swallow a cyanide pill and jump into the harbour to evade capture. The information we need will die with him. At present, he doesn't know we're after him, and we want to keep it that way.'

The guard grimaced at this woman who seemed to have an answer for everything. 'Then show me your papers,' he said gruffly, 'and I will let you proceed with your operation.'

Diana sighed. 'Miles, show the gentleman our papers, would you?'

Miles rolled towards her, agitated puffs of steam spouting from his top hat. He had no papers – had no idea what was expected of him. Yet Diana's ploy worked, because the mere sight of the small, metal-faced man gave the guard such a jolt that he stepped backwards in surprise. The distraction was all Cassie needed. With two quick paces she leapt on the guard from behind, smothering his surprised yell with her left hand while squeezing down on his neck with her right arm. He slumped to the floor.

'*Jean?*' came his colleague's voice from within.

Diana turned and resumed her dash down the pillared arcade, the others following hard on her heels. Arabella knew that this unfortunate episode had put a severe dent in their chances of success tonight. The second guard would soon find his downed partner and sound a harbour-wide alarm. The surprise element of their operation would be over.

The far end of the colonnaded terrace opened onto a vast square, bristling with airship mooring towers like the back of a giant hedgehog. So dense was the fleet gathered at the tops of the towers that they completely blocked out the sky. The square was lit by thousands of gas mantles, which cast an eerie glow on the undersides of the copper gondolas and iron-carapaced gas envelopes clustered a hundred feet up. Arabella gasped at the sight of so many lethal warcraft all in one place. She spotted scores of fast, lightly armoured *Tirailleurs*, *Dessalines*, *Poignards* and *Tornades*; around thirty heavily armoured, big-gunned *Volcans*. And at the very centre, like the queen bee of this aerial swarm, was quite the biggest and most terrifying craft Arabella had ever laid eyes on. She'd heard talk of *Titan*, the flagship of the French fleet, but nothing could prepare her for the diabolical majesty of the real thing: a stately galleon of the air, its golden hull curved gracefully up towards the endless, pointed prow, like the swelling chest of a colossal and very arrogant swan. *Grace, arrogance – and death*, thought Arabella as she took in the brutal snouts of hundreds of cannon projecting from three tiers of gun ports. The entire vessel seemed to sparkle and shimmer in the glow of the gas mantles. It reminded Arabella of that moment just three days ago when Agent Z – Ben Forrester – had demonstrated the Aetheric Shield

on himself. He'd sparkled in just the same way...
Alarm shook her as she realised what this might mean:
was *Titan* already dressed in her shield, then? Were
they too late?

'Come on, Bella,' said Cassie, grabbing her by the
arm. 'We haven't got time to stand here gawping –
we've got a mission to complete.' She began pulling
her towards the others.

'The Aetheric Shield,' spluttered Arabella. '*Titan*'s
already cloaked in it!'

'Then we'd better hurry up and destroy the
generator, hadn't we?' said Cassie.

She'd misunderstood – she didn't realise that
destroying the ASG would achieve little if *Titan*
already had the shield. But Arabella didn't have
time to explain, for just then a bell began a loud and
desperate clanging that echoed right across the square
– the emergency alarm!

All around the harbour, workers, guards and
officers gazed fearfully at the skies. More guards
began pouring out of buildings. Some leapt onto gun
batteries, scanning the heavens for signs of enemy
attack. Others formed into patrol units, rifles primed.

Arabella, Cassie and Miles ran after the others.
Beatrice and Emmeline were on their knees, trying
to lift a heavy iron grating set within a paved area at
the edge of the square. While Diana stood watching
(manual work not being her thing), Cassie and Arabella
lent their strength to the task. Meanwhile, heavily

amplified orders were being trumpeted around the harbour. Workers were instructed to lay down their tools and trolleys and form up into their units for inspection. Steam cranes were halted in mid-hoist. Mooring-tower elevators whined to a stop. Within a few minutes of the bell's first tolling, the only sounds to be heard across the streets and quaysides of Granville Harbour were the tramp of guards' boots on gravel and the bellowed commands of officers. The harbour's entire security apparatus was now dedicated to the hunt for a group of unknown intruders.

By this time, however, the intruders they sought were underground.

CHAPTER SEVEN

THE BLAST

They waited, huddled in the darkness, as the clatter of guards marching in time reverberated through the layer of stone above them. Eventually, Diana managed to locate the valve on her carbide lamp and it flared into life. It revealed that they were in a tunnel with curving, brick-lined walls. The roof was just high enough to allow them to stand.

'Which way, Diana?' asked Emmeline.

'Ma'am,' interjected Arabella, 'before we go any further, I need to speak to you urgently.'

'What is it?'

'I think… I think *Titan* already has its shield.'

'That's impossible,' said Emmeline firmly. 'You must be mistaken.'

'It seemed to sparkle when I looked at it just now. It reminded me of how Ben... how Agent Z looked when he wore the shield.'

'A trick of the light, my dear,' Emmeline assured her. 'That gleaming golden hull illuminated by gas mantles – it must have deceived you. Now come along. We really can't delay any longer.'

Diana led them north, away from the docks. As they advanced, her light beam ate away the blackness, revealing ever more brick-walled tunnel.

Arabella decided to put her doubts aside and focus her mind on the mission. The intelligence reports had said the invasion would be in three days, and there was no reason to disbelieve them. It was also true that the eyes could sometimes be deceived. How many times had she, when flying in *Comanche Prince*, mistaken a cloud for a French airship? As she ran, she could hear Miles humming along beside her, and it gave her an odd reassurance. 'How do you rate our chances, Miles?' she asked him.

'Do you mean our chances of success – or our chances of survival, my lady? You heard what Mistress Emmeline said. They are two quite different things.'

'Both,' said Arabella. 'Either.'

'It's rather difficult to assign a number to such things,' he said. 'There are simply too many unknowns. I'm tempted to say "very poor", but that may be unduly optimistic.'

Diana suddenly stopped and doused her light.

'What's wrong?' asked Emmeline.

'People up ahead,' said Diana.

The others listened, and before long they heard the echo of marching boots, and saw the faint flicker of gas lamps.

'There must be at least ten,' said Emmeline.

'Too many for us to deal with,' said Cassie. 'We'll have to go back – try another route.'

'There *are* no other routes,' said Diana.

'Anyway, we can't turn back,' said Beatrice, who was bringing up the rear. 'Listen…'

Footsteps were approaching from behind them as well. Guards were closing in from both ends of the tunnel. Arabella felt close to despair. This, truly, was the end.

'Any suggestions, Sisters? Miles?' asked Emmeline, with admirable calm.

'I have one, Mistress Emmeline,' said Miles, 'though it has a vanishingly small prospect of success. I only mention it because –'

'It doesn't matter, Miles,' interrupted Emmeline. 'We're desperate. Tell us your plan.'

'First, if someone would be so kind as to remove one of my caterpillar tracks.'

'Of course.' Emmeline got to work, removing the track with a spanner she kept in her utility belt.

Up ahead, the guards were now close enough for their voices to be heard.

While Emmeline worked, Miles said to Arabella:

'My lady, if you would take one of your dynamite sticks, and –'

'Dynamite, Miles?' hissed Diana. 'In a tunnel? Do you want to kill us all?'

'He's right,' said Emmeline, suddenly grasping Miles's plan. 'It's our only chance.'

The caterpillar track was removed. With shaking hands, Arabella detached one of the sticks. Emmeline used her knife to cut off most of the attached fuse, leaving just a couple of inches – no more than ten seconds' worth. She taped it to the side of Miles's caterpillar track.

'You'll kill them,' said Cassie in a dry-throated whisper. 'It'll be horrible.'

Emmeline gave her a grim stare, then rammed her lead fire piston hard against the ground. She extracted the piston from its hollow cylinder and held its now red-hot tip to the fuse. As soon as it began to sparkle, Emmeline set the caterpillar track so that it faced the oncoming guards.

'Get back!' she roared at them in French. 'Run for your lives!' Then she flipped a switch. The track, with its fizzing cargo, raced off down the tunnel.

In tears, Arabella counted to ten. She could hear the fearful muttering of the men's voices up ahead. She and the Sisters dived onto their stomachs and pressed their hands to their ears. At the last second, Arabella remembered Miles and pulled him down next to her.

An instant later, there was a boom so loud it was like a pressure wave inside her skull. A blast of air ripped down the tunnel, almost lifting her from the floor and covering her in hot, blinding, stinging dust. It was even powerful enough to fell the guards closing in on them from the rear, knocking them over like skittles.

Arabella looked up a moment later to see a soot-smeared Emmeline yelling at her – though she couldn't hear a word she was saying. The air was thick with a sweet, sticky smell like burnt toffee. She felt too stunned to move, but Emmeline hauled her to her feet. Diana was coughing and holding her head. Emmeline took the carbide lamp from her and began leading them all down the tunnel. They jogged or staggered as best they could. Miles's trackless foot was having to run hard to keep up with the other one, like a child on a kick scooter. He looked wonky and unbalanced, and kept bumping into the wall.

In the swaying beam of the carbide lamp, Arabella glimpsed dust-caked bodies sprawled across the tunnel floor. She counted six but there may have been more. She felt terrible for the men who had died, and thought about the families who would soon be grieving. When she had joined the Sky Sisters, she'd never imagined it was going to be like this. They were supposed to be the good ones – saving Britain and helping to defeat Napoleon – yet this felt uncomfortably like murder.

Her benumbed ears gradually reawoke to sounds

– their own footsteps, distant shouts. They were still being chased – their pace mustn't slacken. They rounded a bend in the tunnel and she saw dim light up ahead, filtering in from the right.

They reached the source of the light: a ventilator grille somewhat less than two feet square, embedded in the brickwork. A mechanical humming sound emanated from whatever lay beyond.

'We're here!' gasped Diana.

Arabella peered into the blackness behind them. The footsteps of the pursuing guards were louder now. She thought she spotted a flash of a silvery light beam reflected on the curve of the wall. 'We have to be quick,' she muttered.

Cassie stuck her fingers through the iron mesh and pulled, stirring up a cloud of ancient tunnel dust that made her cough.

'Quiet!' croaked Diana. 'There may be people on the other side of that thing.'

Cassie couldn't do much about the low grinding sound the grille made as she pulled it free from the wall.

Arabella could hear running footsteps and Gallic curses coming from further up the tunnel. The guards must have seen their fallen comrades and would now be hungry for revenge.

Cassie was first through the hole in the wall, pushing and wriggling her way into the room that lay behind it. They heard her groan as she crash-landed onto what sounded like a metal floor. Diana went next, followed by Beatrice. Then Arabella lifted Miles and passed him through to Cassie.

'You next,' Emmeline told Arabella.

Behind them, the reflected glow of gas lamps was now playing sharply on the curve in the wall. The guards were just yards away from rounding the bend. Arabella threw herself at the gap, using her arms and legs to push herself through. She landed awkwardly and painfully on a hard floor a few feet below the vent. Emmeline came through a second later, landing almost on top of her.

'Did the guards see you?' asked Arabella.

'I don't think so,' replied Emmeline, 'but we have to block up that gap this second or they'll know we've come in here.'

The Sisters cast around the immediate vicinity for something to cloak the vent with, but the square, steel platform they were standing on was utterly bare. Then Arabella remembered her backpack. Quickly, she removed the dynamite sticks and stuffed the empty canvas pack into the gap, making sure that every part of it was covered.

They crouched there by the covered vent, listening in tense silence. The footsteps of the guards came closer and closer and, to their huge relief, went clattering on by without stopping, before fading into the distance.

'That was quick thinking, Arabella. Well done,' said Emmeline.

Arabella was pleased to have done something to

benefit the mission – she'd been feeling rather like a passenger of late. The others had moved to the edge of the platform, which was about ten feet square and surrounded by a railing. Cassie let out a gasp when she saw what lay beyond the railing. Her face drained of colour, her knees sagged, and Arabella was scared she might be about to be sick. Diana and Beatrice were looking equally nauseous, while Miles was emitting anxious jets of steam. 'Look away, ladies,' he advised. 'Look away right now, or the consequences for your health could be disastrous.'

Beatrice and Diana did so, but Cassie was too late. She retched violently. Arabella ran to join them, frightened yet terribly curious about what they'd seen.

CHAPTER EIGHT

THE AETHERSPHERE

rabella found herself looking down from a high vantage point onto a vast room. It had a dirty concrete floor covered in oily puddles, and smoke-begrimed yellow-brick walls draped in pipes and wires. Standing in the middle of the room, and completely dominating it, was an enormous object. It consisted of a platform, standing perhaps ten feet from the ground, surmounted by five pillars arranged in a circle, each one twenty feet high, and each covered from top to bottom in meticulously wound copper wire. From a pipe in the ceiling there streamed a glittering cascade of deep gold, which ran into the space between the towers.

Arabella noted all this in a vague sort of way, but – like the others before her – what really drew her attention, and made her stomach instantly start to heave, was the shape buzzing, humming, fluttering and flittering in the midst of the five towers – the shape through which the golden cascade ran. She'd witnessed such a shape three days earlier, when Ben Forrester had demonstrated the wonders of the Aethersphere on Taranis. She remembered the feeling of queasiness it had induced then, but this one was at least fifty times more intense – and so much more stomach-churning.

What was it exactly? She couldn't quite say. It was *something*... yet not quite anything – and that was the problem. It was every shape, every colour, every texture and every size you could imagine. It was a yellow, furry cube. It was a green, glossy globe. It was a glittering blue egg. And it was none of them. All at the same time! Being so many things and nothing all at once made it impossible for the eye to work out what it was seeing, and it completely frustrated one's natural desire to pin things down. As Mr Forrester had said at the time of his demonstration, *our human brains weren't built to process the Aethersphere.*

So she quickly closed her eyes – but not before dizziness nearly overwhelmed her. For a sickening moment, she lost her bearings – lost her sense of where floor and ceiling were. It was akin to going into a spiralling dive in an air carriage. Grabbing hold of the railing and squeezing tightly soon brought her sense of orientation back. She opened her eyes and was alarmed to find herself teetering on the very edge of a steep set of steps. If she hadn't grabbed hold of the railing, she'd certainly have fallen to her death.

'Are you all right?' Emmeline asked her.

'Fine,' gasped Arabella, rising to her feet. 'This is it! This is the Aetheric Shield Generator.'

'Are you sure?'

'Yes, though it utterly dwarfs the two I've seen previously... I–I'm sorry, I should have remembered about the Aethersphere – that awful... *thing* buzzing there between the pillars. I should have warned you...'

'It's all right,' replied Emmeline a little brusquely. 'None of us were too badly affected – luckily. Now, let's get down to the ground floor, so we can lay the charge and then make our escape.'

Emmeline picked up the dynamite so that Arabella could carry Miles, and the six of them started down the steep, narrow metal steps to the concrete floor some thirty feet below. As they descended, they noticed for the first time that they weren't alone in the room: a couple of technicians in helmets, goggles and overalls were standing before a large control panel full of dials and blinking lights near the base of the ASG. Luckily, because of the noise generated by the giant machine, the technicians hadn't noticed the intruders. They remained oblivious as Cassie and Emmeline stole up behind them and rendered them senseless with carefully placed blows to their necks.

Arabella quickly set to work, attaching sticks of dynamite to the legs of the platform. She taped three sticks to each of the four legs – easily sufficient to topple and destroy the contraption, she calculated. There was one stick remaining, which she was about to add to one of the legs for good measure when she noticed something. Stepping out from beneath the platform, she peered upwards, using her hand to block out the sight of the Aethersphere.

What she saw alarmed her – it also convinced her that their objective would not be achieved by destroying the ASG. Something more needed to be done. And if Emmeline didn't agree, then she'd have to do it by herself. When she was sure her aunt wasn't watching, Arabella quickly sneaked the remaining dynamite stick under her shirt, pinning it in place with the waistband of her trousers.

'Are you ready to light the fuses yet?' Emmeline asked her.

'Er, yes,' said Arabella, quickly pulling her shirt back into place. 'But have you noticed something odd about the ASG?'

'What do you mean?'

'Well, the humming sound we heard when we first came in here – it's become quieter.'

'I hadn't noticed,' said Emmeline.

'And the liquid gold pouring from that pipe in the ceiling has slowed from a stream to a trickle. The machine appears to be winding down, which can only mean one thing: it's achieved its purpose. *Titan*'s shield must already be in place.'

'You're leaping to conclusions again, Arabella,' said Emmeline sternly. 'Even if you're right about the ASG, there are any number of possible explanations. Perhaps the flow of liquid gold is subject to regular fluctuation, or perhaps it's because the ASG is no longer being monitored by those two technicians – I really have no idea. But what I do see is a young lady who seems determined to prove that our mission here is futile and that we should abort it. If I didn't know you better, Arabella, I'd start to suspect your loyalty!'

Arabella reddened. 'Ma'am, really, I –'

'Enough,' said Emmeline, handing her the fire piston. 'Please light the fuses.'

This was the last response Arabella had expected – she'd only been trying to do her duty, to speak her mind about a very real doubt she was starting to have about the mission, and now Emmeline was virtually accusing her of being a spy!

Feeling numb and bewildered, she moved over to the first fuse and prepared to ignite the fire piston.

'Wait!' said Cassie, gazing at the unconscious technicians. 'We can't just leave these two men to die in here. There's enough blood on our hands already.'

Emmeline looked infuriated by this second challenge to her authority in as many minutes. 'You seem to be forgetting the bigger picture, Cassiopeia,' she said. 'If we hadn't killed those guards in the tunnel, this mission would most certainly have failed.

The invasion would then have gone ahead and untold thousands – both French and British – would have perished. Sometimes you have to commit a small evil to prevent a bigger one.'

'You're right, and I'm sorry, ma'am,' said Cassie, bowing her head. 'But the deaths of these two will not prevent any evil, big or small…'

Emmeline considered this for a moment. Then she shrugged. 'Very well. We'll find a place where they'll be protected from the blast. We can put them in an adjoining room.'

After a quick search, Emmeline could find nothing resembling a door opening off the smoke-stained yellow walls. Finally, her eye lit on an alcove. It was about eight feet across, four deep and four high, and lined with the same dirty yellow bricks. She went over and inspected it, but could find no hint of a hatch or doorway leading off it.

'How strange,' she remarked. 'We appear to be in a completely sealed-off area. The only access is via the ventilator grille we came through, which clearly hadn't been removed in years. So how did those technicians get in and out of here?'

The others looked at her blankly.

'It's a mystery that doesn't concern us,' shrugged Emmeline. 'We know how to get out of here, and that's all that matters. There's no shelter for these men down here, so we shall have to carry them up the steps and deposit them in the tunnel. Arabella: time to light those fuses. Give us five minutes. That should be plenty of time to get clear.'

Arabella cut the fuses to the requisite length, then ignited the fire piston and put its glowing tip to the first one. Meanwhile, the others began mounting the steps to the platform. It was a slow process, burdened as they were with the two unconscious men. As soon as Arabella was sure that all four fuses were sparkling healthily, she began her own ascent of the metal steps. Once she had joined the others on the platform, Emmeline removed Arabella's backpack from the vent and handed it back to her. She was about to haul herself through the hole when she stopped and took a step backwards. She swallowed, and her skin seemed to take on a greenish tinge.

'What's the delay, ma'am?' asked Diana. 'You know, I really don't think we have time to…' Then Diana stopped as well, and she, too, backed up a step.

The muzzle of a rifle was protruding from the vent. It was trained directly at Emmeline's forehead.

CHAPTER NINE

THE ROOM WITH NO EXIT

A light flared from within the tunnel and three more rifle muzzles emerged next to the first. Arabella glimpsed pale cheeks pressed against the stocks of the rifles, and dark eyes glittering next to the gunsights.

'Step out of there, please, mesdemoiselles,' came a gruff, nasal voice from the tunnel.

No one on the platform moved.

'Step out now, or I will start shooting you one by one,' warned the voice. A rifle clicked as a finger began to squeeze more tightly on its trigger.

Emmeline took a short step forward. Unseen by the gunmen, Cassie was moving very slowly towards the wall. When she reached it, she pressed her back to it and began edging closer to the vent.

'Why would you want to shoot us?' asked Emmeline. She had spotted Cassie's manoeuvre and was now stalling to give her time to get into position.

'Because you are British spies and saboteurs, that's why,' said the voice, sounding irritated. The muzzle was thrust further forward, to within an inch of Emmeline's eye. 'You!' snarled the voice. 'You have five seconds to get yourself out of there, or receive a bullet in your brain. Five... four...' Emmeline didn't move. 'Three... two...'

Cassie reached the vent and raised her arm.

'One...'

She shoved her hand hard across the vent so that all four rifle muzzles were forced into the upper corner. The rifle that had been pointing at Emmeline fired with a loud crack, and a trickle of plaster fell from the ceiling above their heads. Cassie wasn't finished, though. Next, she grabbed the four muzzles with both hands and yanked them towards her with all her strength. There were yelps of pain as four skulls collided with the tunnel wall above the vent.

Emmeline pushed the dazed guards back into the tunnel, clearing space to lever herself through the gap. Then she fell back, shock lining her face. Without saying a word, she grabbed the backpack from Arabella and shoved it back into the gap. 'There are more coming,' she murmured. 'Lots more. From both directions. Our duty... our duty, Sisters, is to remain here and prevent them from getting in and deactivating the explosives.

Above all, we *have* to make sure the ASG is destroyed.'

'You're saying we must die in here,' murmured Beatrice.

'No!' cried Diana. 'There must be another way. I refuse to stay here and sacrifice myself like a meek little lamb.'

'How much time do we have left, Arabella?' Emmeline asked.

Blinking tears from her eyes, Arabella checked her chronometer. 'Two and a half minutes, ma'am.'

Diana began running down the steps. 'There has to be another way out of here!' she cried.

Emmeline bit her lip. 'She's right,' she said. 'We should spend whatever time we have left searching for an exit. Perhaps there's a concealed door somewhere in the wall.'

A further minute was eaten up in returning to the ground floor with the men. Diana spent the time running around the room, pushing at random pieces of wall, vainly hoping that one of them would turn out to be a door.

'Miles,' said Emmeline, 'put that extraordinary brain of yours to good use. Where would they hide a door in a place like this? Cassie, see if you can revive one of the men and force him to tell us how to get out of here. Arabella and Beatrice, let's start searching.'

Arabella started towards the wall behind the ASG, but her eye kept slipping back towards those ever-shortening fuses. She saw Diana crouching by one of them, using her knife to try and cut through it. Emmeline saw her, too.

'Put that knife down, Diana!' shouted Emmeline. 'This is no time for cowardice.'

Diana turned to her, red-eyed. 'I just – I just wanted to buy us another minute or two,' she snivelled.

'We cannot afford to delay the explosion,' said Emmeline. 'Any time now those guards up there in the tunnel will find their way in here.'

'You *want* to die, don't you, Emmeline!' Diana suddenly screamed. 'You *want* to be a martyr for Britain. That's what this is all about, isn't it? You want to turn us all into martyrs! Well, *I* don't want to be a martyr! I want to live!'

She began sawing at the fuse, her eyes frightening in their intensity.

Emmeline marched over and punched her in the jaw. The knife flew from her hand as Diana went sprawling to the ground.

Arabella turned away and forced herself to get on with the search.

Then Cassie spoke: 'Ma'am, one of the men is trying to say something. It sounds like *ascenseur*.'

'Elevator,' Emmeline translated. She looked up at the ceiling. 'There must be an elevator out of here. It would make sense, as we're underground. Miles, any thoughts?'

'I'm afraid not, mistress,' Miles steamed unhappily.

'How much time do we have, Arabella?'

'A little over thirty seconds, ma'am.' Arabella was trying to prepare herself for death. *At least it would be quick,* she thought. *Horrible, but quick.* She wondered if she should place herself closer to the dynamite to be absolutely sure she would die immediately. The worst outcome would be a lingering death.

As she moved back towards the ASG, she noticed a thick black pipe, perhaps six inches in diameter, snaking out from beneath the platform, trailing along the floor and up the wall before disappearing into the ceiling – no doubt transporting aetheric energy up to *Titan*. The pipe passed right by that strange little alcove. What could be the purpose of an alcove like that? It had to have a function. Moving closer to it, she saw a hairline crack in the concrete where the floor of the alcove met the main part of the floor. Then the word *ascenseur* popped into her head, and it all fell into place.

She stepped into the alcove and began running her hands over the bricks. It took her just a few seconds to find what she was looking for – a small, scuffed brass button on dirty yellow brick, so easy to miss. She pushed it, and a whine of hydraulics began. The floor of the alcove began to rise.

'Quick!' she shouted to the others.

Cassie, Beatrice and Emmeline looked up, and their anguished faces instantly lit up. The three of them began dragging the dazed men and Diana towards the elevator. As Arabella waited for them, she was acutely aware of the crackling flames coming ever closer to contact with the dynamite. Virtually nothing remained of the fuses – there could be no more than seconds left before they detonated.

'Hurry!' she urged them.

Miles was struggling to lift his legs over the rising lip of concrete, so Arabella reached down and helped him up. As the others clambered aboard, it became a desperate squeeze and Arabella found herself squashed into a tiny perch right in the corner.

The last thing she saw before the elevator disappeared into its shaft was the guards breaking through the vent above the platform. Then the Sisters were inside the shaft and everything went dark. A second later, there came a ferocious boom from below and they were rocked by a wave of heat that burned Arabella's knees and toes where her crouched figure made contact with the floor. She heard the bricks around them crack. There was a dreadful grinding and the elevator slowed to a halt as it caught against the shaft wall, which must have buckled in the explosion.

The heat quickly grew unbearable. The air in the confined chamber felt like fire on Arabella's skin and in her lungs. There were moans and screams in the suffocating blackness, and for those hellish moments it seemed that the elevator would become their tomb – or maybe their oven. She felt a sweat-drenched hand squeeze her arm. 'Cassie!' she tried to yell, but the name felt like ashes in her throat.

Then, with a rasping snap, the blockage came free and the ascent continued. Soon, cooler air began wafting down from somewhere above them, dispelling the heat, and they could breathe again. Cassie's hand was still there on her arm. 'Thank you, Bella,' she said weakly. 'You saved us.'

'That was quick thinking, Arabella,' assented Emmeline.

Pale light began to seep down from above. They were nearing the surface.

'We're not out of the woods yet, of course,' said Emmeline. 'But regardless of what happens now, at least we can take comfort in the knowledge that we have done our duty. The Aetheric Shield Generator is no more...'

CHAPTER TEN

THE FIVE STATUES

A moment later, they emerged into the open air – which turned out to be the main square at the centre of the harbour. The concrete floor of the elevator aligned perfectly with its surroundings, so that it appeared like just another slab of paving. High above them, the golden swell of an immense airship gondola could be glimpsed through an intricate lattice of iron girders that climbed upwards like interlacing branches of a tall metal tree. Arabella recognised the gondola as belonging to *Titan*, which meant they were inside the base of the French flagship's mooring tower. An impressive construction in its own right, the tower rested on four sturdy, sloping legs, each one taller and wider than the pillars of the ASG.

Luckily, despite their prominent location, they hadn't yet been spotted. Guards were positioned at various points along the perimeter of the square, but none were close by.

'Are you OK to move, Diana?' Emmeline asked.

Diana looked very groggy. She touched her jaw tenderly and glared at Emmeline, resentment clear in her face, but refrained from responding with anything more than a nod.

'It'll be hard to get off this square without being seen,' said Cassie. 'The guards seem to have the perimeter covered.'

'What about over there?' said Beatrice, pointing towards an unguarded side road some twenty yards to the north of the mooring tower.

'Good spot, Beatrice,' said Emmeline. 'From there, we can circle back through the smaller alleys to the beach. Once the news hits that the ASG has been destroyed, all hell will break loose, and hopefully we can escape in the confusion.'

They rose to their feet, Diana refusing Emmeline's offer of assistance.

'What about these two?' asked Cassie, indicating the technicians, who were now rubbing their necks and looking around in confusion.

'We can leave them here,' said Emmeline. 'Come on.'

As they moved cautiously out from the shadow of the mooring tower, Arabella spotted a thick black pipe rising vertically from the paving stones and soaring upwards through the tower's centre. It had to be a continuation of the same pipe she'd seen in the ASG chamber, the one that fed aetheric energy to *Titan*'s shield. She looked up once more at the great golden gondola hanging above them like some impossibly enormous Christmas-tree bauble. It was definitely sparkling – Arabella was sure it wasn't an optical illusion. But she wasn't about to point this out to Emmeline, not wishing to inflame her aunt's suspicions about her any further. Arabella had done her duty in trying to warn her, and if Emmeline refused to take heed, it was down to Arabella to take matters into her own hands. The dynamite stick she'd hidden beneath her shirt would help her carry out her plan. But first she would have to find some way of detaching herself from the others.

After a heart-pounding dash across the square, they managed to reach the sanctuary of the side road. Unlike the square, the road was unlit, and tall buildings on both sides kept it in deep shadow. As they advanced along it, Arabella was surprised to discern what appeared to be a row of tall statues – five of them – spanning the width of the street. Emmeline raised her hand to signal the others to stop. The statues were of men on horseback, but they weren't on plinths. They had been placed directly on the road surface, cast-iron hooves on the cobbles.

Intrigued, Arabella was about to go up to the

nearest one when Miles stopped her with a whispered warning: 'My lady… I wouldn't.'

That was when she saw a curl of steam rising from the nostrils of one of the horses, and her heart jumped. It was alive – yet clearly made of metal… *Could it be… an automaton?*

She barely had time to complete the thought, because now the horsemen began to stir. The men themselves were not metal, Arabella now saw, but flesh and blood. Moving as one, they raised their guns and took aim at the Sky Sisters.

Cassie, defensive reflexes taking over, leapt to one side as a shot rang out and a pistol-flash lit the street. A bullet, meant for her, sparked harmlessly against the cobbles. She vaulted towards the shooter and tried to drag him from his iron horse. At the same time, Emmeline charged at the rider nearest her. Plucking a bottle of chilli powder from her utility belt, she threw its contents in his face. He let out a yelp of pain and clutched his eyes.

'Run!' Emmeline yelled at the others, as the street suddenly exploded with gunfire.

This is my chance! thought Arabella as she dashed back down the street with Miles kick-scooting along beside her. *If I can just get away from here…*

She wove from side to side, dodging the bullets that cracked and pinged around her, then she spun down a side alley. She ran for fifty yards until she reached a junction with a street of rundown cottages – dockers' dwellings, she guessed. A grassy track ran between two of the cottages, which led eventually to a disused railway line. A rusty old goods wagon, defaced with painted slogans, sat on the track.

'We can hide under here,' Arabella suggested to Miles.

It may only have been the way he was leaning due to his mismatched footwear, but somehow she read doubt in his posture.

'It will only be for a short while,' she promised him, 'until we're sure the coast is clear.'

'As you please, my lady,' said Miles.

She helped him over the metal tracks and beneath the dirt-encrusted, oily underside of the railway wagon. Then she seated herself on a timber sleeper and leaned back against a wheel, waiting for her heart to return to its normal rhythm. The night breeze ruffled the weeds growing between the tracks, and cooled her brow. They would wait here for a while, she decided, then make their way back to the square – and *Titan*...

Miles's small stature allowed him to remain upright beneath the wagon. He stood beside her, very slightly less than vertical, his face as smooth and expressionless as ever. He was not a creature of moods – she knew that. He was a logical machine, nothing more. Yet tonight, Arabella thought she'd seen all sorts of non-logical qualities in him: stoicism, self-sacrifice, bravery, and perhaps even a touch of sadness.

'You were very gallant tonight, Miles,' she remarked.

'My lady?'

'Sacrificing your caterpillar track like that. You saved the mission.'

'I am here to serve, my lady... And if I may say so, your contributions, especially the discovery of that elevator, were of equal, if not greater, consequence.'

'Thank you,' she said. 'But tell me, Miles, how did you *feel* tonight? Did you feel scared at all? Do you feel satisfied with the success of the mission? Or is it wrong to speak of feelings when it comes to a logical gentleman such as yourself?'

Miles chugged and whirred as he considered these questions. At length, he replied. 'I am logical, it is true,' he said. 'More to the point, I am English. And it isn't the habit of an Englishman to speak of his feelings – not in this century, at least.'

Arabella smiled at this reply. More minutes passed in silence, and she was about to announce her plan to Miles when she heard a noise: running footsteps on gravel. Someone was coming!

She pulled Miles further behind the wheel so they were both out of sight. Peering through the rusty iron spokes, she was dismayed to observe that it was Emmeline, Cassie and Beatrice – and it didn't take Beatrice's sharp eyes long to spot them.

'There you are, Arabella!' said Emmeline when they reached the wagon. 'We've been looking everywhere for you! You can come out of your hiding place – we're safe for now.'

'Oh, Bella,' said Cassie, hugging her. 'I was so worried you'd been killed.'

'I was worried about you, too,' said Arabella, trying to hide her disappointment at being found. 'It's great that we all managed to escape from those horsemen unharmed. Except… where's Diana?'

'We were hoping *you*'d be able to tell *us*,' said Emmeline.

'Do you think she may have been shot?' asked Arabella.

Emmeline shook her head. 'She may not even have been with us when the horsemen attacked.'

'What do you mean?'

'None of us can remember seeing her since we left the mooring tower,' said Cassie.

Arabella stared at them. 'Are you saying she ran off on her own somewhere?'

'It's possible,' said Emmeline grimly – and Arabella could guess what she was thinking: Diana, still furious with Emmeline, had decided to go her own way. Or, worse, she was the spy and had left them in order to link up with her French paymasters.

'We shouldn't jump to conclusions,' said Cassie. 'Perhaps one of those technicians grabbed her.'

'Perhaps…' said Arabella, though she didn't think either of them had looked a match for Diana in a fight.

A thumping sound to their rear interrupted their conversation. It seemed to come from inside the wagon, or from the mess of vegetation growing behind the railway track. A wild animal was Arabella's first thought.

'We'd better get out of here,' whispered Emmeline. 'Hopefully Diana will have made her own way back to *Kraken* and we'll meet up with her there.'

Emmeline, Beatrice and Cassie began making their way south along the side of the railway track. Miles was about to follow, but Arabella put a hand on his shoulder.

'Wait!' she hissed. She led him around the rear of the wagon, over the tracks and into some bushes growing on the far side, which were tall and thick enough to conceal them.

'What is it, my lady?'

'We're not going back to *Kraken*.'

Miles said nothing, merely gazed at her in that expressionless way of his. A brief flicker of his eye-lights was the only clue that a powerful brain was at work behind his doll-like stare. 'I presume this is because you mean to destroy *Titan* with the stick of dynamite concealed beneath your shirt,' he said.

Arabella recoiled, touching the stick defensively. 'How did you know?'

'Bella?' It was Cassie's voice. She had returned to look for them. 'Bella? Miles? Are you there?'

Arabella stared at Miles and pressed a finger to her lips. They waited in silence until Cassie eventually moved away.

'I counted thirteen sticks used,' said Miles, 'so I

knew one was unaccounted for. That is the obvious place for you to have hidden it.'

'But how did you know about my plan?'

'Because you believe that our destruction of the ASG came too late and that *Titan* is already shielded.'

'And do you think I'm right about that?'

'Based on the evidence, I would say there is an eighty-seven per cent chance that you are correct.'

Arabella pursed her lips in annoyance. 'If that's the case, Miles, why didn't you back me up earlier?'

'I am sorry, my lady, but it is not part of my programming to arbitrate on disputes between humans. I am here to advise, and if you or Mistress Emmeline had asked my opinion I would have given it – though I cannot guarantee that she would have listened even then. For some reason, I seem to have acquired a reputation for excessive pessimism...'

'Well, that may be so, but some support might have helped, Miles! – especially while I was being accused of disloyalty. Don't be so shy next time, hm?'

A sharp rattling sound from just behind them made Arabella flinch. It sounded like a sliding door being opened. She turned, but could see no door on this side of the wagon. Cautiously, she recrossed the tracks, Miles trailing behind her. She remembered seeing a sliding door on the other side, which she was sure had been shut.

The door now stood partly open.

CHAPTER ELEVEN

THE SURVIVOR

'Miles,' shuddered Arabella, 'can you see anything… in there?'

The automaton's eyes brightened to become a pair of miniature gas torches, projecting their yellow light into the murky depths of the wagon.

'No, my lady.'

A low growl emerged from the interior. Arabella took a quick step back. 'Is it an animal, do you suppose?'

'My knowledge of zoology is admittedly not extensive, my lady, but I am unaware of any animal that can open a sliding door.'

'Then what is it?'

Miles emitted an anxious puff of steam. 'In the

interests of completing our mission here, may I suggest that we don't stay to find out.'

'Lady Arabella West.'

Arabella gave a start. The dry, masculine voice had whispered to her from the wagon's interior. It was shocking to hear her name spoken in such a familiar way, in such a place. The accent had been English, and distinctly upper class.

Had she heard it? Did she dream it?

'My, how you've grown, little girl…'

'Who's there?' she called, trembling. 'Identify yourself.'

Miles's eye-torches picked up a movement in their beams. 'Move away, my lady,' he said urgently. 'Move away now!'

As he said this, a pale, dirty hand shot out of the darkness and grabbed Arabella's shirt, pulling her hard against the side of the wagon. Pain flared in her cheek.

'I'd be grateful for some water,' said the throaty whisper, just inches from her hair.

Arabella's right arm was pinned against the carriage, so she used her left to fumble with the strap on her utility belt and extract her water bottle. She handed it through the open door. It was instantly grabbed from her. A few seconds later, she heard glugging sounds.

'Let me go!' she demanded.

The glugging stopped and she heard more shifting. Then her captor's face loomed out of the wagon interior – the bruised, heavy, rather handsome face of a man in his late forties. Without relinquishing his hold on Arabella, the man levered himself out of the wagon, landing awkwardly on the stones by the railway track. He grimaced as he hit the ground, and Arabella saw that he had a severe wound. There was a dark red bloodstain across his right shoulder and chest. He wore the uniform of a senior officer of the Royal Air Fleet: red jacket and black trousers. The jacket, though grubby, was resplendent with brass buttons, gold epaulettes and medals over a white, very bloodstained waistcoat.

She tried to push him away, but he clung on to her shirt with brutal, animal strength, pushing her back against the wagon and knocking the breath from her lungs. He had a big, well-fed body – and was surprisingly agile, despite his injury.

'Feisty as ever, I see, Lady Arabella,' he smirked. His chuckle became a prolonged cough.

'How do you know me?' she asked.

'I knew your father,' the man said, wiping blood from his lip. 'We were good friends once, Alfie and I. I was a regular visitor at your house. You were six or seven last time I set eyes on you, and a handful even then.'

'What's your name?'

He smiled, showing blood on his teeth. 'Captain Henry Allenson.'

Arabella stiffened inside when she heard this, but she tried desperately to keep her expression neutral and not show any fear. She'd been hearing a lot of that name recently. Allenson was the sadistic British officer who had tortured the pirate leaders, Sky Magister Odin and Commodus Bane – and turned them into brutes. He'd also killed the parents of the French girl she'd met on Taranis, Marie Daguerre – killed them right in front of her eyes, twisting the girl's mind forever against the British. Arabella could scarcely believe such a monster was human, considering all the hatred and destruction he'd wrought. Yet here he was in front of her, and she was in his grip.

'You're a Sky Sister now, I understand,' said Allenson in his deep, well-spoken voice. 'I suppose you must be here to try and clean up the mess after last night's debacle.'

Arabella didn't reply. Allenson didn't seem to mind. 'I was in command of the *Nelson*,' he went on. 'Picked up this wound in the firefight near Cherbourg. We limped on down the peninsula, leaking gas all the way, then finally ditched the wreck in the Bay of Mont-Saint-Michel. I managed to swim, then crawl my way to this wagon. Not too sure what happened to the others. Perhaps they drowned. Perhaps they were picked off by French snipers. But *I* don't go down so easily. I'm a survivor. Your father knew that. We got into a few scrapes, Alfie and I. Captured once by the French, during a mission in 'thirty-four. Damn near cost us our lives – and our minds. But we survived.'

He coughed again for a long time, until flecks of blood flew out of his mouth. He wiped it away with his sleeve. 'Now what I need is medical treatment,' he rasped, 'and you're going to get it for me, my girl. Call it a favour for an old family friend.'

'I'll get you help,' said Arabella immediately, sensing the opportunity for escape. She tried to pull herself out of his grasp.

'Not so fast, my dear,' said Allenson, tightening his grip on her and making her wince with pain. 'I'd like to trust you, but… in the end, you're a West, aren't you? Your father didn't show me much loyalty. Avoided me like a bad smell after that incident in 'thirty-four. Even though he broke long before I did.'

'My father would never break,' said Arabella coldly. She'd tried to avoid getting into a conversation with the man, but couldn't let this slander go unchallenged.

'Oh, he squealed like a baby,' Allenson chuckled. 'Told Guizot's thugs everything they wanted to know, and more. Gave away secret after secret. I may have betrayed my country, but I was small-time compared to the great Lord Alfred West.'

Arabella wanted to hit him – anything to stop him spouting such filthy lies. 'Shut up!' she screamed. 'Just shut up! My father was noble and brave. He loved his country. He was not a traitor!' Shaking, she tried once more to pull herself free. But from out of nowhere she felt a sharp smack against the side of her face that made her ears whistle and her skin go hot and raw. Allenson's hand remained poised above her for another strike.

'If you prefer to believe those fantasies about your father, that's up to you,' said Allenson, the smile souring on his face. 'But don't you dare try and escape again.' He paused, scrutinising her with his bloodshot eyes. 'There's a doctor I know. Name of Verlet. He lives in Donville-les-Bains, just north of here. Tell your automaton friend to go and fetch him. Explain that if he doesn't return with the doctor in one hour, then I'm going to start doing to you what Guizot's men did to me. Do you understand?'

He pushed her hard against the side of the wagon until her bones creaked and her lungs became painfully compressed. 'Understand?' he bellowed.

'Yes,' she croaked.

He slackened the pressure enough to let her breathe. 'Tell him.'

'Miles…' she began, weakly.

'I understand what I have to do, my lady,' said Miles. 'All I lack is an address.'

'Rue de la Paix,' Allenson said over his shoulder. 'I've forgotten the house number. You'll have to ask.'

'My lady…'

'Just go, metal man!' bawled Allenson. 'The clock's ticking.'

'It's all right, Miles,' murmured Arabella. 'I'll be fine.'

Arabella was not fine. Watching her logical friend kick-scooting away along the trackside, she felt a tremendous welling of sadness and fear. How could Miles possibly get all the way to Donville-les-Bains without attracting hostile attention from soldiers or French citizens? And what if this doctor wasn't even there? She couldn't rely on Miles. She would have to find some way to escape…

As she stood there pondering her options, the air was suddenly shaken by a terrifying noise. It was like nothing she'd ever heard before – a whining, clanking, galloping, hissing roar. She looked up in fright and saw, charging towards them down the grassy track, a man on horseback. But the horse he was riding was not of flesh and blood – it was made of iron, and it emitted great gouts of steam from its nostrils as it came on. This had to be one of the five murderous horsemen they had encountered earlier, and the sight of him here now was the death of all her hopes. Even if she could break free of Allenson's grip, there was no way she could evade the bullets of this equestrian assassin.

Despite herself, Arabella couldn't help but marvel at the graceful movement of the mechanical steed as it approached them. The articulated plates of the neck allowed the automaton to toss its head as if it were alive, and the partly exposed cogs and gears in its joints worked in perfect synchronisation to reproduce the galloping style of a real horse.

The horseman slowed as he drew closer to them. He pulled at the reins of the iron beast and it drew up its great head and gave a high-pitched, echoing whinny.

The rider came to rest in a patch of moonlight. He wore a tricorn hat and a black leather domino mask, but Arabella could see that he was young – a warrior, perhaps, to judge from the scar on his right cheek.

Allenson transferred his grip to Arabella's upper arm and hauled her forward as if preparing to offer her up as some sort of bargaining chip. The horseman drew a large pistol and pointed it at the pair of them. Allenson put a placating hand up, and spoke in smooth French: 'Young sir, do not be fooled by this uniform I wear. I am a friend, a loyal servant of the French Empire. I have been spying on the English for many years now, passing on valuable intelligence to your superiors. This girl, however, is your enemy. I've caught her for you, see?'

Arabella struggled desperately, but Allenson's grip was like steel, his nails digging into her skin. 'She's an English spy,' he said. 'Part of an aerial troupe calling themselves the Sky Sisters. She's here to sabotage the invasion plans. But I managed to stop her in time.' Allenson grinned. 'So perhaps I'm due a reward, eh?'

The horseman said nothing. He swivelled slightly so that his gun was now pointing at Arabella. His face was impassive, his eyes as cold as the barrel of his gun. She knew there was no point in trying to deny what Allenson had said, for the young assassin must know it all anyway – he'd tried to kill her earlier, hadn't he? So instead she relaxed, put on her most defiant expression, and waited for death.

CHAPTER TWELVE

THE CALL OF PROVIDENCE

The gunshot ripped through the night, startling a small flock of crows that had been roosting on the wagon's roof and sending them shrieking and flapping off into the distance. A look of surprise came over Allenson's face. Maintaining his grip on Arabella with his right hand, he clutched at his throat with his left. It couldn't stop the flow of blood, however, which was soon cascading between his fingers. Allenson's hold on Arabella's arm finally slipped as he fell to his knees. He remained like that for a few more seconds, the puzzled look still lodged on his face, before falling forward onto the stones.

Arabella absently rubbed her sore arm as she stared at the back of Allenson's head, observing the blood starting to form a halo around it. She looked up. The horseman was watching her, a wisp of smoke snaking upwards from his gun barrel. Then, to her great surprise, he clicked a switch with his heels, turned his horse around and rode the clanking, hissing thing away.

'My lady, are you all right?'

'Miles!'

She turned, and there he was: the Logical Englishman, gliding and hobbling along the side of the railway track towards her in that endearingly lopsided way of his.

How long had she been standing there?

'I see you managed to kill Captain Allenson. I could not find the doctor. He was out on a house call and –'

'Oh, Miles! Didn't you see what happened?'

A flood of emotion threatened to overwhelm her then. Tears pricked her eyes and her chest heaved, and she did something she never thought she'd do: she went down on her knees and hugged and kissed her little metal friend.

'My lady,' puffed Miles. 'Your eyes are leaking.'

'They're called tears, Miles.'

'Watery secretions produced by the lacrimal gland. Yes, I have heard of them. They are usually produced by humans when they are sad. Are you sad, my lady?'

In truth, Arabella could not hope to explain the confused mixture of emotions that had prompted her tears – least of all to a logical creature like Miles. Relief at not dying was obviously a big part of it. But behind that lay renewed anxiety about her father. That worm of doubt, first planted in her mind by Commodus Bane two days ago, had been given fresh life by Allenson. It was back inside her head, whispering its vile suspicions. *Was her father a cowardly traitor?* Of course he wasn't! He was a hero to her and to Britain, and she would prove it. She'd prove that worm false – squash it under her heel…

'No, Miles,' she said. 'I'm not sad. Actually, I'm very happy. One of the horsemen-assassins came back. I thought he was going to kill me, but for some mysterious reason he killed Allenson instead. Then he rode away. I have no idea why. But I think I've been spared for a reason. I believe I've been spared by providence for the mission that I must now accomplish…'

As if on cue, a deep throbbing sound started up to the west. She raised her head and saw, over a chaotic jumble of rooftops, the French Imperial Air Fleet readying itself for departure. Lights were flashing in the bellies of hundreds of battlecruisers, and thousands of steam-powered turbines were starting to rotate.

'Come on, Miles,' said Arabella. 'Let's go and blow up an airship.'

PART II

20 JULY 1845

CHAPTER THIRTEEN
THE GLUM BUNCH

'Where have you been?' asked Isaac Dreyfus when Jacques returned to the street off the square.

'Trying to chase them down,' said Jacques, bringing *Pégase* to a halt with a flick of his reins.

The other Equestrians cut sorry figures, hunched in their saddles. It was not a good feeling, being bested by a bunch of women.

'Any joy?'

Jacques shook his head.

'May those witches rot in Hell!' muttered Gérard Mesnier, still attempting to wipe his eyes clear of chilli powder.

'Hell's too good for them,' remarked Henri Bilot,

massaging one of his beefy shoulders after the mauling he'd received from the crazy strong Sky Sister.

'The mission has changed,' announced Isaac, switching off his aethercell.

'What do you mean?' asked Jacques.

'I've had a message from Marshal Guizot. The Aetheric Shield Generator has been destroyed. We must now switch our attention to protecting *Titan*. The marshal is already on board, and he wants us to join him there.'

'You think those she-devils are on *Titan*?' gasped Henri.

'We have to assume at least one of them is,' said Isaac. 'After all, only four of them showed up at our ambush.'

'I assumed the missing one was the spy – the friendly one,' said Gérard. 'If so, she won't be a threat.'

'The marshal says that all five must be eliminated,' said Fabien Leloup, the quiet one of the group.

No one said anything, which was a fairly typical response to one of Fabien's pronouncements. His voice, on the rare occasions when he spoke, seemed to have its own echo, as if he was speaking from a crypt. Jacques reckoned that everyone was a little scared of Fabien, who appeared to relish the deadly aspects of their work a bit too much. Most of the time they tended to ignore him and pretend he wasn't there – as one might a ghost.

'Let's go,' said Isaac after a moment's uncomfortable silence. 'We don't want to lose our berth.'

The posse clicked their heel-pedals and trotted into the square towards the mooring tower of *Titan*.

In the elevator taking them up to the waiting airship, Isaac leaned close to Jacques and murmured: 'I heard a gunshot earlier. Are you sure you didn't find anyone?'

'There was a wounded British officer by an old railway track – a survivor of last night's attack.'

'You killed him?'

'Yes.'

Isaac's jaw hardened. 'We might have learned something from him.'

'I had some unfinished business with the man,' said Jacques simply. 'Personal business.'

CHAPTER FOURTEEN

THE CLIMB

Arabella and Miles lurked in the shadows near the base of *Titan*'s mooring tower. From above came the deep throbbing hum of airship engines. Miles detached his left hand. He pressed a button at the base of the middle finger and a small light came on in its tip. Then he placed it on the ground. He drew a retractable aerial from within the same wrist and pulled out a brass toggle from the underside of his forearm.

'My engineers made a few adjustments to my hand before we set out,' said Miles. 'It can now receive aetherwave signals from this aerial.'

'Your hand', breathed Arabella, 'gets more amazing each time you use it.'

She watched in awe as he pushed the toggle forward and the hand chugged away from them. It moved on miniature rollers fitted into its palm, propelled by a tiny steam engine in the base of its thumb. Miles directed the hand towards a pair of dockers who were loading a large pile of boxes into the tower's elevator. It parked itself close by them, but out of sight behind one of the boxes.

From the interior of his handless wrist, Miles drew out a tiny brass nodule attached to the end of a slender wire. 'Place this in your ear, my lady.'

'What is it?' whispered Arabella dubiously, but did as she was told. She was surprised to hear, amid a lot of crackling and hissing, the sound of human voices. 'Oh my heavens!' she gasped. 'I can hear talking. Is it... Is it those men over there?'

'Indeed it is,' said Miles. 'My hand is transmitting signals to that receiver in your ear, so what you are hearing is not a recording but happening at this very moment.'

'Hush!' said Arabella. 'They *were* complaining about their wives, but now I think they're saying something important.' She frowned, listening closely.

'*Eh bien, René, c'est la dernière boîte, n'est-ce pas?*'

'*Oui.* Titan *doit partir à minuit – en dix minutes.*'

She looked at Miles. '*Titan*'s leaving in ten minutes,' she told him. 'We simply *must* get on that elevator.'

'How do you propose we do that, my lady – considering it will be entirely filled with all these boxes?'

Arabella studied the gradually diminishing pile of boxes. The remaining ones were all too small for her to fit inside, but one or two were of sufficient size to accommodate her diminutive friend.

She passed the earpiece back to Miles, and it was automatically sucked back inside his wrist. 'You'll be in one of the boxes,' she said.

The automaton discharged an apprehensive cloud of steam. 'Are you sure, my lady?'

'Absolutely.'

'And what about you?'

'Don't worry about me, I'll find a way on board… Now, I need some sort of distraction. Can your hand manage that?'

Miles nodded. He manipulated the toggle and the hand immediately darted from its hiding place to appear in full view of the two dockers.

One of the men jerked back at the sight. *'Ah – un rat!'* he cried.

'Non, c'est autre chose,' said the other, peering closer. *'C'est une… une main! Une main en métal!'*

Miles guided the hand away from the boxes, past the elevator and under the mooring tower, where it began to pick up speed. The men, fascinated, followed it.

Arabella heard one of them shout as they ran: *'C'est un gadget espion. Il faut l'attraper!'*

'Quick!' said Arabella to Miles, and they dashed towards the pile of boxes. Arabella pulled down the largest one she could find and tore open the top. It was filled with tins of food, presumably for the crew. She emptied the tins onto the ground – the clattering sound eclipsed by the steadily rising volume of engine noise from above – then picked Miles up and deposited him in the box. Miles sat there, still controlling his hand with the toggle, sending the men on a wild chase beneath the mooring tower.

'What about my hand, my lady? We cannot allow such an advanced piece of technology to get into the hands of the French.'

'I shall retrieve your hand, Miles, do not fear,' said Arabella. 'Send it somewhere inaccessible for now.'

Arabella fancied she read unease in the flicker of his eye-lights. But he did as he was told, guiding the hand up a steep iron buttress supporting one of the tower's four legs. The hand soon disappeared into the tower's complex web of iron girders and trusses. While the men tried to seek out its location, Arabella swiftly pushed Miles down inside the box and tossed as many food cans as she could on top of him. Then she forced the box closed and slid it back into the pile awaiting stowage. By the time the two dockers returned to their duties, having failed to find the hand, Arabella had fled back to her former hiding place. From there she watched as the men loaded the remaining boxes. She held her breath as René hoisted up the one containing Miles and shoved it roughly into the elevator. To her great relief, it didn't spring open. She prayed Miles hadn't suffered any damage.

Now she had to get herself aboard. She scooted beneath the tower to the leg where Miles had secreted his hand, and began her ascent. Fortunately, the criss-crossed iron struts were conveniently spaced and climbing was not difficult. She recovered the hand, which was seated precariously in the angle of two struts some twenty feet above the ground. It was warm to the touch and she could feel the faint vibration of its engine in the base of the thumb. She pressed the button at the base of the middle finger, as she'd seen Miles do, and waited for the small light to come on in the finger's tip.

'Miles,' she shouted – for the rising swell of the engines above her necessitated it – 'as you can tell, I have your hand. I'm now going to climb the tower. See you up there.'

A tiny, muffled voice emerged from a speaker in the tip of the hand's ring finger. She thought she heard the words: 'Be careful, my lady.'

Arabella placed the hand in a spare compartment of her utility belt, then continued her climb. The wind gusted hard, flapping at her clothes and blowing her hair into her eyes. She glanced up and was dismayed to note how much further she still had to go. Doubts tore at her mind. *Am I utterly mad? What will I do when I get to the top? How can I possibly get myself aboard?*

A mechanical chugging sound from below told her that the elevator was now on the move. She watched the iron cage glide up the side of one of the southern legs of the tower, powered by a steam engine at the tower's base. It rose quickly on its rope hoist, soon overtaking her. Before long, it was a shrinking black box high above her, moving ever closer to the great golden belly of *Titan*. The time on her chronometer stood at two minutes to midnight.

Now a new doubt overtook her, quickly tripping into something close to panic: *I'll be too late. Titan will cast off before I can get there.* She redoubled her efforts, forcing her weary muscles to move faster – hand over hand, foot over foot. With every yard she climbed, the wind blew harder, as if trying to prise her fists from the struts. She was close to exhaustion. The ache in her legs and arms had become a white fire, consuming her – but she refused to cease, even for a second, the rhythm of movement that was carrying her upwards.

Above her, *Titan* began to loom much closer. The noise of its four gigantic triple-expansion steam engines was so loud she could barely think. The airship's gargantuan bulk filled her horizons so that it was no longer easy to grasp its full extent. It shimmered behind its aetheric force field and Arabella began to appreciate why it had needed three days to construct a shield for such a vessel. The gondola's gold-painted stern rose up steeply in tiers, with each level jutting out from the one below like an old Spanish galleon. The ship had outriggers to stabilise it – thirty-foot-long triangular sails that stuck out from the rear of the hull like aquatic fins, just in front of the enormous engines with their concealed propellers.

The elevator had by now arrived at a small hatchway set into the bottom tier of the gondola's stern. Arabella watched in alarm as crew members loaded the final boxes, including Miles, into the hold, then slammed shut the hatch and twisted home an iron locking wheel. *Now* how was she going to get aboard?

Fresh gouts of black smoke spewed from the funnels as the great skyship achieved the power necessary for launch. The noise and vibrations shaking the tower reached earthquake levels. High up on the gondola's deck, crewmen cast off the mooring ropes that tethered the vessel to its tower. The heavy ropes of twisted wire crashed down against the tower's struts, almost knocking Arabella from her perch. In despair, she watched *Titan* start to move free of the tower, advancing with slow grace into open skies. She was nearing the top now, but the ship was still out of reach. *She was too late!*

CHAPTER FIFTEEN

THE SAIL-FIN

Beneath her, Arabella caught sight of the spreading fan of *Titan*'s enormous sail-fin. This final, trailing wisp of the mighty ship offered her a glimmer of hope. Even as she spotted it, the sail's fluttering hem began pulling away from her at the pace of a galloping horse. Without thinking, she leapt from the tower in a perfect swallow dive, landing with a bounce on the rough sailcloth. She clawed desperately at its surface, trying to gain some purchase on it, but it slipped and fled from her grasp. As she flew off the end, her fingers caught at the flapping edge and her fists grabbed hold with all the frantic determination of a mouse clinging to a twig in a raging torrent.

Her body was forced out at an angle by the hurricane-force thrust of the enormous engines, which lay only yards away to her right. Each engine was the size of a London omnibus and her ears were bombarded by a numbing storm of pure noise from their propellers. With an obstinacy verging on madness, Arabella clung on. But it wasn't enough: she needed to obtain a firmer grip if she wasn't going to be blown off into the sky by forces too powerful to resist. Already, she could feel her fingers starting to slip. So she reached out for the rope that bound the sail to one of its long, down-sloping timber spars. After several tries, she managed to seize the rope. Dragging herself forward, she then clamped her other arm around the mast. Thus, with dizzying effort and infinite slowness, she managed to make her way up the sail and its spar towards the hull. And all the while, her body was being shaken about like a leaf clinging by its last threads to a high branch.

Gradually, the cyclone diminished as she moved in front of the engines and out of range of their turbulence. Yet her struggle was far from over. After her epic ascent of the tower, and now this torturous, arm-wrenching crawl up the sail, Arabella was beyond exhausted. Her biggest fear, as she drew closer to the shimmering golden curve of *Titan*'s hull, was that her muscles, at the last moment, might fail her. She would fall to her death, like the crew of the *Nelson* in the Bay of Mont-Saint-Michel – just another pointless martyr to a doomed cause. Perhaps it was this fear, above all, that sustained her for those last few yards. It had to be something more than physical strength, for that had all been spent.

Finally, Arabella reached the end of the spar, and pressed a shaking hand to the gilded metal surface of the hull. Her limbs were screaming, her face streaked with tears, her lips dry, weakly sucking in breaths. Her mind, barely capable of thought, registered triumph, but also wondered vaguely why the shield did not obstruct her. Did it not sense that she meant harm to the ship it protected?

So now what? she asked herself. And that was when it hit her: so intent had she been on reaching the hull, it hadn't occurred to her that she had no idea how to get inside it!

Arabella allowed her body to rest while her arms continued to clasp the top of the spar. She would need a few moments to think this one through. There might be no solution, of course. She'd come about as far as physical and mental strength could take anyone. She'd achieved things that she wouldn't have thought possible before tonight. Yet she wasn't superhuman. She couldn't punch her way through the hull, or climb its smooth surface like a spider.

After a while, Arabella realised that the sensible thing to do would be to look around and see if she could spot some sort of convenient portal. Looking downwards, beneath the sail-fin, she could see the hull curving rapidly away out of sight with no sign of an entry point. She tried twisting her head to the left, and encountered an endless, unvarying wall of gold-painted, riveted plates. To her right lay a few yards of the same golden wall, which then swelled outwards in a dramatic double curve to house the port engines.

So there were no places of entry beneath her or on either side. Her last hope lay upwards. She craned her neck – and couldn't believe what was there. Just a few feet above her head was a gun port! It was one of forty-five adorning each of *Titan*'s flanks (three rows of fifteen – she'd counted them while on the ground).

Some meagre strength had returned to her by this time and she was able to push herself up onto her knees and raise her arms so her hands lay flat against the hull above her. From this position it required just a small stretch to grab hold of the sill of the gun port. The next stage entailed a great deal of levering, squirming, squeezing and slithering. The port, naturally, had a gun protruding from it – a large cannon with a muzzle that filled most of its cavity. Nevertheless, Arabella was able, eventually, to wriggle past this obstruction and land in an undignified heap on the lower gun deck.

She was in!

But before she had a chance to congratulate herself, she had to quickly scramble beneath a nearby tarpaulin to avoid approaching crewmen. Arabella lay there in silence as voices, accompanied by footsteps ringing hollowly on the metal floor, came closer. The crewmen were talking in coarse, colloquial French.

'I'm telling the truth,' said one. 'Napoleon Bonaparte is aboard this vessel. I saw him with my own eyes.'

'Then we are truly honoured,' said the other. 'It's like in the days of my father, the great days, when the emperor personally led his armies into battle. This means that victory is certain.'

Napoleon on board! Could it be true? In that case, she might be able to do more than bring down a flagship...

CHAPTER SIXTEEN

THE EMPEROR

The footsteps eventually clanged away. Arabella peeped out. She was in a steel-walled room fifty feet long – one of a chain of gun rooms, she guessed, running right around the perimeter of the gondola. The room contained five cannons, evenly spaced along the outer wall, noses jutting through their ports, a pyramid of cannonballs placed alongside each one. The bulkheads at either end of the room contained doors with locking wheels. Everything gleamed as if it had been built only yesterday.

Miles's hand began buzzing in Arabella's belt. She pulled it out and held it to her ear. 'Miles?' she whispered, after pressing the button at the base of the middle finger.

'My lady, are you safe?'

'Yes. I'm on the lower gun deck, near the stern. Will you be able to find me?'

'I will be there as soon as I can.'

Arabella waited for him under the tarpaulin. She wanted to make plans, but her body and mind were so exhausted that she kept nodding off. After an uncertain length of time, she heard the familiar jerky glide of Miles's single caterpillar track approaching along the metal floor.

She popped her head out from under the tarpaulin. 'Over here, Miles.'

He kick-scooted towards her – or rather, hobble-scooted. He looked distinctly off-balance, and more dishevelled than she'd ever seen him.

'How was your journey into *Titan*?' she asked him.

'Most disagreeable,' complained Miles, a self-pitying plume of steam rising from his hat. 'The workers threw my box hither and thither as if I was nothing more than tinned food. As a result, I have sustained damage to the gear wheels in my left shoulder, dents to the bi-articular piston in my right thigh, not to mention a buckling of the ratchet mechanism in my chronometer.'

'You poor chap,' sympathised Arabella. 'I trust it's all fixable.'

Miles nodded gloomily. 'How was your experience, my lady?'

'Oh fine, fine,' replied Arabella, not wishing to start him worrying about her in addition to his own troubles. 'Miles, I've just heard that Napoleon himself is on board *Titan*. So our little stick of dynamite might be able to end both the invasion and the entire war – if we use it effectively. Now, where would be the best place to detonate it?'

Miles's analytical brain chugged. 'The gas envelope,' he concluded after a moment's thought. 'If we can place the charge within the iron exoskeleton, then the blast should be sufficiently powerful to pierce both the outer skin and most of the internal helium-filled gas bags, which would certainly be enough to bring the vessel down.'

'What about the Aetheric Shield?'

'The Shield surrounds the exoskeleton and the gondola, protecting them from external attack. But, as our friend Mr Forrester proved a few days ago, it can do nothing to protect a vessel against an explosion from within.'

'Then let's do it,' said Arabella. 'Our first challenge will be to get to the gas envelope unseen.'

'I would not advise going the way I came,' said Miles. 'There are too many crewmen about. Only my modest stature saved me from being spotted.'

Arabella moved cautiously sternwards. She turned the locking wheel and opened the door a few inches – just enough to peep inside. A loud, rhythmic hissing and clanking filled her ears, and she was struck by a wave of smoky heat. She stared, blinking, into the dark, noisy cavern of the port-side engine room.

Two blazing furnaces dominated the far wall, fed with coal by six sooty-faced men with shovels. The wall surrounding the two fires was a giant relief sculpture of intricately coiled pipes, like a nest of oil-black vipers. Among the vipers were dials the size of church clocks. More grimy-cheeked men stood before the dials, studying their flickering needles, moving brass levers or twisting red wheels to open and shut valves. Machinery hissed and steamed and chugged and whistled.

An unguarded iron cage elevator lay just inside the room, to Arabella's left. The elevator shaft scaled the entire height of the room – about thirty feet – and there were doors set into the back wall of the shaft at regular intervals. If they could take the elevator to the topmost door, that should get them very close to the upper deck. After making sure that none of the engine-room crew were looking, Arabella beckoned to Miles, and the two of them sneaked in.

Five minutes later, they slipped quietly out through the top-floor doorway, emerging from the loud, sweaty, smoke-filled world below into a clean-smelling, timber-floored vestibule, fitted with coat rails and boot racks. An archway led from here into highly contrasting surroundings: a long, luxurious room furnished with Persian rugs, Louis XV sofas and chairs, ornamental brass-framed portholes and rosewood-veneered panelling. The room was illuminated by a soft greenish glow, which seemed to emanate from its vaulted ceiling, made up of glass panels embellished with swirling floral patterns.

'Where are we, do you suppose?' asked Arabella.

'It appears to be an officers' mess, my lady.'

Arabella glanced back towards the engine room. 'If we can't make it to the gas envelope, perhaps we should blow up that engine room instead. That would stop *Titan* in its tracks.'

'May I remind you, my lady, that *Titan* has *four* engines? With one stick of dynamite we could disable, at most, two of them. But the vessel is perfectly capable of flying on two, or even one.'

Arabella sighed. 'Gas envelope it is, then,' she said. 'Which door do you recommend we take?' There were two to choose from – one set in the longer wall to their right, the other in the short wall straight in front of them. 'The one ahead of us looks more promising, wouldn't you say, Miles?'

Before he could respond, they heard the sound of footsteps approaching the door that Arabella had been on the point of selecting. She was now tempted to make a run for the other door, but decided it was too far away to reach in time. Instead, she hurriedly secreted herself behind an armchair, while Miles reversed into the vestibule. The elegantly slender, gilded legs of the chair scarcely hid Arabella, and she silently cursed herself for not following Miles's example. But it was too late to swap hiding places now, for the door was already opening.

In came four very tall men wearing blue jackets with gold braid, red trousers and high peaked caps – the uniform of French army officers. They were followed by a short, stout man in an immaculate National Guard uniform, his right hand tucked inside his waistcoat, his left clutching a walking stick. The man's hair was as white as his waistcoat. His features – ebony eyes, slender nose and small mouth – were somewhat lost in the broad expanse of his ageing, fleshy face. Yet Arabella instantly recognised him from a thousand portraits, and the sight sent ripples of fear and fascination running through her.

She clasped her knees tight, trying to make herself as tiny as possible behind the hopelessly spindly chair. If just one of the officers glanced in her direction, her life would be over in a second. They'd cut her down with their ceremonial swords before she could crawl two feet. She risked another look at the short, stout man. For almost half a century, British children had suffered nightmares about this man. Thousands had died fighting him. He was Britain's eternal nemesis: Napoleon Bonaparte.

One of the men handed him a glass of wine. He withdrew his hand from his waistcoat and took the glass. More wine was poured and passed around. As Arabella crouched there and watched, the breath tumbled softly from her lips and was quietly, carefully drawn back in. Her limbs had turned to stone, the blood no longer circulating.

'Gentlemen,' said Napoleon. 'Let us raise our glasses and drink a toast… to the Phoenix.'

'The Phoenix!' the other men echoed.

The Phoenix? Could that be the code name for the invasion?

'Soon, very soon, it will be within our grasp!' continued Napoleon, after taking a sip of his wine. 'I can hear it calling to me.'

She couldn't stay in this position for much longer. Her legs were shaking. She could feel herself losing her balance.

Eventually, Napoleon put down his glass. 'On with the tour!' he said.

'This way, Excellency,' said one of the officers, guiding him across the room. 'From this vantage you will be able to review Engine Room One.' The emperor and his retinue passed beneath the archway and out onto the little platform overlooking the engine room.

Seconds later, Miles emerged from his hiding place. Arabella knew that this was their only chance to escape. They had seconds at most, before the officers returned. She could see a guard with his back to them stationed at the door at the far end of the room, which left just one escape route: the door set in the long wall to their right. With a silent nod towards the door, she communicated her plan to Miles and the two of them made a dash for it.

They found themselves in an armoury filled with weapons and equipment: armour, helmets, swords, guns and a large black pack containing a parachute.

Arabella grabbed a pistol and the parachute. She planted the pistol in her waistband and strapped the parachute on her back. 'This will be our means of escape once we've burst the gas envelope,' she declared. 'I'll hold you very tight when we jump, I promise!'

'Very good, my lady.'

'Now we need to find some stairs to the upper deck.'

There were three new doors leading off this room. Arabella picked one at random and pulled it open – then gasped and took a step backwards.

'Miles,' she said, 'forget the gas envelope. I've just seen what we need to blow up.'

CHAPTER SEVENTEEN

THE IRON ARMY

The room was full of barrels and boxes with frightening labels like GUNPOWDER, NITRATED COTTON, BALLISTITE, CORDITE and DYNAMITE.

'My lady,' said Miles, 'if ignited, this will blow the entire airship to pieces. It will vaporise it.'

'I know,' said Arabella, her eyes shining. '*Titan* will disappear. Napoleon will disappear. It will be a new world!'

Then her shoulders slumped and her smile faded. 'Hundreds will die...'

'True.'

'Oh Miles, if *Titan* is allowed to continue on its journey, all these explosives, and the weapons next door, will be used against *our* people. The ninety cannon on board will blast our aircrews from the sky. Yet I still find it hard to do this.'

She sniffed and wiped an eye with the back of her hand. Then, steeling herself to the task, she removed the dynamite stick from her waistband and placed it near the barrels of gunpowder. She unravelled the fuse to its full length so that it trailed along the floor. 'This will give us half an hour,' she said. 'Time enough to get away, I should hope.'

Blinking away her tears, Arabella took out the fire-piston and lit the fuse. 'I do this in the name of all the soldiers who died in Operation Zeus,' she whispered, 'so that you did not die in vain.' Then she stood up. 'Now let's find an escape route, Miles. That gun port I came in by should suit our purposes.'

They tried retracing their route, but could get no further than the armoury. There were voices coming from the officers' mess.

'We'll have to find an alternative way down,' said Arabella, and she tried one of the armoury's other doors. This led onto a balcony that ran around an enormous hall, a hundred feet long, fifty wide and three storeys deep – they appeared to have reached the very heart of *Titan*.

Arabella stared, open-mouthed, at the scene below her, very much wanting to believe it was an illusion. She was looking at an army, sizable enough to fill the entire hall – not only the ground floor but the balconies, too – wide, spacious balconies, on five different levels.

There were even troops on the balcony where she stood. None of the soldiers moved, none said a word. They were dormant, still. For this was no ordinary army. It was an army of metal: rank after rank of iron soldiers, upon iron horses – the men were made of the same stuff as their mounts. And, looking more closely, she saw they weren't astride their horses, but growing out of them. For these soldiers had no legs, and their horses had no heads. The soldiers' bodies emerged from the necks of their horses like centaurs! Automaton-centaurs!

They were all identical, as if cast in the same mould – all huge, fierce-looking and crudely formed. Their bodies were made up of iron plates and cylinders formed into the rough anatomy of a human–horse hybrid, with cogs, springs and gears visible at the joins. They didn't have proper faces, just round black holes for eyes, bumps for noses and slits for mouths. They didn't even have hands – their forearms ended in guns. There was nothing elegant about these warrior-beasts. They'd been put together with brutal efficiency.

Individually, they would have been daunting enough, but together like this – so many of them, assembled in such perfect lines, with their identical bodies glinting in the cold blue overhead light – they scared Arabella to her core. Their uniformity seemed evil, inhuman. Was this the future? Was this Napoleon's dream? To send a tide of deadly metal sweeping across her country, wiping out towns, communities? There would be no mercy from these brutal machines with black holes for eyes. Suddenly she was grateful for the flame quietly burning its way through its fuse in that powder keg of a room next door. So, some people would die. It was worth it – to save Britain, to save the human race, from a future with black holes for eyes...

She had been staring at this scene for no more than a few seconds when the light in the hall suddenly changed from blue to shimmering gold. The new light didn't come from above, but seemed to radiate outwards from the far end of the room. And it didn't act like normal light. It didn't spread through the air evenly, but clung to the objects it touched – the iron centaurs – surrounding each one with a glistening golden halo. Arabella recognised the light. And when she peered into the shadows at the far end of the hall, she identified its source: raised up on a high platform were five pillars bound in copper wire, and a strange and nauseating shape hovering between them – *another Aetheric Shield Generator!*

It was smaller than the one they'd destroyed at Granville, yet looked fully equal to the task of shielding this metal army. And now the full diabolical scale of Napoleon's plans emerged: he hadn't been satisfied with creating an invulnerable airship raining terror from the skies. He wanted to launch an indestructible army, too! It made the Sky Sisters' operation to destroy the Granville ASG seem futile. Now that Napoleon had the technology, he could build any number of these machines. But the ASGs drank gold – great quantities of the stuff. How much did he have? And was he prepared to use it all up to fulfil his dreams of world domination? It appeared that he was.

From somewhere in the ship came the faint grinding sound of a door opening.

As Arabella watched, the light gradually faded back to blue. She glanced back at Miles, who had not ventured beyond the armoury doorway. He had gone quite still as his eyes processed all this new and startling information. 'I'm only thankful,' she murmured to him, 'that in less than half an hour, everything we see here will be superheated dust... Now, Miles, how do we get out of here?'

'You're going nowhere, lady!'

The sneering voice spoke English in a heavy French accent.

Arabella whirled around and surveyed the centaurs sharing their balcony. They looked as still and lifeless as those everywhere else in the hall – *so who could have spoken?* She began walking slowly down the line, examining the man–horse hybrids one by one. There wasn't a flicker of animation in their hollow black eyes. It made her skin crawl to think that any of them might actually be alive.

'STOP right there!'

She jerked to a halt.

There was a drumming of hooves and a shadowy movement from the rear lines. Suddenly, five horsemen burst through to the front rank, knocking aside any centaurs in their way. With a sinking heart she saw who they were: the masked assassins who'd tried to ambush them in Granville. Three of them drew long silver pistols from holsters beneath their jackets and levelled them at her.

Arabella couldn't fight like Cassie or Emmeline, but she was fast. Before they could take aim and fire, she turned and ran back towards the armoury. She had almost reached the door when the air behind her was filled with a high-pitched whipping sound and a rope circle appeared as if by magic above her head. The rope descended and, in less than the blink of an eye, it had enclosed her, twining itself tightly around her waist.

A twitch on the rope forced her backwards. Desperately, she reached out for the doorway, but could do nothing to avoid being hauled to her knees and dragged back before the horsemen. A couple of them laughed, but not the one with the lasso who had her captured. He had black, curly hair and seemed the oldest – perhaps the leader of the bunch. She stared up at him defiantly, refusing to show any fear.

'We should kill her now,' said one of the gun-toters – the biggest boy in the gang. Arabella recalled him as the one who Cassie had attacked.

'I completely agree,' said another with a whining, nasal voice. Arabella couldn't help noticing that his eyes were still bloodshot from Emmeline's chilli-powder assault. He turned to the older boy with the lasso: 'Let's kill her, Isaac.'

The lassoer nodded. He used his other hand to draw his gun. There was a volley of clicks as four spring-loaded hammers were pulled back, ready for firing.

Arabella went rigid with shock. 'No!' she started to say.

'Wait!' said the only one who had not yet drawn his gun. 'Let's not do this yet. She may have some information. And the metal man could be useful technology for our scientists.'

Arabella recognised this one from the scar on his cheek – it was the boy who had spared her life by the railway track. Now he was trying to save her once again. *Why?*

The other four kept their guns trained on her, seemingly unpersuaded by his argument.

'Our orders were to kill them, Jacques,' said Isaac.

The scarred one shrugged. 'You said yourself, our orders have changed. Our duty now is to protect *Titan*. And the best way of doing that is to question this woman – find out what she knows and what she may be planning.'

Isaac stared at her for a moment longer, then put away his gun. 'Very well, we'll take her to the marshal,' he said.

'But Isaac…!' protested the big one.

'Shut up, Henri!' said Isaac.

Reluctantly, Henri holstered his pistol, as did the

red-eyed, whiny-voiced one. That left one more, who maintained his aim on Arabella's heart.

'Put it away, Fabien,' Isaac ordered.

'You are making a big mistake,' said Fabien. His thick, deep voice seemed to emerge from the bottom of a well. His eyes, as they studied Arabella, were cold and dead – not so different from those of the automata lined up behind him.

'Now, Fabien!' roared Isaac.

Grimacing, he put away his gun.

The young men dismounted. The whiny-voiced one searched Arabella with rough hands, and immediately found the pistol. He took it from her, and wrenched the parachute from her shoulders. Isaac retrieved his rope from her, and she and Miles were then led at gunpoint along the balcony and out through another door at the far end of the hall. Henri took pleasure in pushing and prodding her from behind, frequently causing her to stumble.

They were led through room after room, and Arabella couldn't help but gape at the grandiose luxury on display: hand-carved oak furniture with crimson upholstery, mahogany panels inlaid with mother of pearl, portholes covered in silk curtains and lamps carved to resemble cherubs. A grand staircase rose sixty feet to a glass ceiling painted with an airship battle in the clouds. She saw a palm court with trellises covered in climbing plants where groups of officers relaxed over cups of coffee, and even glimpsed a steamy Turkish bath decorated in Arabian mosaic. Was *Titan* a warcraft or a luxury airliner? It seemed to be both.

Somewhere in the background a chamber orchestra played soft, smug tunes. Arabella shuddered to think of all the millions lavished on this ostentatious dream ship when so many of the French were struggling to find food to eat. Well, all this mahogany, silk and ornamental glass would soon be smoke and ash, and a good thing, too!

She tried to catch Miles's attention. There could only be another twenty minutes or so before the ship blew up. Somehow, before that happened, they would have to give their captors the slip and make a run for it. But Miles was having troubles of his own. The whiny-voiced one with the sore eyes was picking on him, kicking him in the legs. 'Hurry up, metal man!'

They were both pushed unceremoniously into a room that was brutally plain – steel walls and floor, like the gun decks, with a metal desk and a couple of metal chairs for furniture. A single porthole showed a view of night sky and clouds. Standing in the room were two people. One was a short man with a powerful build and a narrow, bullet-shaped skull streaked with black, greasy hair. Arabella immediately recognised him from secret service files as Marshal François Guizot, head of the Bureau de la Sécurité Intérieure. The other person was even better known to her, and it shocked and saddened Arabella to see her here.

CHAPTER EIGHTEEN

THE
KNIFE

Diana Temple was still in the black outfit that Emmeline had issued them with a few hours earlier, but while Arabella's was grimy and torn, Diana's looked pristine. And from the look of her shiny, bobbed hair, dark red lips and painted nails, she could have just finished a modelling shoot for a top fashion daguerreotypist.

'Traitor!' Arabella hissed at her through bared teeth.

Diana smiled distantly, but said nothing.

'Marshal,' said Isaac, saluting, 'we found this woman and her automaton in the Central Chamber. She matches the description of the one named Arabella West.'

'*Lady* Arabella West,' Guizot corrected him amiably. He came closer, smothering her in the rich, greasy scent of his garlic breath. 'I'm impressed at your ingenuity, Lady West – getting aboard our flagship. Do you like what you see?'

'It seems like a fitting symbol for the gargantuan ego of your emperor,' answered Arabella.

Guizot's simper turned to a scowl. 'Well, you won't have a chance to enjoy it for much longer. You will be dying very soon.' He glanced up at Diana. 'As will you, my dear.'

Diana gave a start. Her lips fell open in surprise. 'But, Marshal! After all I have done for you – for France!'

'And we're grateful to you for that,' said Guizot. 'But now that you have outlived your usefulness, your continued existence can only be a liability. Gérard…'

The thin, whiny-voiced one grabbed Diana. With a lascivious grin, he ran his fingers lightly over her arm.

'Shoot her,' said Guizot.

Gérard pulled out his pistol and ran its muzzle through her hair, letting it come to rest at a spot on her temple. Arabella felt she was going to be sick.

'Wait!' groaned Diana. 'Wait! You still need me.'

'Why?' snapped Guizot.

'Because I'm sure Arabella has planted an explosive device somewhere on this airship. You're going to need me to find it for you. You know I'm the best finder there is.'

Guizot swivelled his steel-grey eyes on Arabella. 'Is this true?'

'No,' gasped Arabella, her cheeks aflame.

'She didn't use all the dynamite on the ASG at Granville,' gabbled Diana. 'I counted the sticks. She had one extra, which she didn't use, and which she must have brought aboard *Titan*. She hasn't got it with her now, so she must have placed it somewhere already. I doubt we have more than ten minutes before this whole ship goes up in flames.'

Guizot's eyes widened and his face purpled until it seemed he might explode. He moved in close to Diana, trembling with fury. 'If you're lying, my girl, I'm going to rip out your tongue with my bare hands.' He turned to Gérard. 'You go with her! Don't let her out of your sight for one second. Now go, both of you! Find that explosive and deactivate it.'

Diana and Gérard left the room.

Guizot turned on Arabella. 'So, you thought you could destroy the greatest ship ever to take to the skies, hm? I think you were being a little optimistic thinking one stick of dynamite could take down *Titan*. Still, I don't like the idea of the damage it may do… So why don't you be a good girl and tell me where it is?'

'I have no idea what you're talking about,' said Arabella.

Guizot merely smiled. He took her left hand in his. 'You have fine hands,' he muttered. 'Soft and white, like an English rose.' Then he nodded at Fabien, who immediately stepped forward and pushed her hand down hard on the surface of the desk. Guizot unsheathed a knife from his belt. It was a big, vicious-looking blade, with a curving tip that ended in a sharp point and a serrated section along its edge. He ran a thumb over the serrations. 'Most people start talking after the first finger comes off,' said Guizot. 'A few brave souls hold out until the second. Only one I have heard of remained silent after three of his fingers had been severed, and the experience apparently unhinged his mind. His name was Commodus Bane. I have no idea what became of him…'

Arabella tried to tug her wrist free, but Fabien used his weight to keep it pinned there. The boy smiled, a gold tooth glinting as he did so. She could feel beads of sweat rolling down her forehead as Guizot placed the saw-toothed edge against the base of her little finger.

'Do you feel like talking yet, my dear?' Guizot breathed, 'before you say *adieu* forever to your little pinkie?'

'I have nothing to say,' she cried, squeezing her eyes shut and bracing herself for the pain.

'Sir!' came a voice from behind her. 'If you cut her finger off, she'll faint. They always faint. And by the time she comes round, it may be too late. Give me five minutes with her. Alone. I'm sure I can extract the information you require.'

She recognised the voice. It was Jacques – the boy with the scar on his cheek. Why did he keep trying to save her?

Guizot was breathing heavily in her ear, suppressing his rage, his urge to be violent. 'You can have *three* minutes,' he grunted. 'And *then* I'll start slicing off her fingers. Isaac! Bind her.'

Isaac expertly twisted and knotted a length of rope around her wrists, then Jacques led her from the room. He guided her across a concourse, past the grand staircase to a set of wicker chairs by the arched entrance to the Turkish baths. Here they sat, partially shrouded by steam wafting from the baths.

To her surprise, as soon as they were seated, Jacques took her hands in his. 'Lady,' he said, face flushed and voice trembling, 'I so wish I could help you. I hate this war and I know that Napoleon must be stopped. But I have a sister who's very dear to me – she's all I have left in this world. And she's in a British prison. I probably won't ever see her again unless this invasion succeeds and she can be liberated. I'm so torn. I don't know what to do.' He looked imploringly at her. 'I know for one thing that I don't want to die... Can't you tell me where the dynamite is and we can figure something else out – some way of stopping this madness that will leave us both alive?'

Arabella had been willing to trust him until that moment. 'You're clever,' she said. 'Cleverer than your boss. But I can see through your game. This is just your way of getting me to spill my little secret.'

'No!' cried Jacques. 'I spared you over by the railway track, didn't I? And again, just now, when my fellow Equestrians were going to shoot you. I really *am* on your side…'

'In that case, maybe we can help each other,' said Arabella. 'The dynamite will explode in about ten minutes. That still gives us time. Get me, my automaton and yourself to the upper deck, with parachutes, and we'll escape together.'

Jacques gazed at her wretchedly. 'How am I supposed to do that with Guizot watching my every move? What you ask is impossible!'

'We have to try,' she said.

Henri appeared. 'Has she confessed yet?' he asked Jacques.

'It's not been three minutes!' Jacques protested.

'The marshal says you've had long enough,' said Henri. 'Has she told you where the dynamite is?'

'No! Now let me –'

But Henri grabbed Arabella and dragged her back to the room, with Jacques trailing helplessly behind.

The rope was removed from her wrists and, a moment later, Arabella found herself once again with Guizot's knife blade hovering close to her finger.

She caught Jacques' eye with a sad smile. A last-minute escape with the kind-hearted French boy would have been nice, but it wasn't to be. *Ah well! Very soon now, all the suffering will be over.*

Then Diana's voice piped up from the doorway: 'You can relax, Marshal. I've found the dynamite, and I've defused it.'

'Wh–?' grunted the marshal, looking up in surprise.

It was a moment of distraction – an opportunity Arabella had been praying for – and she grabbed it. She curled her right hand into a fist and slammed it as hard as she could into Guizot's jaw.

He let out a sharp cry and staggered backwards. The knife fell with a clatter to the table. Arabella was quick – she'd always been quick. She picked up the knife and, in the same movement, slipped behind Guizot and hooked her arm tight around his neck. He was shorter than her, but a lot stronger. Before he could throw her off, she pressed the side of the knife hard against his neck.

Guizot gurgled curses. His lips were bright red – he must have bitten his tongue when she'd punched him. Looking up, she saw four pistols trained on her head, the only part of her not concealed by Guizot's bulk.

Diana stood in the doorway looking appalled, her eyes flicking between Arabella and the guns trained upon her. The stick of dynamite was in her hand. *The traitor!* She'd just foiled the only chance Arabella would ever get to destroy *Titan*.

'Shoot her!' Guizot screamed at the boys. 'Shoot her in the head and she'll die before she can hurt me… Jacques, why aren't you taking aim?'

Jacques wasn't moving, wasn't meeting anyone's eyes.

Arabella saw Fabien's finger squeezing down on the

trigger, and she pressed harder with the knife, making Guizot squeal with pain.

'They have located *one* of the sticks, but not the other, my lady?' said Miles suddenly.

Everyone stopped and stared at the automaton.

'What?' murmured Arabella.

'You remember the other one we planted in the… Well, perhaps I shouldn't say where we planted it…'

'The automaton's lying,' said Diana. 'There was only *one* extra stick of dynamite.'

'Automata cannot lie,' said Arabella, trying to conceal her surprise at Miles's new-found ability. 'It's not allowed in their programming, as you very well know, Diana… I wasn't going to tell you about the other one. But now he's mentioned it, I might as well.'

'Shoot her!' shrieked Guizot.

'Then you'll all die,' said Arabella, calmer now.

The boys kept their muzzles trained on her, but she could read the hesitation in their eyes. She reminded herself to kiss Miles if they ever got out of this. *But how had he managed to lie?*

'Tell us where it is,' demanded Isaac.

'I give you my word that I will,' said Arabella. 'I'll tell you as soon as my automaton and I are leaping off the upper deck of this ship with parachutes strapped to our backs. When that moment comes, I'll shout out the location… But not before.'

'She's lying!' foamed Guizot. 'The British always lie, as do their automata! Just kill her!'

Isaac put away his pistol. 'No, sir.'

'Are you disobeying me, boy?' growled Guizot.

'With all due respect, sir, I... yes, I am,' answered Isaac. 'It is my understanding that the emperor is aboard this airship, and as a BSI agent I am sworn, above all else, to protect the emperor's person. If there's the remotest chance that this woman placed a second live explosive aboard this vessel, then we can't kill her until she tells us where it is.'

'Remind me to roast you over hot coals when this is over, Isaac,' snarled Guizot. 'Fabien, shoot this woman for me.'

'A pleasure, sir,' said Fabien, taking aim once more. As his finger began to squeeze down on the trigger, Arabella made a decision. Maybe she had failed in her quest to destroy Napoleon's flagship, but at least, in the final second or two remaining to her, she could kill his most evil henchman: Marshal François Guizot.

And this was exactly what she would have done, given the chance. However, at that moment, the room exploded...

CHAPTER NINETEEN

THE
ROCKETEER

To be precise, the room didn't *actually* explode – it just seemed that way to those standing there at the time. What in fact happened was that the entire outer wall caved in. There was a deafening screech of tearing metal, a shattering of glass and a roaring cyclone of freezing night air that swept everyone off their feet and caused Fabien's bullet, which had been destined for Arabella, to bury itself in the ceiling above her.

The desk and chairs went tumbling, cracking Henri in the head and slamming Isaac in the ribs. Marshal Guizot tumbled from Arabella's grasp and belly-slid into the wall, while Diana went spinning right out of the room. Gérard's elbow collided with Fabien's face, Jacques was stabbed in the leg by Guizot's falling knife and Arabella inadvertently kicked Miles in the chest as she flew across the floor and crashed into the corner.

Her neck ached, her arm groaned, her knee cried out in misery – Arabella felt like a broken doll. Peering through the swirling, dusty maelstrom that had until recently been Guizot's office, she noticed that the space was now filled with an entirely new object. It was a machine, she supposed, perhaps a transport device – it was hard to say for certain, so mangled was it after its collision with *Titan*. Bits of metal, wood, wire and springs hung off a vaguely tubular frame. Shorn-off stumps on either side of this frame might once have been wings. From the midst of this strange wreckage emerged an extremely dusty figure. The figure fought its way out and slid awkwardly to the floor. Picking itself up, it stumbled through the screaming air towards Arabella. As the figure came closer, she saw that it was a male in a full-face helmet, completely caked in dust.

She was too shocked to resist as he lifted her from the floor and began dragging himself, and her, towards the jagged hole that his flying machine had ripped in the hull. She was vaguely aware of other figures in the room crawling ineffectually about – but they scarcely seemed real. Nothing actually seemed real in that moment. It was so like a dream, she wasn't even alarmed as the mysterious figure stepped out of the hole in *Titan*'s wall, pulling her with him into the night.

It was only as they were plummeting through the darkness, with the giant underbelly of *Titan* receding from them at great speed, that she began to return to her senses. They were falling, which meant that at some stage they would be landing – and with great force and violence. She glanced down. It was impossible to make out whether they were due to hit land or sea, but whatever lay below them, she guessed they'd be hitting it soon – possibly in a matter of seconds – and at this speed, whether land or sea, it was bound to be fatal.

'Do you have a parachute, good sir?' she shouted.

He shook his head.

'Then you didn't really think this through, did you?' she yelled.

He held up a hand – the one he wasn't using to pin her to his chest. A pair of goggles was flapping around in it, and she guessed he wanted her to put them on. Odd, this concern for her eyes, when any second now their bodies were going to be smashed to smithereens. Nevertheless, she obliged him and with some difficulty managed to manoeuvre the goggles over her head and onto her face.

Then his hand moved across the straps of some sort of harness he was wearing. His thumb sought out a brass button, which he pressed. Arabella heard a tremendous roaring. Flames began shooting out of the bottom of his backpack – two long jets of silver-yellow fire. Suddenly they were no longer falling, but rising. Instinctively, as the fiery momentum built beneath her, she clamped her arms tighter around him. She looked up and the wind pummelled her face. The stars were spinning. Such speed, such power – it was as if they were riding the slipstream of an explosion. It took her breath away. Intense, exhilarating, more thrilling even than air-carriage flight, this was *real* flying! No machine enclosed her. Nothing separated her from the wind and sky. She was an eagle arcing through the heavens. She was Icarus, Iris, Pegasus…

They were no longer heading straight up, but levelling off. A few hundred yards to their right, she could see *Titan*, moving through shreds of purple cloud, bathed in the faint glow of the Aetheric Shield. She wondered what they must look like to the people on board: two figures riding a tiny rocket. She thought about Miles, still there, and prayed he was all right. He was small, and would be able to hide, she hoped, until she managed to figure out a way of rescuing him. *Miles had lied!* The shock of it struck her anew. He'd used deception in a very human way, to save her life, or at least prolong it. What kind of programming had enabled him to do that?

They were flying more or less parallel with the airship, and the tear in her gondola was visible – a tiny black scar in the dark gold expanse. How had this mysterious rocketeer managed it? How had he penetrated the shield? That was just one of a thousand questions she had for him – but she would save them for later. Right now she wanted to enjoy her reunion with the air, with the wind in her face and the astonishing power at her feet. Coming so soon after the nightmare on *Titan*, it felt like liberation in every sense – almost as though Guizot had achieved his desire and she'd died and gone to heaven.

She would have been happy to fly on like this for ever, propelled by an inexhaustible flame through endless skies, but far sooner than she desired, Arabella noticed they were sinking. The roar of burning fuel became a hiss, and the flame dwindled to a feeble flicker, which finally blinked out. They were freefalling again, though this time it was an angled dive and from a far-from-deadly altitude. Beneath them black waves were visible, laced with foam, coming up fast...

Splashdown was a cold, wet shock, knocking the breath from her lungs and turning her body rigid. The impact separated her from her rescuer. Now she was floating free through an ice-dark, silent world. Her need for air broke the tranquillity. Her limbs began to struggle, but the momentum of her fall and her heavy belt were carrying her ever lower. She could see glinting ripples above her, a silhouette approaching, arms enclosing, carrying her upwards into moonlight. She broke into the air with a cough and a splutter, trod water as waves swelled like small hills around her, dragging her up and down like a cork in their currents and spitting their salt-foam in her face.

She heard a rasp of canvas or India rubber and a mechanical hiss. Her companion had pulled something from his rocket pack – a shapeless piece of black fabric, which was now filling with air and transforming itself into a boat. He heaved himself in, then helped her up and over its fat, tubular side.

For several moments she lay there in the bottom of the inflated boat, catching her breath and gazing at the stars as the water sloshed and swayed beneath them. She could see *Titan*, the sparkling aerial galleon beneath its giant gas-filled sail, drifting past the moon. It looked so peaceful and unthreatening from this distance. How she wished the moon would snatch the airship into its orbit and keep it and its monstrous mecha-army imprisoned up there in the heavens where they could do no harm.

Titan flew in the vanguard of a huge and shadowy fleet, which now emerged from a cloud. The dark ovals fanned out behind their flagship in a long arrowhead that seemed to go on forever – a deadly swarm.

'How're you doing, ma'am?'

Startled by the familiar voice, Arabella immediately switched her attention to her companion. He had removed his helmet and was studying her with a pair of intense, dark eyes.

CHAPTER TWENTY

THE FOOLISH, GALLANT IMPULSE

'Mr Forrester!' she cried, her heart pounding, 'is it really you?' It *was* him, and she could do nothing to prevent a huge smile surging onto her face. When they'd said farewell to each other at Weymouth two days ago, Arabella had entertained little hope of ever seeing Ben Forrester again. Yet here he was, crashing back into her life in the most dramatic and unexpected fashion.

'Mr Forrester…' she said again, but could not think how to go on. The thousand questions she had put aside earlier now crowded back into her mind, but it was difficult to know which one to begin with. She was distracted by his hair, which matched his eyes in colour and was sticking out from his head in tufts. She felt a ridiculous urge to pat it back into place.

From his rocket pack, Ben extracted a rectangular metal plate with a short tube at one end. He tugged at the tube and it telescoped outwards to form the handle of a paddle, which he now applied to the water.

'How did you know where I was?' Arabella asked him, deciding to start with the most perplexing question of all.

Ben took his eyes off the sea to glance at her. 'By surfing the secret aetherwave channels.' He grinned sheepishly. 'Call it a hobby… Did you know, all you ladies have your own individual call signs, known only to the guys at the monitoring stations – and me?'

Arabella shook her head.

'It's true. And when I heard yours, I knew that you must be on another mission. So I took off in my back-up air carriage and went to investigate.'

He took a hand off the paddle and reached under the hem of her shirt.

'What are you doing, sir?' said Arabella, alarmed.

Ben tore off the pearl-sized aetherwave transmitter that she'd pinned under there and held it up before her eyes. 'This tiny thing led me to you.' Then he added, after a cursory examination: 'Sadly, it didn't survive its dunking in the sea.' He tossed it overboard.

A frown broke through her smile. 'And what made you think I needed rescuing?'

'That much was obvious,' said Ben. 'I had a copy of *Titan*'s deck plans, having stolen them some weeks ago for your government, and when I saw that your signal was emanating from Marshal Guizot's office, I figured that you might just have run into some trouble. Didn't know for sure, of course, but I... Well, let's say I've got a nose for that kind of thing.'

'As it happens, I had everything under control,' said Arabella.

'Is that so?' said Ben, looking a touch less pleased with himself.

'Why, yes!... In a manner of speaking. By which I mean, you... you saved my life, sir, and I thank you for that. But you also saved Marshal Guizot's, whom I was just about to kill.'

'Well, how about that!' said Ben, digging at the sea angrily with his paddle. 'Perhaps I would have done better in that case to leave you to it! After all, a world without Lady Arabella and the marshal has got to be a better place than the one we've ended up with, with both of you still alive! Thanks to my meddling, an evil man still walks, and a churlish and ungrateful woman now sits in my boat!'

'That is not fair!' cried Arabella. 'I am neither churlish nor ungrateful. I am simply saying that I prefer to be in control of my own destiny. If I choose to sacrifice my life for the greater good, I want to feel that I am free to make that choice without any danger of being rescued at the last minute!'

Ben's upper lip twitched in the way it always did when he was angry – as if he was doing his best to control the volcano raging within. 'Well, I'm grateful to you, ma'am, for putting me straight on this matter. And if I ever get the urge to rescue you again, I shall immediately chastise myself for entertaining such a foolish impulse, because now I know that the Lady Arabella must, in all circumstances, be in control of her own destiny!'

'It was a *gallant* impulse,' said Arabella placatingly, for she was disturbed and upset by the rage she'd stirred in him. 'And I *am* grateful to you. But I confess I'm also confused as to why you even attempted it. After all, on Taranis you said it would be better if we didn't see each other again.'

'And I still hold to that view – even more so now than before,' said Ben, his face contorted as if he were being forced to eat a lemon. 'I am a prize ass,' he declared, 'who wishes he'd never embarked on this damn-fool errand,' before adding under his breath, 'as if I ain't got any better place to be than the English Channel at this godforsaken hour...'

An uncomfortable silence reigned in the boat. Arabella shivered in her wet clothing. She listened to the swish of Ben's paddle and the soft, deep roar of the sea and waited for her heart to regain a more normal rhythm. She was surprised and disappointed by Ben's attitude – how he seemed to demand meek gratitude from her after he'd blundered blindly into the airship. It was true that his timing, if she had cared only about herself, could not have been better. But at the same time, thanks to his intervention,

Marshal Guizot – torturer and killer of hundreds of her compatriots – still lived. Surely Ben could see that this was a less than desirable outcome?

'It so happens,' said Ben after a time, 'that I had another reason for rescuing you – aside from my idiotic notion that it might be a good idea in and of itself. I've been working on a system in my workshop – a system for defeating the Aetheric Shield. And when I discovered you were on board *Titan*, it gave me an idea…'

'But I thought the shield was impenetrable,' said Arabella.

'Not entirely,' said Ben. 'You remember back on Taranis, when I demonstrated the shield to the sky pirates, and Odin managed to touch me even while I was wearing it?'

She remembered the moment vividly. 'You said it's sensitive to negative energy. It knows when we mean harm.'

'Right!' said Ben, who seemed to have recovered a little of his earlier good humour. 'So?'

'So if you can trick the shield into thinking that you don't mean any harm, then you can break through it.'

'Exactly!'

'Is that how you managed to crash your air carriage into *Titan*?'

'I can't say it was easy,' said Ben. 'I mean the shield ain't easily fooled. But after several experiments in my workshop, I figured out a way… See, the mind's a subtle thing – too subtle by half for the Aetheric Shield. The mind can think two contradictory things simultaneously. It can perform aerobatics that would make an analytical engine blow a fuse. And sometimes the mind can believe something while knowing, deep down, that it simply ain't true.

'I realised that to fool the shield, I first had to fool myself. So, when I was approaching *Titan*, I convinced myself that I was merely visiting, dropping by to see my old friend Lady Arabella. I said to myself that I would fly by the portholes and see if I could catch a sight of you, maybe waggle my wings and say howdy, then be on my way.

'But when I got to within forty, fifty yards of *Titan*, lo and behold, my air carriage developed a fault. The rudder jammed, and so did the ailerons on my wings. Of course, I'd planned this to happen before take-off, but the Aetheric Shield around *Titan* didn't know that. I did everything I could to break out of the collision, to no avail. When I crashed into *Titan*, I can honestly say, I did so unintentionally. Deep down, of course, in the depths of my – what do those psychologist fellows call it? – my *subconscious*, it was a different story, but like I say, the Aetheric Shield – it ain't that subtle, and it ain't that deep.'

CHAPTER TWENTY-ONE

THE TEXIAN

here was a buzzing in the depths of Arabella's utility belt. *Miles's hand!* Hastily she pulled it out, as Ben stopped paddling. From the miniature speaker in the tip of the ring finger, she heard a muffled crackling. She pressed it to her ear. 'My lady...' came a tiny voice, barely discernible above the hiss of static.

Arabella pressed the button at the base of the middle finger. 'Miles, are you all right?'

'Yes, my lady.' He sounded like a small dog yapping in a storm. 'I am most relieved that you are still alive.'

'What is your situation, Miles?'

'I have managed to procure a parachute and have secreted myself within the airship's exoskeleton. I plan to jump as soon as we reach the coast, and will contact you again with my coordinates once I am on the ground. I would be most obliged if you and your companion could collect me.'

'Of course,' said Arabella. 'It's Mr Forrester, by the way.'

'I beg pardon, my lady. It's a little difficult to –'

Ben grabbed the hand. 'Howdy, Miles!' he yelled. 'We'd be delighted to pick you up. It'll be swell to have the old gang back together!'

'That is most gracious of you, Mr Forrester, sir,' said Miles faintly. 'I look forward to renewing our acquaintance.'

Dawn was breaking when Ben and Arabella made landfall. The clouds to the east glowed a vile yellow – like a swarm of sinister jellyfish, thought Arabella. A cold sea with a surface like beaten copper rippled around black rocks covered in seaweed – severed heads, they seemed to her. There was no joy in reaching the shores of her homeland, only trepidation. Was it even her country any more? By now the French fleet would be blasting London from the skies and unleashing their ground forces. Her skin crawled at the thought of those hideous automata sweeping through Pall Mall, Piccadilly, Leicester Square. For all she knew, the British Parliament had already surrendered and the French Tricolour was waving from Buckingham Palace. She tried to push such negative thoughts from her mind as she helped Ben haul the boat through the surf and up onto the beach.

They had landed to the north of the coastal town of Selsey. Miles had contacted them earlier with his landing coordinates at Middleton-on-Sea, ten miles east. Ben was all for hiking there immediately, but Arabella, after a night of being hurled from one life-threatening situation to the next, could go no further. Exhausted and freezing cold, she insisted on the need for rest and some dry clothing.

Ben coaxed her to walk a short way inland to find some shelter. They passed a row of houses, and he stole some sheets and feminine attire from washing-lines in the back gardens – Arabella was too tired to make more than a token protest at this blatant theft. She followed him to a grassy mound, the remains of a Norman castle, near the village of Church Norton. Beneath the mound was an old smugglers' tunnel with a soft, earthen floor. He left her there to change her clothes and make a bed for herself with the sheets. Within minutes of lying down, she was asleep.

Hours later, with the sun pouring through the mouth of the tunnel, Arabella awoke to smells of roasting meat. Her stomach growled, and she realised that she was quite astonishingly hungry. She staggered, blinking, from the tunnel and was confronted by the sight of Ben turning a skinned rabbit on a makeshift spit.

'Ready for some breakfast?' he called out cheerfully.

Soon enough, they were both eating.

'Delicious!' said Arabella between mouthfuls of succulent rabbit flesh. After eating her fill, she rinsed her tin plate in a bowl of water that Ben had fetched from a nearby stream.

'Mr Forrester, I have a question for you. You build air carriages and rocket packs and home-made aetheric shields. You speak French like a native, and provide expert intelligence for the British government. You can trap and skin rabbits and survive for days in the wilderness. Is there *anything* you can't do?'

Ben stirred a pot of black coffee hanging over the fire. 'I'm a lousy piano-player,' he said as he poured the coffee into a tin mug. After taking a sip, his face lit up. 'Yes sir! A mighty fine brew! Here you go, ma'am...' He poured some into a chipped china cup and handed it to her.

The coffee was hot and on the bitter side of lovely, but would certainly do.

'I grew up in a place called San Antonio in Texas,' said Ben. 'Have you heard of Texas, ma'am?'

'I believe it's a country in the southern part of North America.'

'Indeed it is – although I hear that it's recently become incorporated into the United States. Anyways, I lived there with my pa. It was just me and him, my mother having died when I was born. He fixed up steam carriages for a living, and I spent my childhood in his workshop. Spanners and wrenches were my playthings. I could strip an engine and rebuild it before I was ten.' He took a swig of coffee. 'In those days we were ruled by Mexico. Pa tried to steer clear of politics, but then the War of Independence started and he joined a local militia of the Texian Army. Got himself killed in a siege at the Alamo Mission. That was nine years ago.'

'I'm sorry,' said Arabella.

'I had no one to look after me, so I had to learn to fend for myself.' Ben poked at the fire with a stick, lost in reminiscence. 'I turned wild. Learned to trap beaver, raccoon, muskrat. I fished in streams for perch and speckled trout. Made my clothes from animal skins.'

'And how exactly did that lead to a career as a spy based in France?'

'That was an accident. It came about through impressment.'

'Impressment?'

'Yes, ma'am. When I was fourteen, I was drugged and kidnapped by a gang of French air troopers. Forced to join the French Air Fleet... Not an uncommon fate for young drifters like me. You Brits do it, too. How else do you keep replenishing your aircrews for this never-ending war of yours? I swear, a lot of Texian blood has been spilt over the years, fighting this side of the Atlantic.'

'I had no idea,' said Arabella, shocked.

Ben chuckled, as if to say *There's a lot you don't know, Lady Arabella.*

'I escaped as soon as I could,' he said. 'Fell in with a band of anti-Bonapartists in Rouen. I learned French, and pretty soon found myself infiltrating local army bases and sending reports to your superiors in London. Before I knew it, I was Agent Z.'

He seemed amused by her amazement. 'It's not so very different to my life as a wild boy in Texas,' he chuckled. 'You have to think on your feet, stay focused, learn the habits of your prey – French officers in this case, rather than raccoons... The only difference being that if I made a wrong move back in my days as a trapper, the raccoon wouldn't turn around and shoot me.'

By midday they had reached Middleton-on-Sea, where they found Miles sitting on a bale of straw in a cattle shed, his parachute a mess of silk around him. He did not get up when they came in, but merely vented a forlorn sigh of steam from his hat.

'Miles!' cried Arabella warmly, running to him.

'Good to see you, old buddy!' said Ben.

'You have been many hours,' Miles remarked to both of them before returning his attention to his damaged right leg. He'd opened up a panel in the dented limb and was trying, one-handedly, to repair some inner circuitry.

Arabella cast an anxious look at Ben. She'd never seen Miles looking quite so morose.

'Her ladyship needed rest and breakfast after her long night,' explained Ben. 'We humans have to recharge occasionally, you know, Miles.'

'Speaking of recharging,' said the automaton, 'I require some coal dust for my burner. I would be obliged if one of you would go and procure some for me.'

'Certainly,' said Arabella, making her way out of the shed. The farmhouse was sure to have a coal cellar.

'Let's take a look at that leg, Miles,' she heard Ben say.

Then she turned back. 'Miles…' she began.

The logical gentleman looked up, his eyes as innocent as those of the cows patiently watching them. 'Yes, my lady?'

'On *Titan*, just before Mr Forrester arrived, you…'

Miles waited for her to go on, but she found she couldn't. It was too strange even to express it. Automata were becoming more advanced and more complex every year – this she understood. Yet none had, so far as she knew, ever been programmed to speak an untruth. This was a line that ought never to be crossed – the scientists, the Church and the politicians were all agreed on this point. For, once machines had learned to lie – so the argument went – they could no longer be fully trusted, even by their human friends. Once they had learned to lie, and discovered the power this gave them, who was to say they would continue meekly to serve their masters, and not start pursuing their own interests?

'What is it, my lady?'

'Nothing, Miles.'

She turned and left the shed.

The farmer and his wife proved most friendly, inviting Ben and Arabella for lunch and offering their 'little automatic friend' as much coal dust as he desired. While they ate, the farmer switched on his wireless receiver, hoping for news, but none of the regular stations were broadcasting. There was nothing but ominous static on the aetherwaves.

After they had said farewell to their hosts, Arabella, Ben and Miles set out on the road to London.

'I need to reconnect with my colleagues and find out what's going on,' said Arabella as they walked. 'Do either of you have a working aethercell?'

Miles's internal cell had broken during the parachute landing, but Ben had one in his rocket pack that was still functioning.

They found a secluded area behind a hedgerow and, after several minutes of trying, Ben managed to set up a link with London HQ. He passed the headphones to Arabella. At first all she could hear were whistles and crashes.

'Major Stuart!' she cried into the mic. 'This is Arabella! Come in, please!'

Whistle, fizz!

'Major Stuart, do you read me?'

Crash!!

'Auntie!'

'Who is this?' came a man's panicked voice. He could only just be heard above the background of incendiary noises.

Arabella breathed a heavy sigh. 'It's Lady Arabella West of the Sky Sisters. Where is Major Stuart?'

'She's in Hades.'

'Hades?'

'HQ has been evacuated!' bellowed the man. 'Bombs are falling all around us! I'm the last one here, and about to head down there myself. Let me try and patch you through to the major.'

Arabella jammed the headphones to her ears, waiting through the static. Finally she heard her aunt's voice. It was like a cooling rain on her frazzled nerves.

'Arabella? Is that you? This is very good news! I thought you were dead.'

'Auntie! I mean m-ma'am. I'm so pleased to hear you. What's going on? What is Hades? Is London destroyed? Have we surrendered?'

'Please calm down, Arabella. It's not as bad as you fear. We're under heavy bombardment, but we're holding out. The government and the military high command are directing operations from bunkers below ground, as are we. Hades is the code name for our new HQ, behind Charing Cross Underground Station. What is your situation? The trackers lost contact with your transmitter somewhere over the Channel. We all thought you'd drowned.'

'I made it to Sussex, ma'am, thanks to Agent Z. I'm with him and Miles.'

'That's wonderful! The three of you must make your way here as soon as you can and by whatever means you can devise. It may be difficult. All roads to the capital are closed and all transport links suspended. Do you have any other means of travel?'

'Uh…' Arabella eyed Ben's rocket pack. 'There is one possibility that occurs to me, ma'am.'

CHAPTER TWENTY-TWO

THE ATTACK ON LONDON

The invasion force, consisting of 348 battlecruisers of varying classes, appeared over London an hour after dawn on 20 July. The drone of thousands of engines created a gradually thickening wall of sound that no witness on the ground was ever likely to forget. The morning sky dimmed as the enormous fleet cast its shadow over the city, and so densely packed were the incoming craft that it seemed to many that London had acquired a roof.

The bombs began to fall, and for the next day and night the capital suffered an aerial onslaught on a scale unknown in the history of any city. Buildings exploded. Rubble cascaded. People, horses, omnibuses and steam carriages were scorched, burned and buried. The bombs started fires wherever they fell, whipped up by the wind into flames hundreds of feet high. The fires tore through government buildings, transport termini, manufactories, office blocks, shops, churches, schools and hospitals. They devastated neighbourhoods, destroying mansions and slums with equal ferocity.

Army units patrolled the rubble-strewn streets, helping the injured, arresting looters and trying to maintain some semblance of order. And while firefighters did their best to contain the conflagrations, most residents took shelter in the subterranean stations of London's newly built network of underground railways. Families held on to each other on the gloomy, gaslit platforms and children cried as the constant *crump-crump-crump* of heavy bombs shook the earth and sent tunnel dust and soot down on their heads.

The city's defence forces hit back as best they could. Nine- and twelve-pounder anti-airship guns, mounted on armoured steam carriages, fired smoke-trailing incendiaries into the guts of the attacking craft. They could scarcely miss such plump targets. Yet so well protected were the gas envelopes within their iron shells that few were downed.

The Royal Air Fleet had gambled on Operation Zeus, and its failure had left Britain's air defences dangerously weak. The RAF's remaining battlecruisers were scattered in different parts of the country, defending its coastlines, and it would be days before they could be mobilised into a force capable of hitting back against the invaders, by which time it could well be too late. So the RAF's High Command was obliged to turn instead to its tiny, fledgling force of aerial steam carriages to mount an aerial defence of London. Its one and only squadron of fighters was scrambled from its base at Northolt on the edge of the city, but they were too few in number, and the pilots too inexperienced, to make much impact, and they were soon wiped out by the big guns of the French *Volcans*.

The invaders seemed unstoppable, like a force of nature or agents of divine judgement, raining fire and brimstone on the capital. Londoners cowered in their shadow and prayed for them to go away. But this was only the beginning. In the early hours of 21 July, the flagship of the French fleet began to descend…

CHAPTER TWENTY-THREE

THE TAKING OF HYDE PARK

Search beams wandered the night sky – pale blue shafts of light that cut through the blood-coloured smoke. Tracer fire made bright curving lines through the air. The wind carried a stench of burning.

Jacques' right lower leg, where Guizot's knife had stabbed him, seethed with pain beneath its bandages, but he was trying his best to ignore it. His leg was a minor discomfort compared to the hell most people were going through down there. Jacques leaned forward to get a better view of the devastated city as the wind whipped at his clothes and hair. London was wreathed in smoke and stabbed by fires that gleamed like fresh wounds. The Thames was aglow, its ships and bridges burning, its waters lit in lurid colours and frothing like a witch's cauldron.

A projectile from an anti-airship gun whistled as it soared towards *Titan*. It exploded in a blinding flash just yards from where Jacques was standing. He didn't feel a thing. When he opened his eyes, he saw the starburst, with its white-hot centre and bright streamers. It hung motionless in the sky before him like a frozen chandelier. The gondolas of airships much further away were still rocking from its reverberations. A fire had started up in one of them, and crew members were racing to put it out. But *Titan*, safe behind its shield, continued to descend.

Isaac emerged from a doorway in the forecastle. He held on to his battered tricorn as he made his way, falteringly, towards where Jacques was standing. When he reached him, he clasped Jacques by the shoulder. 'What are you doing out here, friend?' he bellowed.

'Witnessing the glory of conquest,' Jacques replied, fairly confident his sarcasm would not be detectable amid all the wind and pyrotechnics.

'We've been given a new assignment,' Isaac roared in his ear. 'When we land, we're to act as the personal bodyguard of the emperor. It's a great horror.'

'*Horror?*' queried Jacques.

Isaac looked at him aghast. 'HONOUR!' he yelled. 'A great HONOUR!' He pulled him away from the railing. 'Come back inside. We have much to discuss.'

Reluctantly, Jacques followed Isaac below decks, limping as he went.

The monster airship, *Titan*, sank steadily towards London, hissing as it jettisoned lift-gas and sucked air into its compensator tanks. Its ninety guns blasted British artillery on both sides as it made its final descent into Hyde Park. The sail-fins were folded neatly into its sides and crew members flung hundreds of sandbags on ropes from the upper deck to secure the ship, as the keel of the galleon-shaped gondola hit the turf. The 900-foot beast landed between the eastern end of the Serpentine lake and Hyde Park Corner, crushing trees, bushes, flowers, benches and a statue of a dead British general.

As soon as it landed, a section of the gondola's tiered, steeply angled stern began to open. With a groan of hydraulics, the hatch door descended to form a gently sloping ramp that rested on the grass, not far from the Serpentine's shore. British cannon continued to pound the ship from all sides, to absolutely no effect. The shield stopped the shells in mid-air while still yards from their target. Thereafter, the shells moved forward as if through dense, invisible oil at about a yard a minute.

Meanwhile, the interior of the gondola began to rumble ominously. The air was suddenly filled with the echoing thunder of hoofbeats as hundreds of horsemen exploded out of the rear of the ship, clattering down the ramp and galloping across the grass.

British troopers watched dumbfounded as the tightly disciplined French *cavaliers* fanned out with perfect uniformity, rounding the lake on both sides and surging across the open spaces to the north. It was hard for witnesses to tell for sure, in a gloom lit only by sporadic bursts of shellfire, but many agreed that there was something slightly inhuman about these mounted troops. Indeed, they seemed almost antlike in their utter sameness, in the way they swarmed across lawns and pathways, engulfing the park in a gleaming black mass. Some began to doubt their own eyesight: was it possible that the French cavalrymen were actually growing out of their own horses?

As the black mass drew closer to the defending troops, the hideous truth of what they were suddenly became clear. With a mix of fear and revulsion, the defenders let fly at the oncoming horde with field guns, mortars and howitzers, but the four-legged iron warriors didn't even break their stride. It was as if the barrage had struck a wall of thick, transparent jelly – not a single shell reached its target. The soldiers could see their projectiles like metal splinters spidering the air around the advancing legions, but never reaching them. The Aetheric Shield! It was not only protecting *Titan*...

Shocked and beginning to panic, the British troops fell back in disarray, but not before the enemy opened fire. The centaurs' handless gun-barrel arms blasted death on all sides. Hundreds of troopers were killed before their commanders were able to sound the retreat.

Jacques watched all of this from *Titan*'s hatchway with growing horror. He was mounted on *Pégase*, his iron steed, alongside his fellow Equestrians. Beside him, Henri fist-pumped the air. 'Go, mecha-swarm! *Vive la France! Vive la Révolution!* Down with the *rosbifs*!'

Metallic hoofbeats sounded behind them. The Equestrians immediately parted as Emperor Napoleon Bonaparte cantered up to join them at the top of the ramp, flanked by Marshal Guizot and Diana Temple. All three were riding iron horses. Jacques had met the emperor on a number of occasions in the course of his duties as an Equestrian, and he felt the usual dizziness, bordering on vertigo, as Bonaparte halted his steed less than two metres from him. It was as if he was breathing not air, but history. So legendary were the man's achievements, it scarcely seemed possible that he was a real human being. Yet here he was, in his eighth decade, still cutting an impressive figure on horseback.

Jacques laughed at himself for being so starstruck. In truth, it would have been better for everyone if Napoleon had died years ago. It would have saved the world a great deal of bloodshed. And how many more litres of blood would be spilt tonight and in the days and weeks to come, to satisfy the cravings of the man's monstrous ego? Wouldn't it be best for someone to kill him now?

Jacques could feel the weight of the gun in his holster. He could reach for it, aim and fire in one quick movement. In two seconds, the emperor would be dead. He might even be able to kill the monster Guizot, too, before the soldiers or crewmen cut him down. It would be a worthy martyrdom. The world would sing praises to his name. So who or what was stopping him?

Marie, that was who.

Foolish Marie, who worshipped the ground Napoleon walked on, would never forgive such an act. It might even drive her mad. And Jacques, who loved his sister with the same unthinking devotion as she lavished on the little general, couldn't bear the thought of that. Guizot had told him that Marie was imprisoned here in Britain, and, even more than he wanted to see Napoleon dead, Jacques wanted to see Marie alive and safe again.

'What I would like to know is how the shield was penetrated by that airman.'

Napoleon addressed this statement to no one in particular. His eyes remained glued to a pair of binoculars as he studied the one-sided battle between his mecha-army and the British.

'It is a mystery, Excellency,' said Guizot. 'We ran tests on that part of the ship later, and the shield was working fine. As you can see, it is impervious to the British artillery.'

'Nevertheless, the incident bothers me,' said Napoleon. 'And also the female spy. How is it that you let her escape?'

Guizot shot a poisonous glance at Isaac. 'That was not my intention, Excellency. Unfortunately, one of my officers saw fit to disobey a direct order to kill her. I will deal with him when this mission is over.'

Napoleon put down his binoculars and turned to Guizot. 'Which officer?'

'Isaac Dreyfus,' said Guizot, pointing a crooked finger at the accused.

Isaac straightened in his saddle as Napoleon fixed him with a dark stare. Jacques was impressed by Isaac's calm demeanour.

'Explain yourself,' Napoleon said to him.

'Sire, the female spy claimed there was another live explosive on board *Titan*, besides the one we had managed to find and defuse. It was my view that we ought to force her to tell us where it was before killing her.'

'It was obvious to me that she was lying to save her skin,' said Guizot, 'and so it proved. There never was a second explosive.'

Napoleon inclined his head. 'No... but there might have been. Dreyfus was doing his duty to protect

Titan, and me. He should not be punished.'

Guizot made a growling noise in his throat, but managed to force a smile. 'Very good, Excellency.'

The mecha-army had driven back the British and secured the southern perimeter of the park. It was now advancing beyond the gates into the streets of Kensington, Knightsbridge and Belgravia. The view to the north was obscured by trees and darkness, but there was no reason to believe the French push hadn't been equally successful there. Overhead, the rest of the fleet continued its bombardment. Explosions shook the ground and air, and lit the night in frequent flashes.

'Nevertheless, Excellency, we must deal with the consequences of the female spy's escape,' said Guizot. 'Diana Temple's status is now compromised. It will inevitably get back to British Intelligence that she is working for us. I suggest that we jettison Mademoiselle Temple immediately.'

Diana glared at the marshal. 'There is no way Arabella survived that fall,' she said.

'I saw a flame from some sort of human fire-arrow,' said Gérard. 'It flew alongside us for a while…'

'Yes,' said Diana. 'And then it fell into the sea. Arabella must have drowned, along with the airman who rescued her.'

Napoleon's mind already seemed to be elsewhere. 'Let us keep her for now, Guizot.' Then his lips curled into a small smile. 'If all goes to plan, I shall have the Phoenix in my hands by the end of this day. It is close. I can almost hear it, can't you? Once I have the Phoenix, the war will be as good as won, and all your petty fears will melt away.'

PART III

21 JULY 1845

CHAPTER TWENTY-FOUR

THE SECOND ROCKET TRIP

As it turned out, Arabella's plan to 'rocket' herself to London was not quite as straightforward as she had initially imagined. For one thing, Ben was 'all out of rocket fuel'. For another, no matter how much she willed it, he wasn't about to 'let her loose on such an expensive, dangerous and cutting-edge piece of tech' without supervision.

'You'll kill yourself,' he predicted solemnly. 'More importantly, you'll damage my rocket – and there's a lot of very pricey kit in there.'

'Well, *you* fly me there, then,' said Arabella, feigning indifference to his callous words.

'And leave Miles behind – again?' She glanced guiltily at Miles. Of course that would be impossible.

'Can't you carry us both?'

Ben shook his head. 'Impossible. The thrust-to-weight ratio will be all wrong.'

In the end their only option was to hike ten miles up the Arun Valley to Ben's 'English residence' near the village of Amberley, where he kept his spare rocket pack and enough fuel to get them to London.

Arabella was quite surprised that Ben *had* an English residence, having assumed he was based permanently in France. For some reason she pictured it as an idyllic cottage nestling at the foot of the South Downs, with a white fence and a climbing rose and perhaps a cat sunning itself on the doorstep.

It turned out to be an abandoned and dilapidated carriage-house at the end of a long, heavily rutted driveway. An encirclement of tall, dense trees obscured any view of the Downs and kept the building in permanent gloomy shadow. Few of its windows contained glass, and the only thing climbing on it was bindweed. There was a cat, at least – a scrawny, half-wild creature that Ben called 'Alamo', which hissed at Arabella as she went to stroke it.

The interior of the carriage-house, lit by cobwebbed gas lamps dangling from the roof beams, was an Aladdin's cave of mechanical wonders. Arabella spotted among the debris of tools, cogs and springs a clockwork spider, a camera disguised as a book, a one-wheeled steam bike, an aethercell hat, a helmet with a propeller and a self-rocking armchair, as well as innumerable absurd-looking gadgets she couldn't begin to put a name to. The only vaguely homely features in the entire place were the camp-bed and stove in one corner.

'Your "English residence" is a workshop,' said Arabella.

Ben acquiesced to this description with a shrug. 'For me it's home,' he said.

It took Ben the rest of the day and most of the following night to get both rocket packs into working order and to lay his hands on enough liquid oxygen and methane to get them to London. As he worked, Arabella went into Amberley and bought some bread, a chicken and some carrots and peas from the village shop. After supper, as Ben went back to work, she settled herself down in the self-rocking chair, with Alamo stretched out on her lap.

'If there is nothing else, my lady, I will power down for the night,' Miles said to her.

'Miles?'

'Yes, my lady.'

'You… um… lied, didn't you? About the second explosive on *Titan*.'

He stared at her, and it was as though a shadow passed across his eyes.

'Don't worry, I'm not cross or anything,' she quickly

added. 'Actually, I'm grateful... and curious. How did you manage it?'

Miles clicked and whirred for a while. Eventually, he said: 'It was where logic led me. My programming demands that I try and protect my human mistress by any means necessary. I explored every possible way of doing so, and deduced that the only pathway left to me, in the circumstances, was to say "a thing that wasn't" – a *lie*, as you humans call it. I do not anticipate this happening again. I realise it is... unorthodox behaviour for an automaton, and I would be grateful if you didn't mention it to Professor Storm, my chief engineer. It is liable to be... misunderstood.'

'Come closer, Miles,' said Arabella quietly.

He trundled towards her. When he was within range of her lips, she leaned forward and planted a kiss on his cheek. 'That's to say thank you,' she whispered. 'And don't worry, your secret is safe with me.'

'Thank you, my lady.'

Arabella closed her eyes. The chair, with its gentle creaking motion, was very relaxing, but her head was too full of thoughts to surrender to sleep. After a time, her eyes opened. Miles stood sentry-like nearby, his eyes dark. She could see shadowy silhouettes of giant cog wheels, brass pipes and pulley systems. In the far corner crouched Ben. He was wearing a pair of goggles as he held a welding torch to a rocket-engine nozzle. Blue-white sparks fountained off the metal, lighting his cheeks.

She thought about the incredible story he'd told her that morning, of growing up wild in the badlands of Texas and then being thrown straight into the Franco-British war at the tender age of fourteen. What a survivor he was! And what an odd life he'd carved out for himself, between tinkering in this isolated workshop and spying in France. He had no friends, so far as she knew, and seemed content with that situation. Yet he'd risked life and limb to rescue her from *Titan*. Why had he done that? He was certainly a puzzle, and an intriguing one. She wondered if she'd ever work him out.

The following morning, Arabella, Ben and Miles went out into the weed-infested forecourt of the carriage-house and Ben strapped the rocket pack to Arabella's back. He showed her how to steer it using body movements, and how to adjust her speed by means of the thrust controller. Then he heaved the other pack onto his shoulders and picked up Miles.

'To London, or bust,' said Ben.

'Godspeed,' said Arabella.

'Taking all factors into consideration, I calculate we have at least a fifteen per cent chance of surviving this journey,' said Miles cheerfully.

Ben frowned at him.

'Those are good odds from Miles,' explained Arabella.

She and Ben closed their helmet visors, pressed the ignition buttons on their belts and shot vertically into the air. Their trajectory gradually tilted during the first few hundred yards of flight until they were moving parallel to the ground. For Arabella, the experience was even more satisfying than her first rocket ride, for this time she was flying solo and was in charge of the controls. As they roared through the sky a hundred feet up, meadows, trees, roads, farms and villages sped by beneath them at an unbelievable speed. Farmers gawped at them from their steam tractors and Arabella waved back merrily. The helmet Ben had given her helped reduce the effects of wind and air resistance, but even so the battering to her head and shoulders was only slightly less violent than the one she'd received near *Titan*'s engines.

In just fifteen minutes they hit the outskirts of London, and farms were replaced by suburban neighbourhoods. Ahead of her Arabella could see a pall of smoke shrouding the city centre. The black shapes of enemy airships lurked within the smog, which occasionally shimmered with silver flashes. The thud of heavy ordnance was like a faint, irregular drumbeat growing steadily louder. Soon they were hurtling over Wimbledon Common and Putney. They swung left over the Thames, following the course of the river as it snaked east, heading ever deeper into the war zone. Arabella's heart wept as she took in the black, smoking shells of houses, churches, high streets and whole neighbourhoods. The smoke stung her throat and eyes as she flew, more slowly now, towards the burning heart of her city. Dimly, through the yellow-brown haze, she glimpsed above her the hulking leviathans wreaking death from the skies. How she longed to get up here in *Prince* and hand them a taste of their own foul medicine!

They flew past the chemical works, the mills, malt houses and foundries of Battersea and Vauxhall. Ahead, through a sickly veil of smoke, she could see the hollowed-out ruin of Westminster Abbey. A smoke-blackened Clock Tower still stood proudly amid the gutted remains of the Houses of Parliament. But, as Arabella watched, it took a direct hit from a *Tirailleur* hovering above its spire. The proud tower crumbled in upon itself and fell with a roaring avalanche of brick and limestone.

'Look out!' cried Ben.

Arabella made a reflexive dart to her left just as a projectile from a nearby *Tornade* whistled close. It exploded like a thunderclap behind her, sending her somersaulting through the sky.

Despite her best efforts to stabilise herself, she continued spinning, the ground veering closer with every rotation of her body. Then she felt Ben's hand on her arm, and the spinning stopped. The sky was no longer beneath her, the streets no longer above.

'Thank you,' she said, and couldn't help adding: 'I never knew you cared!'

'Just looking after my equipment,' he said coolly. 'Perhaps it's time we landed. It's not very safe up here.'

Arabella scouted the scene below and spotted a cobbled square and an underground railway entrance. Above it hung a familiar sign. 'There's Charing Cross underground station,' she said.

They sank gently to the square, their flame-tails dwindling and vanishing as they landed. There was no one about, but sounds of war filled the air. As well as the thudding of bombs, they could hear blasts of artillery fire and volley guns on streets not far away. Arabella feared that a ground war might already have started.

Ben looked at the bland station entrance. 'The British Imperial Secret Service is in *there*?' he said dubiously.

'Come on!' said Arabella, running into the station ticket hall.

The hall was deserted, the turnstiles all open. There was no one selling tickets in the booth. From below, they could hear the muffled sounds of large numbers of people.

'What now?' asked Ben.

'We go down to the platform,' said Arabella.

The westbound platform of the Metropolitan District Railway was a pitiful sight. People were huddled together in their hundreds, pale and dirty, both on the platform and down between the tracks. There were so many crammed down there, it made her shiver. Arabella was a girl of space and light – she loved nothing better than an empty, sunlit sky. This place was the very opposite of that.

There were some sad, frightened souls, but others who were laughing and cracking jokes. They'd lost their homes, some had lost loved ones, and no one had any idea what the future held. They didn't even know if their city would still be British when they finally resurfaced. Yet they laughed. She found that inspiring, and it gave her hope.

A woman with a trolley was serving hot beverages and snacks. There were nurses offering medical checks, and uniformed employees of the MDR dispensing advice. Arabella approached one of the men in uniform. 'We are ready, Mr Charon.' Emmeline had given her this phrase at the close of their aethercell conversation.

The man looked at her, startled. '*What* did you say?'

She repeated the sentence.

He looked her up and down, and then noticed her companions. He gave a start when he saw Miles, but quickly calmed down.

'Follow me,' said the man, and he led them down a short corridor to the eastbound platform, similarly crowded with refugees of the bombing. At the end of the platform was a longer corridor leading to the platforms of the Baker Street and Waterloo Railway. Before they reached the steps that would take them down to those platforms, they came to a plain door set into the wall. The man extracted a set of keys from his pocket and fiddled with them until he found the one he was looking for. He waited for a group of people to drift past, then inserted the key in the lock and opened the door. 'You'll find the place you're looking for down there,' said the man, nudging them forward into another, much darker corridor. As they moved into the passage, the door closed and locked behind them.

The corridor ended in a door. In the light cast by Miles's eyes, it looked like a very sturdy slab of steel. Arabella pressed a button in its centre and a speaker crackled to life. 'Identify yourself,' said a voice.

'Lady Arabella West,' said Arabella.

There was a pause.

'Is Miles with you?'

'Yes.'

'Miles, can you confirm?'

Miles said: 'I am with Lady Arabella and Ben Forrester, an American citizen with full security clearance.'

After another, longer pause the door hissed and slid slowly open. The door, like the wall it disappeared into, was more than a foot thick.

The room on the far side was brightly lit and very white. It hummed with the sound of hard-working analytical engines. A portly, grey-haired man in glasses rose from his desk to greet them.

'Albert!' said Arabella warmly.

'Lady Arabella! You made it! Can't have been easy. Welcome to Hades! And Miles, too!' He turned to Ben. 'Pleased to meet you, sir.'

'And you, Albert,' said Ben.

Albert turned to Arabella. 'You'll find Major Stuart, Cassie and Beatrice in the Lab. Just go through there and follow the signs. They'll be thrilled to see you.'

'Thank you, Albert.'

The three of them headed through the doorway Albert had indicated. Yet more corridors awaited them – a whole warren of them. There were signs to CODE-BREAKING, COMMUNICATIONS, COUNTER-ESPIONAGE, DORMITORIES, FIELD OPS, FLYING CORPS, INTELLIGENCE GATHERING, LAB, RECREATION ZONE, REFECTORY, TOILETS and TRAINING.

'It's like a duplicate of our old HQ at Millbank House,' gasped Arabella. 'All the same departments.'

'An alternative HQ inside a bomb-proof underground bunker,' nodded Ben. 'Mighty sensible, if you ask me.'

'I understand they have enough supplies down here to sustain them for more than twelve months,' said Miles.

This gave Arabella hope. Napoleon could do his worst above ground – the British would hold out down here.

CHAPTER TWENTY-FIVE

THE LAB

The Lab was the department dedicated to trying out new spy weapons and gadgets. As they entered, they were hit by strong smells of burned rubber, gunpowder and sweet doughnuts. The room was busy with technicians in white coats at work stations, tinkering with and testing new devices. Ben's jaw dropped at the sight of so much fascinating technology on display. They watched as a female technician fired a gun and the muzzle ejected a thin stream of yellow sticky stuff, which coated a dummy figure standing a dozen yards from her. One of her colleagues pressed a button and a paperweight on a desk exploded. Another twisted the top of a fountain pen and a dart flew out, embedding itself in a cork target.

Arabella advanced cautiously into the room, refraining from touching anything for fear it might blow up or shoot a missile. She heard a buzzing sound above her head and had to duck as a miniature aerial steam carriage, not much bigger than a paper dart, missed her by inches before crash-landing into a work station.

'Sorry! Sorry!' cried a loud voice. 'We're still fine-tuning the, er, dihedral angles on the wings!'

Professor Brayden Storm, clutching a bulky aetherwave transmitter with a long aerial, came charging towards them from the far side of the room. The professor's stained white coat flapped wildly as he ran. His hair stood straight up from his forehead like a cliff of dense black curls.

'Lady Arabella!' he said breathlessly, when he reached them. 'How stupendous!' Then his face crinkled in paternal pride when he caught sight of Miles. 'I see you've got yourself into a few scrapes, dear boy.' He wiped a tear from his deep brown cheek.

'I am in need of one or two repairs, Professor,' said Miles.

'Yes, yes, of course, of course. We'll see to you in a minute.' He turned to Arabella and muttered under his breath: 'Tell me, my dear, has he been, er, behaving himself?'

She glanced at Miles. 'He's been perfect, as usual,' she said with a wry smile.

'Ah, good, good!' The professor took a doughnut

from his pocket and bit into it. Then he noticed Ben, who was examining the crashed air carriage, and his bushy eyebrows shot up. 'Young man, do you mind?' he bellowed, powdering everyone near him with sugar. 'That's highly classified, er –'

'It's the elevators on your horizontal stabiliser, Professor,' said Ben, pointing to the flaps on the tail section. 'You'll need greater variation on the angle of attack if you want to achieve more lift.'

Professor Storm ran a sticky hand across his cliff of hair. 'Is that so? Let me take a look. An aeronautical fellow, are you?'

'Well, I do like to dabble…'

The two of them were soon lost in discussion over the aerodynamics of the little air carriage.

'Bella!'

She turned to see Cassie approaching from another part of the Lab, with Emmeline and Beatrice close on her heels. She felt a warm thrill of pleasure on seeing Cassie again, and a flicker of guilt that she could ever have suspected her of being the spy.

Cassie embraced her. 'What happened to you, Bella? Tell me you didn't run away on purpose as Beatrice keeps saying. Tell me you got lost or – or kidnapped.'

Arabella saw the tears welling in her friend's eyes and wished she could be the simple, obedient girl Cassie so wanted her to be.

'She lost herself on purpose,' said Beatrice.

'No,' insisted Cassie, 'there has to be another explanation.'

'I'm inclined to agree with Beatrice,' said Emmeline, looking sternly at Arabella. 'First you fail to follow us back to *Kraken*, then our trackers pick up your signal aboard *Titan*. Now unless you're planning to tell us you were press-ganged onto the French flagship, I think the only possible explanation is that you and Miles purposely sneaked aboard.'

Arabella nodded meekly. 'You are correct, ma'am.'

'Oh, Bella,' murmured Cassie.

'I thought as much,' said Emmeline. Then her stern expression faded. 'I must apologise, Arabella. You were right, and I was wrong. *Titan* did already have her shield. Even so, I'm disappointed that you felt the need to go behind my back like that. Why couldn't you at least have tried to persuade me of your view instead of embarking on yet another reckless solo mission?'

'I *did* try,' said Arabella, feeling her face start to burn. 'I told you twice that I believed *Titan* was already shielded, and both times you refused to believe me. Worse, you even began to suspect my loyalty. I didn't feel I had any choice in the end but to act alone.'

Emmeline bowed her head. 'For that I can only apologise,' she said. 'I admit I can be a little... single-minded at times. However, I had been given one very clear instruction before we set out and that was to destroy the ASG, and all I seemed to be getting from you was objections. As it turned out, the destruction of the ASG proved insufficient to thwart the invasion. Nevertheless, its loss will, I'm sure, prove a significant setback for the French, and our mission was worthwhile for that reason alone... I take it that your plan in boarding *Titan* was to destroy it from within?'

Arabella nodded.

'Well, clearly you failed, because *Titan* is here in London... Did you discover anything of use while you were aboard?'

'Yes, I...' Arabella hesitated. She glanced at Cassie and Beatrice.

'You can say whatever you like in front of these two,' said Emmeline.

'Diana was on board,' said Arabella, her lips suddenly very dry. 'She's a traitor. She's working for the French.'

Emmeline nodded.

Arabella couldn't believe how coolly she took this news. Had she already suspected Diana?

Beatrice was outwardly calm, but her jaw muscles were working hard. Cassie looked horrified. 'I don't believe it,' she muttered. 'Diana!'

'Thank you,' said Emmeline. 'Did you discover anything else?'

'Napoleon was also on board. I heard him mention something called the Phoenix. At first I thought it was the code name for the invasion, but then he said it would soon be in his grasp, as if it was some sort of object.'

Emmeline frowned. 'The Phoenix. I can't imagine what that might be. However, I shall pass this information on to my seniors. Thank you, Arabella. That was good work!'

'One other thing, ma'am,' said Arabella. 'I saw an automaton army on *Titan*.'

'Yes, we know about that,' said Emmeline. 'Our troops are fighting them right now for control of the streets. They seem to be shielded, just like *Titan*, which is making things a great deal harder. We assume they acquired their shields at the same time as the flagship.'

'I'm afraid it's worse than that,' said Arabella.

'What do you mean?'

'There's a second ASG on board *Titan*. That's what supplied them with their shield.'

'A second ASG...' Emmeline's voice turned brittle. The colour vanished from her face. 'Oh my, our enemies *have* been busy. I suppose this makes our little operation in Granville appear somewhat pointless after all.'

'You weren't to know, ma'am,' said Cassie.

'No...' For a few seconds, Emmeline seemed lost for words. Then she turned back to Arabella: 'Well, this puts a new complexion on things. It means that our current project is more urgent than ever.'

'And what is our current project?'

'We're looking at ways of penetrating the Aetheric Shield so we can destroy *Titan* and fight back against these automata.'

'Maybe I can help with that,' said Arabella. 'Or rather, maybe *he* can.' She pointed at Ben, who was still engrossed in conversation with Professor Storm.

Emmeline looked, then stared. 'Oh my word, is that…?'

'Agent Z,' Arabella finished for her. 'Have you not met him before, ma'am?'

'He's a lot younger than I imagined.'

The three women fastened their eyes on Ben.

'You know Agent Z?' whispered Cassie. 'I want to hear all about this, Bella. How did you meet?'

'None of that is relevant now,' said Emmeline, and she strode over and interposed herself between Professor Storm and Ben. 'Mr Jefferson Blakewood,' she said. 'I assume that's your name.'

'One of them,' said Ben. 'Though I currently go by the name of Ben Forrester.'

'I am Major Emmeline Stuart.'

'Truly honoured to finally meet you, Major.' He bowed his head.

'Likewise,' said Emmeline. 'And thank you, by the way, for helping our agent, Lady Arabella, defeat the sky pirates of Taranis.'

'It was a pleasure,' said Ben, bowing once again.

'And also for agreeing, belatedly, to hand over the formula for the Aetheric Shield Generator after you'd stolen it from the aforementioned agent.'

Ben was in the process of bowing for a third time, when he froze.

'What did you say?' Ice seemed to form over his words as he uttered them.

Emmeline didn't appear at all flustered by Ben's change of demeanour. 'I wanted to thank you for giving us the formula for the ASG.'

'I did no such thing,' said Ben. 'I would *never* do such a thing. Don't tell me you Brits have it now, too? Who the hell gave it to you?'

'Why, Miles, of course,' broke in Professor Storm. 'He gave us the formula three days ago on his return from Taranis, and we've worked round the clock to build a scale model of it here in the Lab.' He pointed to a roped-off section where a small ASG, about the size of a steamer trunk, was currently running.

When Ben saw this, his fists clenched and his shoulders hunched up like a bear about to go on the rampage.

'Miles!' he growled. 'What did we talk about? What did you swear to keep secret?'

All eyes now turned to the automaton. A cloud of steam spurted from his hat, but apart from that Miles remained still and quiet.

'I'm waiting, Miles,' said Ben.

'Mr Forrester,' said Miles, 'may I remind you, sir, that I am the Logical *Englishman*. Loyalty to my country is deeply embedded within my programming. My country needed the Aetheric Shield Generator. You had the formula but were not willing to pass it on. Logic dictated that I could obtain the formula by offering to help you build the ASG, while swearing that I would keep the formula a secret.'

'You double-crossing rat!' fumed Ben. 'What of decency? What of honour? Aren't those supposed to be English virtues? Didn't they build any of that into your precious programming?'

'Fine words, Mr Forrester,' said Emmeline, 'from a man who tricked my agent into stealing the formula, only to snatch it from her straight afterwards. How exactly was that decent or honourable behaviour?'

Ben was momentarily lost for words.

'We would all like to be honourable,' continued Emmeline. 'But in the end we are spies, and spying is not an honourable profession. We lie and steal for our country, if we have to. Miles did the right thing, and for that I congratulate him.'

'Yes, but I never thought he *could* lie,' spluttered Professor Storm. 'It's not in his programming.'

'You made me logical, Professor,' said Miles. 'And you made me patriotic. These are what led me to say the thing that wasn't – to lie to Mr Forrester when I swore to him I wouldn't pass on the formula. You didn't program me to lie. I had to invent lying for myself in order to do my duty.'

'Fascinating!' breathed the professor. 'Yet also a little worrying.'

'Miles's lie has helped restore the balance of power between Britain and France,' said Emmeline. 'I would hardly call that worrying.'

'Oh, I would,' grumbled Ben. 'A dangerous technology has now spread to a second superpower. My country has only just won its independence from Mexico. How long before you Brits start threatening it again?'

'You have the formula, Mr Forrester,' said Emmeline. 'And your country has hitched itself to the USA, which has plenty of gold, so I hear. Why not build one yourself if you're that worried? Alternatively, perhaps you'd care to help us figure out a way of defeating it, so none of us ever have to worry about this technology again. I understand from Lady Arabella that you have discovered a method.'

Ben nodded. 'I guess that would be the best way in the end,' he said in a more conciliatory tone. 'But I ain't too sure my method is practical. I mean, it's psychological, and it involves flying directly at the shielded object. I can't imagine how it would work using a missile.'

'But you're willing to give it a try?' said Emmeline.

Ben shrugged and sighed. 'I am.'

'Thank you, my boy,' said the professor warmly, leading Ben over to the ASG.

Arabella smiled, relieved that Ben had been won over. Now she started wondering what she could do to help the war effort.

She didn't have long to wait.

'Arabella, Cassie, Beatrice,' called Emmeline. 'You three must take to the air immediately.'

'What is our mission?' asked Cassie.

'To shoot down as many French warcraft as you possibly can!'

CHAPTER TWENTY-SIX

THE DOGFIGHT

'All ready for you, ma'am,' said the engineer, with a nod towards *Comanche Prince*. He wiped his hands on an oily cloth and checked off the items on his clipboard. 'Engine, steam condenser, air intake, cowlings, access panels, propeller blades, bracing wires, struts, control surfaces, vents, shock absorbers, tyres, brakes, aetherwave aerial, gimplets and the Jennings magnetic steam cannon. They're all in perfect working order. And I've filled you up with enough coal dust for an hour's flight.'

'Thank you,' said Arabella as she ran her fingers over *Prince*'s immaculate red gloss.

They were standing at the start of a 300-yard underground runway located down a corridor from the Lab. Alongside *Comanche Prince* were Cassie's green Steam Glider, *Sultan of Mandara*, and Beatrice's newly repaired blue Double-Wing, *Rani of the Madurai*. Cassie and Beatrice were already seated in their cockpits, propeller blades spinning. At the far end of the runway a huge hydraulic door was grinding open and smoke and daylight were flooding in, along with sounds of distant explosions. A monstrous roar echoed around the hangar as Cassie opened up *Sultan*'s throttle.

Arabella hopped up onto *Prince*'s wing and climbed into the cockpit, instantly feeling at home in the snug seat surrounded by familiar controls. The engineer gave her propeller a spin and the engine coughed into life. Cassie was first off, quickly picking up speed as she tore along the concrete tunnel, becoming smaller and smaller until she finally disappeared up a ramp into the bright rectangle of sun. Beatrice followed her, wobbling slightly as she accelerated, almost scraping a wingtip against the tunnel wall. Once she was safely airborne, it was Arabella's turn. Excited to finally get a chance to engage in some aerial combat with the enemy, she thundered down the tunnel at breakneck pace and flashed into the sunshine, a scarlet arrow.

Prince rose high above the river into a smoke-filled sky studded with sleek grey shapes like basking whales. The whistle and thud of incendiaries was in Arabella's ears as she climbed to two thousand feet. Beneath her, the city was a hellish mosaic of fires and charred buildings. Only one sight cheered her: a fallen

French warcraft, a *Tornade*, presumably downed by ground-based anti-airship fire. It was big enough to fill a whole street, and people were swarming over its surface like ants over the corpse of a beetle.

Above, the enemy ships loomed close. She could see the snouts of their cannon and the little black cylinders of death spilling from their gondola bomb-bays. The giant sky-beasts might be hard to miss, but they were also lethally equipped with their own defensive weaponry. They could sustain any number of strikes to their armoured carapaces and survive, but just one direct hit from a *Volcan*'s *Téméraire*- or *Centaure*-class cannon would blow an air carriage right out of the sky. On her port side, Arabella caught sight of Cassie engaging with a hundred-foot, wind-powered *Poignard*. Just beyond her, Beatrice was challenging a larger *Dessalines*-class vessel. They were buzzing around the battlecruisers like insects, constantly changing direction – soaring and diving, pitching and rolling – trying to present as slippery a target as possible as they unleashed their shells at the metal-plated hulls of the enemy.

Arabella set her sights on a *Tirailleur*, steaming away from her at about half a mile's distance. The 210-foot monster would be a prize indeed! She felt like a baby dolphin hunting a shark as she accelerated towards the elegant and sinister warcraft. It was a Mark IV *Tirailleur*, with gondola and gas envelope fused into one sleek, ironclad vessel – a true battleship of the air! She approached from below – always the safest option with a *Tirailleur*, whose most effective weapons, its four rotating Michaux guns, were situated on the upper deck.

The ship's ANODE detectors must have spotted the danger: already she could see its lower-deck Minion guns swivelling towards her. At a range of two hundred and fifty yards, Arabella fired a short burst from her steam cannons. At the same time the airship's guns crackled and little explosions peppered the air around her. The gunners were shooting hurriedly, and wide. Minions were designed to repel boarding parties and were not accurate at range. Arabella's volley was similarly ineffective, ricocheting harmlessly off the ship's darkly glinting armour. She would have to get in closer, and put herself at greater risk, to have any chance of causing real damage.

The gas envelope was too well protected to be pierced by her steam guns. Her best hope of crippling or destroying the vessel would be to use her gimplet. This was a small rocket with an explosive tip, launched from beneath *Prince*'s fuselage. The gimplet's magnetic casing would ensure that it stuck fast to the *Tirailleur*'s iron hull, and it certainly packed enough incendiary power to rip through the plating. The *Tirailleur*'s thinnest armour, and therefore the best place to aim the gimplet, was along the ship's upper flanks. Unfortunately, that would also put Arabella within range of the mighty Michaux guns.

And there was more bad news: the gimplet's rocket was notoriously inaccurate. To be sure of hitting the target she'd need to come in very close, so even if she evaded the guns, she might well be destroyed in the resulting explosion. Fortunately, the gimplet was not designed to detonate on impact, but by means of a fifteen-second clockwork fuse, hopefully giving her time to flee.

Arabella flew to a safer distance, then executed an extended half-loop, taking her high above the *Tirailleur*. She approached the airship in a 'falling leaf' manoeuvre, using delicate rudder control to side-slip one way, then the other, presenting a dodging, weaving target to the gunners. The Michaux guns were rotating into position, lining her up in their sights. As she came to within five hundred yards, she gave the upper decks a burst of steam cannon and watched in satisfaction as the shells hit home, smashing the rigging, snapping a mast, shattering a conning tower. Tiny figures on deck scampered for shelter. By now within two hundred yards, she moved her finger towards the gimplet launcher. The thinnest armour-plating, just below the guns, was in her sights. She would have to move like lightning once she'd fired.

She was about to press the launch button when there came a double boom from the *Tirailleur* and a blast of smoke from the big guns. Arabella banked steeply. An ear-splitting explosion just beneath her shook *Prince* from propeller boss to tail fin. The ribs in his fuselage and wings creaked alarmingly, as if the whole structure had been warped out of shape. The second explosion, near her starboard wing, jolted her so much, her head collided with the canopy window.

Dazed, she sensed that *Prince* was spinning out of control. The inclinometer, which showed the angle of the wings, was seesawing from one side to the other, and the needle of her compass was swinging wildly. *Prince* spun into a grey, wet cloud. It probably saved Arabella's life, obscuring *Prince* from the airship's gunners just as they had him in their sights. Arabella shook her head to clear it and tried to coax *Prince* back onto an even keel. Her starboard engine had been damaged by the blast and had cut out, causing the spin. She switched off the port engine. This brought the air carriage under control, but left her with only the centrifugal propeller engine keeping her airborne.

She emerged from the cloud more determined than ever to destroy the *Tirailleur*. This time she approached the stern of the vessel, just behind its rear gun battery, hoping to launch the gimplet before they spotted her and rotated the big guns into position. Arabella opted for the direct approach this time – no falling leaves, just all-out speed. She urged the now single-engined *Prince* faster, and her ears were filled with the shriek of the propeller and the howl of the wind. At less than two hundred yards, she spotted the tiny figure of a man on the upper deck, peeping from behind the remains of a conning tower, pointing a volley-gun at her. The gun crackled before she could take avoiding action, and several bullets ripped into her engine cowling with vicious thuds. The engine screamed its pain, and black smoke began pouring from it. Alarmed, Arabella dived. The dive became an inverted loop as she pulled *Prince* level just beneath the *Tirailleur*'s stern. She was close enough to see the ANODE aerials and the rivets on the iron plating.

Prince was leaking strength, but she forced him into a steep ascent on the far side of the vessel. Flying upside down now, she spied the lone gunner with his back to her. He was leaning over the gun-deck railing, trying to catch sight of her below. She fired her steam-cannon and blew him over the side. A second later, with the deck just tens of yards from her propeller, she unleashed the gimplet, and heard the rocket's roar beneath her. Without even checking to see if it had hit its target, she pressed down hard on her aileron pedal, corkscrewing her way to safety.

As she flew on a shallow descent, Arabella counted to fifteen in her head. At the end, she waited.

Nothing.

Then… *BOOM!!!!*

The sky turned a deep pink around her and the shockwave, like a solid fist of air, struck *Prince*, sending him bouncing and yawing around the sky. Arabella, grappling with the controls, twisted to look and saw the *Tirailleur* enveloped in black smoke and tangerine flames, plummeting earthwards. The gimplet must have found its mark and pierced the hydrogen-filled gas envelope. She shuddered inside – a strange mixture of intense happiness and giddy horror. She remembered her father's words about war: *Sometimes glorious, often sad, always horrible.*

Prince's one remaining engine was rattling and juddering unhealthily. Arabella would have to put down very soon, or crash. She had lost her bearings – easily done when her home city lay under a blanket of ash and smoke – and had no idea where the underground runway was, or if she could even make it back there. But she could discern the gleaming snake of the Thames through the haze, and it gave her an idea.

Arabella had never tried landing on water before, but she remembered her father telling her about the time he was once forced to ditch his air carriage in a lake in Brittany. Could she do the same in the Thames? *Slow down*, was the first thing he'd said. She circled into the wind and extended her wing flaps to reduce her speed.

If there's time, Lord Alfred had advised, *burn as much fuel as possible to reduce your weight and increase your buoyancy.* Not a chance! Already she could see a *Poignard* heading ponderously towards her from the southeast. Time was not a luxury she possessed.

As she began her search for a clear stretch of river to land in, a dreadful thing happened: the engine gave a final dying cough and cut out. The propeller stopped turning, and suddenly all she could hear was the whistle of the wind in her wires as she began plunging towards the ground.

Only it wasn't quite a plunge yet. She had just enough momentum to glide, but her choice of landing zones was now limited to whatever patch of river *Prince* could reach from here.

Down and down she fell. Buildings and bomb sites became bigger, more real and solid. Pungent smells of smoke and charred timber filled the cockpit. Her flaps were extended to maximum, but she was coming in fast – too fast? *Both wings must be level with the water*, her father had advised. *The tail should be lower than normal. The nose should be at twelve degrees, higher than for a normal runway landing.* She applied pressure to ailerons and elevator to try and achieve the necessary position, conscious that she would only get one chance at this.

She was coming in now, and everything would have been just about OK – except for a bridge. The bridge was on a bend in the river, and the stretch of river she was aiming for lay just beyond it. She could clear the bridge, just, but there was a line of British armoured gun chariots slowly crossing it. If she'd had a working engine she'd have climbed a few yards to clear the tops of the vehicles. As things stood, it was going to be close – very close!

As she approached she could see soldiers waving frantically at her from the turrets of the AGCs, yelling at her to climb.

'Get down!' she screamed at them.

At the last second, they did. She had to bank slightly to negotiate the bend in the river. As she zoomed over their heads, she felt a dull clunk beneath her starboard wing. Its tip, she guessed, must have skidded off the top of a gun turret. She straightened out to get her wings level for landing. The next second, there was a violent bump and a splash and she was planing along the river, sending up huge curtains of spray on both sides, bouncing along and skimming the surface like a pebble. Gradually *Prince* slowed and drew to a halt near the northern bank. A perfect water landing! Her father would have been proud of her.

CHAPTER TWENTY-SEVEN

THE CENTAURS

rabella soon began to recognise her surroundings: on the opposite bank was Whitehall Gardens, near Charing Cross station. By complete chance she had landed very close to her launching place: just a hundred yards to the north was the 'mouth of Hades', where the underground runway opened to the sky.

Before too long a couple of tugboats headed out from a jetty near the runway's ramp to tow *Prince* back to base. Arabella climbed out onto the wing and leapt aboard one of them.

'I saw what you did up there, m'lady,' said the tug's pilot, 'bringin' down that big Frenchie airboat. It was one of the most spectacular and stirrin' sights I ever saw. Thank you for makin' my day!'

'It was a pleasure, sir,' replied Arabella. 'Just doing my bit.'

'You've given us hope, m'lady,' said the pilot, as he steered for shore.

A massive *boom* sounded on the far side of the river and a jet of water and steam shot fifty feet into the air. *Another bomb!* Waves radiating from the explosion rocked the little tugboat. The pilot muttered a curse. 'Hope is really what we need right now,' he added.

Emmeline met Arabella on the jetty. Next to her was Miles, whose eye-lights seemed to be glowing with a little more vitality than they had of late. The dents to his body had been repaired, and attached to his feet were two brand-new caterpillar tracks.

'Welcome back, my lady,' he bowed.

Emmeline seemed tense. 'Beatrice just called,' she said. 'She was forced down in St James's Park after a tussle with a *Dessalines*. I understand Napoleon is currently on the march in that vicinity. I want you and Miles to get yourselves over there with all speed and link up with her. Then the three of you must follow Napoleon and see what he's up to. It could have something to do with this "Phoenix" thing you mentioned. But take care, will you? It's dangerous out there.'

'I will, ma'am,' said Arabella. 'Any news of Cassie?'

Emmeline paused. 'Nothing as yet.'

Arabella didn't want to imagine what might have prompted that pause.

Her aunt turned to leave, then stopped as if remembering something. 'By the way, well done on bringing down that *Tirailleur*,' she said. 'You've improved morale immensely.'

'Thank you, ma'am.'

Arabella and Miles moved stealthily through the cratered, debris-filled streets of Whitehall. The area had been so heavily bombed, it was no longer recognisable. This had been the administrative heart of the British Empire. Arabella recalled it only days ago as a place of sturdy, granite edifices that seemed as robust and eternal as mountains. Now it was a shattered landscape of blackened, broken stone and glass. A shard-like outcrop was all that survived of a wall; a dust-coated wheel, the sole remnant of a horse-drawn cabriolet; a dented hat, the only remaining evidence of a man. It was a landscape that belonged to the end of times – the apocalypse – when civilisation would give place to savagery. It was impossible to imagine it rebuilt.

The sky raiders had moved on to other parts of the city, fresher targets. Between the ground-shuddering whumps of distant explosions, all that could be heard in these once-vibrant streets was the low moan of the wind. It was a strange and horrible sound, so alien to this city. Arabella wished she could block her ears from it, yet its mournful song seemed to tell her something – something desperately sad. She stopped walking.

'Miles,' she said, 'what happened to Cassie?'

Miles, who was using his tracks to negotiate his way over some rubble, stopped and turned. 'I cannot say, my lady.'

'You cannot, or you *will* not?'

'I am bound to secrecy.'

Arabella felt a tremor beginning deep inside. She went closer to him and dropped into a crouch so she was staring directly into his eyes. 'Miles,' she said, 'I think Emmeline bound you to secrecy because she was worried that the truth might upset me. She wants to keep me focused on the mission and she thinks I won't be if I'm sad. But, you see, I can't possibly focus on the mission if I don't know what has happened to my best friend. If Cassie is dead, you must tell me. I promise I won't have a breakdown or anything. I know I must keep going, no matter what, and I will. But I'm not taking another step until I know the truth.'

Miles vibrated uncomfortably. He gushed a hesitant cloud of steam. 'My lady, you make things difficult for me. Human affairs can be... complicated. First I learned that it is sometimes necessary to lie, and now...'

'You broke your promise to Mr Forrester, remember? You've done this before.'

'There was a clear need in that case. I did it for my country.'

'And you will do this for your mistress… and your friend.'

Miles emitted a soft clicking sound, which Arabella recognised as a sigh. 'Cassie's Steam Glider was hit during a skirmish with a *Poignard*,' he said. 'It was last spotted spiralling to the ground, trailing smoke from one wing. It seemed out of control.'

'Did anyone see a parachute?'

The automaton fell silent.

'Did she bale out, Miles?'

'I don't think so, my lady.'

Arabella bit her lip – hard – until she tasted blood.

'Come on,' she said, her voice harsh in her ears. 'Let's go.'

They found Beatrice standing by the lake in St James's Park. She'd taxied *Rani* beneath a large willow tree to keep her out of sight of enemy airships.

'I damaged the *Dessalines*,' Beatrice said when she saw them. 'Partially deflated it – forced it back to France. I doubt it'll make it.'

'Nice work,' responded Arabella, barely aware of what she was saying.

'I saw you take down that *Tirailleur*. It crashed in Lincoln's Inn Fields.'

Arabella stared at her. 'Did anyone die on the ground?'

'Don't know,' shrugged Beatrice, and she stared out across the algae-covered lake. 'We didn't make much impact,' she muttered. 'There were too few of us. We need eighty or a hundred air carriages with guns and gimplets. That would –'

Beatrice broke off. The ground beneath them was trembling with a rhythmic thudding, as of hundreds of hoofbeats in perfect step. The ominous sound was getting louder and more insistent with every second.

'Centaurs,' said Beatrice.

'What?' said Arabella, feeling as though she was waking from a dream.

'Quick! We have to hide.' Beatrice grabbed Arabella by the arm and pulled her under the willow tree.

Miles trundled after them and joined the two women beneath *Rani*'s fuselage.

Centaurs! Arabella recalled the horrid things she'd seen on *Titan*, with black holes for eyes and guns for hands... The world was swiftly turning into a nightmare. Perhaps it was better that dear, sweet Cassie would not be around to witness it.

She crawled forward and peered through the curtain of overhanging willow branches. Her breath grew sharper as she saw a dense blackness emerging from the trees at the northern edges of the park. The lawns and pathways were being consumed by this deep, unfolding shadow. The thudding of thousands of hooves was like hammers in her head.

As the shadow drew closer, she started to make out

individual galloping figures: brutal metal automata, part man, part horse.

'I don't think they're coming this way,' murmured Beatrice.

Arabella began to breathe more normally when she saw that Beatrice was right. The centaurs were progressing along the Mall – the traditional ceremonial route used for state occasions. But there were so many of them, some had spilled into the park that bordered it.

As she watched, a battalion of British infantry and armoured gun chariots broke through the trees from the east.

"They are attempting to prevent an attack on Horse Guards Parade and Army Headquarters,' said Miles. 'It is futile. More soldiers will die. Yet I understand that it is necessary. Surrender will send out the wrong message to the people.'

The infantry formed into a thick red wall in front of the trees. They discharged their volley-guns into the centaurs' right flank. Behind them the line of chariots fired their large-calibre guns at the same targets. Arabella looked on in stupefied fascination and dismay as the rounds and shells snagged in the invisible, syrupy wall surrounding the enemy. A column of centaurs broke away from the main body to confront their attackers. They raised their arms and blasted the British lines, cutting them down as casually as a child's hand knocking over a row of tin soldiers. The surviving infantry fell back, but the gun chariots stood firm, firing again and again on the advancing centaurs – to no effect. The centaurs' return fire on the gun chariots' steel plating appeared similarly ineffective.

When the two forces were just a hundred yards apart, the centaur hordes halted. Their front ranks parted and a very strange-looking machine rolled forward into the open space between the armies. At least twice the size of the other automata, it looked like the upper part of an elephant, but instead of legs its body was supported on four wheels. Its mighty trunk pointed straight out in front like a big gun. Arabella noticed that a fuse had been lit above the elephant's ear. She could see it sparkling its way towards the rear of the trunk, and she cringed at the thought of what would follow. The sparkling stopped and there was an eerie hush. Then, *BAM!* – a huge cloud of smoke and flame erupted from the trunk's muzzle. The elephant rocked back on its wheels, and the nearest gun chariot exploded.

After this display, the AGCs began reversing as fast as they could into the trees, and the centaur detachment rejoined the main troop. For just a second, as they carried out this manoeuvre, a gap opened up in their ranks, and Arabella glimpsed other shapes moving among them – smaller, human figures on horseback. One of them was wearing a bicorne hat. The profile was instantly familiar to her.

'Napoleon is there,' she told the others. 'He's protected

by his centaur shield.' She started forward, abandoning the sanctuary of their willow hideout. 'Emmeline said we should follow him. Come on!'

They made a furtive dash across the park, darting from tree to tree to avoid being seen. When they reached the edge of the park, they saw the rearguard of the centaur swarm surging through the huge ceremonial gates leading into Trafalgar Square.

'There is something rather odd about this invasion,' remarked Miles.

Arabella turned to him. 'What do you mean?'

He hissed and clanked a little, as if thinking. 'Firstly, why has Napoleon's air armada struck only London and ignored the rest of the country? Secondly, why has only *Titan* landed, and with a relatively small force? Thirdly, why has this force bypassed the centres of power – Buckingham Palace, Downing Street, the Palace of Westminster, Army HQ, the Admiralty – and made instead for Trafalgar Square, a place of mere symbolic importance? Is his purpose really conquest… or just to give us a very bloody nose?'

'I have no idea, Miles,' said Arabella, 'but our orders were to follow him. So let's go.'

'I would urge caution, my lady.'

'If we go out there, we'll almost certainly be seen,' agreed Beatrice, surveying the empty expanse of the Mall.

But misery had made Arabella reckless. On the far side of the road she noticed a row of buildings with pillared porticoes supporting first-floor balconies. 'Those pillars could give us cover,' she said to Beatrice and Miles. Without waiting for a reply, she raced into the Mall.

When she was about halfway across the road, one of the rear centaurs stopped. Its head rotated 180 degrees on its neck, so it was looking directly at her. The dead black holes stared at her without curiosity, without hatred – just cold evaluation. *Here is a new target,* they seemed to say. Twin jets of steam burst from the holes where its ears should have been. It turned its horse body around and began galloping towards her.

CHAPTER TWENTY-EIGHT

THE STEAMBIKER

'Run!' screamed Beatrice, as the centaur raised one of its gun-arms. Her voice came from close behind Arabella; she must have decided to join her. As Arabella began sprinting for shelter on the far side of the road, she could hear Beatrice's footsteps and the whirr of Miles's tracks just behind her.

They made it to the portico of one of the buildings opposite, just as a gunshot cracked the air. Black lines zigzagged through one of the graceful, cream-painted columns that were giving them cover. Another gunshot, and a second pillar started to splinter. A loud rumbling from above warned them that the balcony over their heads, no longer supported, was collapsing. There was no time to escape. Brick and plaster began tumbling around them. Arabella pulled Miles and Beatrice towards a large sash window next to the building's main door. They squeezed themselves onto the window ledge just as the pillar finally gave way and a roaring avalanche of masonry began pouring down from above. Perhaps it was the general structural collapse or the pressure of their own bodies, but something caused the window behind them to shatter and they all fell backwards into the room behind. A second later, the ledge they had been sitting on was crushed to pieces by a falling iron girder.

Arabella lay in the dusty darkness for a while, just breathing and listening. With Cassie gone and London so smashed up, she wondered how it was that life persisted. Yet it did.

She thought back to one of her last conversations with Cassie, as they were walking along the Thames embankment two days ago: they'd talked about what they wanted to do when they were older. Cassie had spoken cheerfully of her ambition to study Egyptian hieroglyphics. A tear had run down her cheek after she'd said that, and she'd blinked it away, thinking Arabella wasn't looking. Of course, Cassie knew that it was just a dream: she would never grow older.

Arabella heard Miles moving around. She opened her eyes. He was busy exploring their new environs, examining objects with his eye-lights. Beatrice was climbing gingerly to her feet, dusting herself down.

They were in an office in the Admiralty, filled with teak desks with leather surfaces and fancy brass lamps. A couple of tall wooden filing cabinets stood against one wall. The only illumination was dusty daylight streaming in through the top third of the window – the rest of it was blacked out by a mound of balcony debris.

The restful silence was punctured by shattering glass and the noisy clatter of hoofbeats on a hollow wooden floor.

'The centaur,' whispered Beatrice. 'It's come in through another window. Probably wants to make sure we're dead.'

Arabella got to her feet. She discovered she was filled with loathing for the machine, in some crazy way blaming it for Cassie's death. 'I want to kill it,' she said.

'That is impossible,' said Miles. 'It is shielded. Our only option is to hide from it.'

He and Beatrice found a hiding-place. In the corner of the room, near the window, was a semi-concealed space formed between the side of one of the filing cabinets and the angle of the walls. Reluctantly, Arabella joined them there. *This was the future, then,* she thought – *hiding out from metal killers in the ruins of her city.... You died at the right time, Cassie dear!*

The clip-clop of the hooves halted.

Arabella risked a quick peek around the corner of the cabinet. The centaur filled the office doorway. She could see its blank, dead eyes surveying the room and heard the breathy sigh of hot steam escaping from its vents. She quickly hid again as it trotted forward, gun-arm raised.

BANG!!!!

She bit down a scream of shock at the suddenness of the report.

Rubble behind the shattered window shook. A small cascade of dust and debris tumbled to the floor. *Why had it fired?*

And then she saw what it had seen in the freshly fallen pile: her leather flying hat. It must have come off when she'd toppled in through the window.

The centaur trotted closer to the window. Now it was just yards from them. It would see them if it turned its head ninety degrees to the left. She knew it could swivel it at least twice that distance. The metal creature stared down at the hat with cold scrutiny. Arabella could almost hear the cogs turning in its dull brain: *hat, but no woman under hat. Where is woman? Woman still alive. Woman in this room…* More hot steam sizzled from the side-holes in its head. The wheels in its flexible neck started to shift, and its head began to rotate towards their hiding-place.

Arabella pushed back against Miles and Beatrice. There was space – just – for them all between the back of the filing cabinet and the wall behind it, if they could clamber in there in time. Beatrice and Miles squeezed themselves in as the centaur's head completed its turn. Arabella fought to get in beside them, but was too late. The centaur's eyes locked onto her disappearing form.

The barrel of its gun-hand took aim and fired, just as she managed to push the rest of herself behind the cabinet. Wall plaster exploded an inch from her left arm.

She gritted her teeth, wanting more than ever to kill the thing. It was positioned directly in front of the cabinet. Placing her hands flat against the cabinet's back, she pushed with all her might. The tall, heavy unit teetered and then began to topple, gaining speed as it fell. When it had fallen some thirty degrees through its arc, it suddenly stopped – or appeared to. The cabinet was now within five inches of the centaur's head and had hit the creature's shield. It was still falling, but at a tiny fraction of its former speed.

Something flashed deep in the centaur's eyes and Arabella briefly smelled burning. It retreated a few steps, and the laws of gravity reasserted their grip on the cabinet, which duly crashed to the floor.

Arabella, Beatrice and Miles made a dash for the second cabinet just as the centaur fired again, and a large chunk of the wall where they'd been standing caved in. A fury seemed to possess the creature now, and it began firing round after round at them. Ferocious sounds of splintering wood and exploding paper assailed Arabella's ears as bullets buried themselves deep in the guts of the cabinet now shielding them.

It seemed that the firing would never stop. But then, quite abruptly, it did. Into this unexpected silence crept a faint chugging sound. It was like an engine

– but different from the engine driving the centaur. And it was slowly increasing in volume. The sound had an echo, as if it was inside the building, and beneath it could be heard the squeal of pneumatic tyres on parquet flooring.

While Arabella was wondering what new nightmare might be coming their way, the centaur recommenced its assault. This time the attack was more physical. It butted the unit with its head and used its gun-muzzle arms to smash the frame and drawers. The cabinet jerked backwards with each strike it received, delivering bruising bumps to Beatrice and Arabella. The frenzied battering of iron against wood and the excited rasp of the centaur's steam-breath scraped at Arabella's nerves.

Just as she was contemplating ending it all with a suicidal full-frontal attack on the creature, there came a booming gunshot, much louder than the earlier ones, followed by a rowdy clatter as if someone had dropped a tray full of metal plates on the floor. Everything stopped once again. No more banging and crashing on the cabinet, no more steam-breath. Even the strange engine sounds had stopped. Just silence.

Arabella was the first to poke her head around what remained of the cabinet to see what had happened. The centaur was spreadeagled across the floor, completely still. It no longer had a head. A few yards behind the creature's corpse, in the doorway of the room, was a figure with a shotgun sitting astride a huge steambike.

Arabella's jaw dropped open in wonder and relief. 'How did you kill it?' she managed to ask. 'How did you get through its shield?'

'I have no idea,' replied a deep female voice – a voice Arabella knew very well. Her mouth widened still further as the figure removed her full-face helmet.

It was Cassie.

CHAPTER TWENTY-NINE

THE DESTRUCTIVE INGREDIENT

Cassie had some cuts on her face, but otherwise seemed OK. She smiled as Arabella ran to her and hugged her tightly. They embraced for a long time without speaking. Eventually Arabella sniffed and wiped her eyes. 'Tell me everything,' she said.

'I will, Bella dear,' said Cassie. 'It's been quite an astonishing few hours.' She glanced up as the other two emerged from the wreckage of the cabinet. 'Hello, Beatrice. Hello, Miles.'

'How did you survive that crash?' asked Beatrice.

'I still can't quite believe that I did,' said Cassie. 'It was such a disaster! I was hit in my port wing. The engine and most of the wing were blown right off. *Sultan* was a goner, I knew it immediately. I went into a death-spiral. It happened so fast I could barely think. Smoke was filling the cockpit. It was a struggle just to stay conscious. One of the straps for my chute was trapped under my seat and I couldn't yank it free.'

'Oh, Cassie,' murmured Arabella. She could imagine the scene all too clearly. She'd had nightmares about such things happening to *her*. 'What did you do?'

'I baled out,' said Cassie. 'What else *could* I do? I was about fifteen hundred feet up. I decided I'd have a better chance outside my machine than in.'

'So you were falling,' said Beatrice. 'Towards streets and buildings, I assume? Then what?'

'I spread my arms and legs out, as we were taught to do when freefalling, to create air resistance and reduce velocity. I searched the ground for something, anything, that could soften my landing or at least break my fall: a body of water, a mound of hay, even a glass roof. But there was nothing beneath me except hard roofs and hard streets... And then I saw it.'

'What?' cried Arabella. 'What did you see?'

'You remember that *Tornade* that crashed in the Strand? You must have seen it shortly after take-off.'

'I remember it,' said Arabella excitedly. 'Oh my goodness, Cassie, you *didn't*? Did you?'

'I certainly did. I found that by twisting and rolling my body I could actually steer myself, and I began to steer towards the downed airship. I narrowly missed being impaled on the spire of St Clement Danes, but I made it. I landed feet first, as vertically as possible, into the *Tornade*'s slowly deflating gas envelope. I couldn't have found a more perfect landing place. It was so cushiony and soft. I suffered a few cuts and bruises. But apart from that, I was fine!'

'Cassie, you're indestructible!' laughed Arabella, and she hugged her again. 'Now you must explain what you're doing here, and how you were able to destroy the centaur.'

Cassie opened her mouth to explain, then stopped and smiled as a rumble filled the air and two more steambikers entered the room, one behind the other. 'I went back to Hades,' said Cassie over the roar of engines. 'I was given a bike and a gun and told to go and find you. As for how I destroyed the centaur, perhaps I should leave that part to the professor... and his new assistant.'

'*Associate*,' came a muffled, American-accented voice from beneath the helmet of the second biker.

'Associate, sorry,' said Cassie.

Professor Brayden Storm and Ben Forrester removed their helmets and nodded their greetings.

Arabella thought Ben looked rather dashing astride the long, low-slung, high-handlebarred machine, yet endeavoured to keep her attention on his older companion. 'Professor,' she said, 'have you really discovered a means of penetrating the shield using a...' – she glanced at the weapon nestled under Cassie's arm – 'a *shotgun*?'

Professor Storm was trying to coax his cliff of hair, which had been flattened by the helmet, into some approximation of its former shape. He beamed proudly at her. 'Indeed I have, my dear.'

'*We* have,' corrected Ben, with an even prouder beam.

'That is true,' acknowledged the professor. 'My assistant...'

'Associate.'

'My associate and I, by painstaking scientific deduction...'

'By a complete fluke, in other words,' Ben said, flashing a grin at Arabella.

The professor frowned. 'Not a *complete* fluke, young man. We knew the mineral contained traces of copper, which...'

'...*conducts* aetheric energy, so cannot possibly be the destructive ingredient in this case.'

'But may nevertheless have served to convey the destructive ingredient to its target.'

'Though we still don't know what that destructive ingredient is,' said Ben.

'Not as yet, it is true. Even so, it can only be a matter of time...'

'Time we don't have,' said Ben.

'Would one of you please explain what you're talking about instead of arguing?' cried Arabella impatiently. 'How did Cassie just blow the centaur's head off?'

'We've found something that can penetrate the shield,' said Ben.

'But that's great, isn't it? Why aren't you looking thrilled about this?'

The professor looked at Ben, and Ben looked at the professor. 'Shall I tell her?' said Professor Storm. 'Or do you want to?'

'Tell me what?' asked Arabella.

Ben cleared his throat. 'We've found *something*... but we don't quite know what it is yet.' He drew his own shotgun from a long holster attached to the bike. He cocked it and took out one of the rounds, then held it up so everyone could see it. 'Inside here,' he said, 'is a mineral containing a number of different elements. One of those elements penetrated the shield and blew the head off that centaur. We don't as yet know which one. The element probably only exists in trace amounts, which limits our power to inflict real damage.'

'We can take down an individual centaur more than a mile away from *Titan*,' added the professor, taking a dejected bite from a doughnut he'd found buried in his pocket. 'But that's about our limit right now.'

'Why does the distance from *Titan* matter?' asked Cassie.

'The ASG from which the shield draws its power is aboard *Titan*,' said Ben. 'The further the shield gets from the source of that power, the weaker it is.'

'If we're going to defeat the centaurs *en masse* and destroy *Titan* itself, we're going to need a purer form of that elusive element,' muttered the professor.

'But, gentlemen, logic suggests that the shield must be growing weaker,' pointed out Miles. 'The invaders cannot have brought enough gold to keep it powered for more than a few days.'

Instead of cheering them up, this comment only seemed to make Ben and the professor gloomier than ever.

'Shall I tell them, or will you?' said Professor Storm.

'Let's show them instead,' said Ben.

The professor nodded, and they dismounted their bikes.

'Step this way, please,' said Ben, as he and the professor headed out of the room.

Arabella looked at Cassie. 'Do you know what this is about?'

'No idea,' said Cassie.

Arabella, Cassie, Miles and Beatrice followed Ben and the professor through the dim halls of the Admiralty, with its gloomy portraits of ancient mariners. They headed up a steep spiral staircase with ship's-wheel balusters. From an upper-floor balcony, Ben showed them a view of London in ruins. To the north lay Trafalgar Square. The small figure of Napoleon was visible there, standing on the steps at the base of Nelson's Column. He stood between two of the bronze lions, delivering a speech to a small assembly of officers and troops. They were greatly outnumbered by the centaurs, which surrounded them, filling the whole square in ranks at least ten deep.

Arabella couldn't hear what Napoleon was saying, but she could see that Nelson no longer stood atop his column. His statue lay shattered at the French emperor's feet. Meanwhile, a crane was slowly winching another statue towards the summit of the column. The new statue bore a distinct resemblance to the man delivering the speech. Arabella was appalled by the sight, but also puzzled. Did Napoleon's defeat at Trafalgar four decades ago still rankle so deeply that he was prepared to expend time and effort on this ridiculous display of petty revenge? She was struck again by Miles's observation that this did not feel like a proper invasion – more like an exercise in humiliation.

'Look over there, ladies and gents,' said Ben, pointing northeast. They all looked and saw a long line of steam wagons moving slowly towards them down the Strand. Each wagon was flanked by marching centaurs and piled high with gleaming bars of gold. 'They're emptying the vaults of every bank in the city,' said Ben. 'There's no chance of the ASG running out of fuel any time soon.'

'That is English gold,' said Arabella furiously. 'Why, he's nothing but a common thief!'

Beatrice stared at the wagons and licked her dry lips. 'I've never seen so much gold,' she whispered.

As they watched, Napoleon began leading his men, with their centaur escort, out of the square. They headed down Northumberland Avenue towards the river.

'We'd better get after them,' said Arabella.

'And me and the Prof had best get back to the Lab,' said Ben. 'See if we can create ourselves some benite.'

'Benite?' queried Arabella.

'It's our provisional name for this mysterious element that can penetrate the shield.'

'Of course he means braydenite,' laughed Professor Brayden Storm. 'Braydenite will be the name of this element, once I have identified it.'

Arabella turned to Ben and smiled sweetly at him. 'So, if you're going to be busy in the Lab finding this element, I don't suppose you'll be needing your steambike?'

CHAPTER THIRTY

THE
CHASE

Arabella felt the power surge up like a wave beneath her as she twisted the throttle of the steambike. It was a beautiful machine, easily ten feet from prow to stern, with fat black pneumatic tyres, brass-riveted leather trim, huge swept-back handlebars, extended forks and a front end raked at forty-five degrees. She moved slowly forward through the open gates into Trafalgar Square, the engine no more than a gentle throb, like a lion disturbed from slumber. Miles was riding pillion on a little seat behind her. Beatrice (on the professor's bike) and Cassie rode on either side of her and just behind as she crossed the now-empty Trafalgar Square. A crudely painted sign had been left hanging around one of the lions' necks. The words 'Trafalgar Square' had been daubed on it, then crossed out, and above this was written the square's new name: 'Place Napoléon'. Arabella resisted the urge to shoot the sign down. They couldn't risk drawing attention to themselves.

They headed east along Northumberland Avenue in the direction Napoleon had gone. When they reached the north bank of the Thames, they caught sight of the tail end of the emperor's centaur entourage on the same side of the river, half a mile further east. They began following them, keeping their distance. They rode along the dirty, cobbled embankment, past abandoned wharves and boatyards, past looted warehouses, under echoing railway arches. They rode in the shadows of cracked coalstacks and wrought-iron cranes that leaned over the water like prehistoric birds. Barges sat heavily in the river, dark and sludgy with the raw sewage tipped in there. Rats skittered along the piers and jetties.

The road bent away from the river at Blackfriars, and they continued to shadow the centaur army east along Upper, then Lower Thames Street, passing tiny courts, yards, lanes and narrow alleys where they glimpsed the frightened faces of beggars and street urchins. There were surreal sights: a cow wandering through the smoke, having escaped its destiny at the slaughterhouse; a line of geese crossing the road; the rear end of an omnibus emerging from a giant bomb crater. Arabella could not help wrinkling her nose at the filth and the slums.

Perhaps this is an opportunity, she thought to herself. *If London ever rises again, they might think about cleaning up the riverside...*

Napoleon and his centaurs drew to a halt outside the walls of the Tower of London. A determined British army unit had holed itself up inside the ancient fortress and was firing from the battlements of the outer wall. Arabella had no idea how many there were, but silently saluted them for their bravery. She and the others could only watch as the centaurs blasted them mercilessly.

After a quarter of an hour, Napoleon ordered up his elephant gun. The enormous cannon was duly wheeled into position. It unleashed a heavy, high-velocity shell, smashing a huge hole in the western side of the outer wall. The centaurs poured through the breach, galloping clumsily over the fallen stones, and even trampling each other in ungainly desperation to get inside the castle. There were sounds of gunfire and groans of pain. Red-uniformed corpses cascaded into the moat. Within ten minutes, the siege was over and the French Tricolour flew over the White Tower. Napoleon and his escort entered the castle through the outer gatehouse.

'Again, my lady,' said Miles, 'the emperor conquers a site of no strategic importance.'

'But it does contain the Crown Jewels,' Arabella pointed out. 'It would appear that Napoleon may be more interested in grand larceny than conquest.'

'What do you think we should do, Bella? Stay here and keep watch?'

'I think we should hide our bikes somewhere and try to sneak into the Tower,' said Arabella. 'We need to find out what exactly Napoleon is up to.'

'Shouldn't we call Emmeline first?' asked Beatrice. 'Tell her what we're doing?'

Arabella glared at her suspiciously. Had Emmeline told Beatrice to keep an eye on her, knowing her maverick tendencies? Then she smiled. 'Our orders were clear, Bea. We should follow Napoleon and find out what he's up to. I don't think Emmeline needs to be informed of every stage of the mission.'

She began looking around for a place to conceal their vehicles.

'Bella,' said Cassie, 'I –'

She never got any further. A whispering, whistling sound filled the air – a sound Arabella recalled from her time on *Titan* – and three whirling rope circles descended from the sky. Instinctively, Arabella opened her throttle and jetted forward, just as the rope aimed at her skimmed her shoulder. Twenty yards on, she braked and threw her bike to the left, causing the rear wheel to skid in a ninety-degree arc. She looked behind her. Cassie, struggling like a wildcat, and Beatrice had both been caught securely in lassos flung by two Equestrians – she recognised them behind their domino masks as Henri and Gérard. The hoops of rope bound the Sisters tightly, pinning their arms to their sides. The men clicked their heels, backing up their iron horses and dragging the two Sisters from their machines, which fell with a clatter to the street.

Two more Equestrians were also there – Isaac and Fabien. Jacques, Arabella's only friend among them, was nowhere to be seen.

'After her!' yelled Isaac, quickly gathering in his lasso, and he and Fabien took off towards Arabella.

'Hold on to your hat, Miles!' she shouted, aiming her front wheel north. Then, yanking open her throttle to its maximum extent, she screamed away from her pursuers and down an alleyway, leaving a smear of burned rubber on the cobbles. She flashed past tenements, taverns and dingy merchants' dwellings. She skidded round corners and splashed through filthy puddles, clogged with dung and slaughterhouse offal. Yet however fast she went, and however many corners she turned, she couldn't escape the rattle of hooves and explosive hissing of iron horses coming up behind her.

At length she found herself in Billingsgate Fish Market, an open square bordered by sheds and stalls next to a wharf that surrounded three sides of a small inlet of the Thames. The place was abandoned, its wares left to rot in crates, creating a stench that nearly induced Arabella to faint. She could no longer hear her pursuers and allowed her bike to drift quietly into the shadow of an awning.

'Surrender, Lady Arabella,' said a calm,

French-accented voice behind her. 'We have you surrounded.'

She whirled around. Isaac was sitting placidly atop his horse, guarding one of the roads leading away from the square. Fabien, she quickly saw, was guarding the other. Arabella searched desperately for a means of escape. The only unguarded exit from the marketplace was onto the wharf, where boats delivered their catch. She eyed a smack – a decent-sized fishing boat – berthed at the northern end of the wharf. After hastily calculating the distance, she revved her engine and accelerated towards it.

'My lady...' was all Miles had time to say as they smashed through a wooden barricade and flew out over the edge of the wharf into empty space. They landed on the deck of the fishing boat with a bump that jarred her bones and hurled Miles at least five feet into the air. He fell back in his seat just as she took off again, slaloming along the deck to avoid getting snagged in nets and rigging. The front of the boat sloped gently upwards towards the bow, providing her with a perfect lift-off for her next manoeuvre.

Building up to maximum speed, Arabella roared up the improvised ramp, shot out onto the bowsprit, somehow maintaining her balance on the narrow beam, and sailed out over the water towards the western side of the wharf. She soared over the wall of pilings that formed its foundation and, to her joy and relief, felt her bike's wheels make skidding contact with the quayside. Laughing, she screeched away in the direction of the main river.

But the river arrived sooner than expected. More brakes and screeching tyres, and Arabella was forced into a ninety-degree turn, at speed, to avoid plunging straight in. She leaned right, bringing the bike down at such a low angle that her right knee almost scraped the cobbles. Miles failed to hold on and was flung from his perch, hurtling head first into a pillar of an arcade. Unaware of this, Arabella straightened out her bike and resumed her escape along the embankment.

Before she had covered twenty yards, a detachment of centaurs rounded a corner just ahead of her. She squeezed her brakes, but too late. The next second, she hit something that felt like an invisible wall of thick, dense, heavy glue. Arabella tumbled over the handlebars in super-slow motion, somersaulting through the jellied air towards a row of fifteen identical metal faces with black holes for eyes. In perfect synchronisation, they raised their gun-arms towards her. Smoke and flame burst from the gun-arm of the nearest automaton. It flashed blindingly before her face. Something very hard and hot punched into her forehead and she went flying backwards into darkness.

CHAPTER THIRTY-ONE

THE PRISON

Jacques stared up at the high, forbidding walls and iron-barred windows of Newgate Prison. Even the Bastille in Paris, which he'd seen depicted in numerous Revolution-era paintings, had never looked quite so bleak. He shuddered to think of Marie languishing in a cell behind one of those windows.

'Forward!' Jacques barked at his soldier-automaton escort. The metal creature jerked to life and began trotting towards the prison entrance. Jacques kept pace with it on *Pégase*. It had been the work of fifteen minutes to capture and tame the deadly automaton. Although he hadn't gone to engineering school like his sister and would never possess her genius with machines, he had taught himself the basics by working on *Pégase*. He knew how to reprogram their analytical engines. The mass-produced soldier-automata were very simple-minded, luckily – he wouldn't have known where to start with anything so complex and intelligent as Lady Arabella's automaton. A few new lines of code was all it took. Using his portable keypunch machine he'd pierced fresh holes in the machine's number cards, causing its gear wheels to move in slightly different directions. Now the automaton would obey only him.

Jacques and his escort passed the high black platform with its crossbeam and its row of nooses: the gallows where criminals were hanged – so much more barbaric than the guillotine. They rode up the steps to the main entrance. His escort raised its gun-arm and bashed on the iron-studded door. To Jacques' surprise, the door creaked open. Had even the prison been abandoned by its guards? It seemed so. The building rang with the groans and cries of trapped inmates, but there was no sign of any staff. From the chief warden's office, he obtained a large iron ring of keys. Jacques and his metal companion slowly rode the length of the high, echoing central hall. He observed the prisoners in the cells on either side. Many yelled at him, demanding or begging for their freedom. Others simply stared. All were men, and many looked violent.

Iron staircases rising from the hall led to cells on the upper galleries. Jacques abandoned *Pégase* and his companion on the ground floor and mounted the steps alone.

He saw some women up here, as well as men.

'Marie!' he called out. 'Marie Daguerre!'

Plenty answered: a cacophony of yells and cries that made no sense.

'*Y a-t-il quelqu'un de* La Fayette?' he demanded. 'Anyone here from *La Fayette*?'

The same confused babble was the only response he got.

He tried to recall the name of the sky pirates' flying city. 'Anyone from… Taranis?' he cried.

'Me!' a woman shouted from the gallery above. 'I was on Taranis!'

Heart racing, Jacques clambered up the stairway to the next level. He charged down the gallery, boots clanging on the metal floor. 'Who spoke?'

A pale fist reached out and grabbed him on his way past one of the cells. He turned. The woman was tall, with brown eyes and long, matted chestnut hair. Her grubby face seemed oddly familiar. He'd seen someone similar, and not long ago.

'You were on Taranis?' he asked.

'The floating pirate city, yes!' she said.

'Did you know someone called Marie Daguerre? She was a passenger on the *La Fayette*.'

'Marie?' she said, so quietly he could barely hear her above the general din. 'Yes, I knew Marie.'

CHAPTER THIRTY-TWO

THE
TOWER

Arabella awoke to sounds of creaking oars and gently lapping water. Her forehead burned and her neck and skull ached. She blinked a few times. Images of sky came to her and sounds of distant bombs. Airships floated above her like ghosts in the mist. She was lying in a rowing boat, breathing in the rank smell of the river.

Near her sat a young man. She recognised him as one of the Equestrians – the silent, scary one who took delight in killing: Fabien. He seemed almost monochrome – beige skin and blond hair so dull it was virtually grey. Like Beatrice, he would never stand out in a crowd. Fabien's eyes were trained upon her, as was his gun. The gun barrel shifted slightly with the rocking of the boat, but the eyes never moved.

Behind him sat the oarsman, rowing with steady strokes. She recognised him as Isaac. He had curly black hair and a firm, strong jaw: the look of someone with no doubts about the world or his place in it.

'What happened?' Arabella murmured. 'How am I alive?'

Fabien ignored the question and just kept staring at her.

'I have no idea,' replied Isaac. 'You should be dead. You were shot in the head at point-blank range.'

Arabella touched her forehead tenderly. It felt sticky with blood and puffy with bruising, but there was no bullet hole. *What had happened?*

He stopped rowing. A large wooden gate set into the stonework of the embankment behind him was slowly opening. Arabella recognised it as Traitors' Gate. 'Where are you taking me?' she gasped.

'To the Tower,' Isaac said simply. 'Isn't that where you British traditionally imprison spies and traitors?'

'I'm not a traitor,' said Arabella.

'Not yet,' said Isaac. 'But it might serve your interests to become one.'

With the gate now open, he rowed through the vaulted tunnel to a small docking point at the bottom of some stone steps.

'The war is over now, anyway,' Isaac said as he tied the boat to a wooden post. He pulled her up out of the boat and pushed her onto the moss-covered lower steps. 'The airships are running out of targets to bomb in London. It's the same story in the other cities.'

'No!' cried Arabella, horrified. 'Only London has been hit. I was in Granville. I saw the size of your armada. There weren't enough of them to strike anywhere else.'

'You were in Granville,' said Isaac, 'but not in Le Havre, Dieppe, Boulogne or Calais. You have no idea how many armadas we have sent!'

'You're lying!' said Arabella. 'Our intelligence, our ANODE stations would have picked it up...'

Isaac just smiled. He began walking backwards up the steps ahead of her, gazing down at her as he went. Fabien was pressing the muzzle of his gun into the small of her back, forcing her to climb.

She clenched her jaw, blinking back tears. *He had to be lying!*

'Your government will soon surrender,' said Isaac. 'This is now just a mopping-up operation. Old London will become New Paris. Britain will become a colony of the French Empire. You have no country to betray, so you might as well tell us everything.'

They passed beneath the spikes of a portcullis, up a sloping cobbled street, through a doorway in a wall, up some steps, along another path and into one of the towers. Isaac led the way up a steep and narrow corkscrew staircase. Arabella, with Fabien's gun prodding her, followed. At the top lay a short passage leading to an iron-studded wooden door. Isaac banged three times on the door. Gérard Mesnier, the tall, thin, weasely one, opened it. 'Welcome to the Bloody Tower,' he said with a sickly smile. 'What took you so long?'

'Never mind about that,' said Isaac, barging past him.

Fabien pushed Arabella into the room. She was relieved to see Cassie and Beatrice there, unharmed.

But where was Miles?

She guessed he must have fallen from her bike just before she'd crashed into the centaurs' Aetheric Shield.

'Where's my automaton?' she demanded of Isaac after she'd embraced Cassie and Beatrice.

'No idea,' he replied. He turned to Henri, and gave a start of surprise when he saw him. Henri had dressed himself in the fancy red-and-black costume of a Beefeater, or Yeoman Warder – one of the ceremonial guardians of the Tower of London. The big hat was placed at a jaunty angle on his head. He was kneeling on a ledge and leaning out of the window, lining something up in the sights of his pistol. 'You look ridiculous,' Isaac said to him. 'What do you think you're doing?'

Henri fired the gun, then cursed. 'Missed! I'm trying to shoot those pesky ravens, or at least scare them away.' He turned to Isaac. 'Don't you know the legend? If the ravens leave, the kingdom falls. Trouble is, the damn things don't seem to want to go…'

Isaac gave him a withering look. 'Did you get any information out of the prisoners yet?'

Henri spat on the floor. 'What information were you hoping to acquire?'

'Where the underground base is located, for example!' Isaac's lips were tight with impatience.

'Guizot's not too bothered about extracting information from these girls,' said Gérard. 'He wants to execute them. He says he wants a traditional British execution on Tower Green. All we need now is an axe. There must be one somewhere in this castle.'

Arabella's neck hairs bristled at this. Cassie gave an audible gulp.

Even Isaac looked upset. 'He means to behead them? What are we, medieval monsters? I thought he wanted us to bring them here for questioning.'

'If those are the marshal's orders, then we must obey them,' said Fabien in a voice that seemed to drip like blood into a bucket.

Isaac shuddered. Glancing at Arabella he said: 'I'm not even sure if that one is capable of dying.'

'What do you mean?' asked Henri.

'She was shot by a soldier-automaton from less than a metre away, and all she got was that bruise on her forehead.'

Cassie cried out. 'Bella, is it true?' Arabella nodded.

'The automaton's aim must have been off,' said Fabien. 'The bullet glanced off her head. When I wield the axe, I will strike the target.'

'Guizot said nothing about *you* wielding the axe,' said Henri.

Fabien stared at him. 'Are you volunteering?'

Henri looked down at his hands, which were now trembling. 'No,' he said.

'I don't think the automaton's aim was off,' muttered Isaac – but only Arabella heard him.

She crossed to the mullioned double window where Henri was lounging and looked out onto Tower Green. A scaffold was there, and on top of it an executioner's block.

She felt a warm gust of fish-scented breath against her neck and spun around. Gérard had sidled close to her. 'I suppose you are dreaming that the rocket man will come and rescue you again, eh?' he sniggered. 'Well, dream on, lady. These walls are three metres thick.'

'I don't need anyone to rescue me!' Arabella told him. 'I was perfectly prepared to die that day, as I am today!'

Gérard laughed. 'Such anger! Such defiance! I wonder how long it will last.' She shuddered as he began to stroke the back of her neck. 'I look forward to watching you beg for mercy as Fabien prepares to chop off your pretty English head.' He bent forward and kissed her cheek.

In a fury, Arabella slapped him hard on the face. Gérard simply laughed.

'Let her be!' shouted Isaac, pulling him away from her.

Gérard wrenched himself free of Isaac's grip.

'Get your hands off me!' he growled, showing his teeth. 'You can't tell me or any of us what to do any more! The marshal has it in for you after what you did on *Titan*. You are finished, Isaac Dreyfus.'

He turned to Henri and Fabien for support. 'Isn't that right, boys?' He scowled when they didn't react.

Isaac stared at him pityingly for a moment, then turned on his heel.

Cassie went over to Arabella and gently dabbed the bruise on her forehead with a handkerchief. 'Are you all right, dear?'

'Fine,' said Arabella.

'I will go and speak with the marshal,' said Isaac. 'There's been some misunderstanding – I'm sure he didn't mean what he said. We are not butchers, after all.'

'Good luck with that,' said Henri with a yawn. 'I think I'll stay here and keep an eye on our prisoners.'

Isaac looked thoughtful. 'I think not,' he said. 'They can't escape from this cell. Now we've rounded them up, we should resume our primary duty, which is to protect the emperor. Come with me!'

But before he could reach the door, it opened. Filling the entrance was the tall, brooding figure of Jacques. His eyes were red, his cheeks dark with anger or misery. When he saw Arabella, his lips tightened into a snarl.

'You!' he said, striding towards her. *'You* killed my sister!'

CHAPTER THIRTY-THREE

THE BOY WHO LOVED

Arabella was shocked into temporary paralysis. 'What?' she mumbled as he reared up before her, his shaking finger pointing at her chest. 'My sister, Marie Daguerre!' he said. 'You killed her three days ago, on Taranis.'

'That… That's not true…' Arabella gasped. Then she frowned. 'Was Marie your sister?'

Someone else had entered the room behind Jacques. Arabella recognised her as Sally, the girl she'd briefly impersonated on the floating city.

'She saw you kill Marie!' roared Jacques, pulling the reluctant girl forward so she stood in front of Arabella. 'Tell her what you saw!' he ordered the girl.

Sally looked confused and terrified. Her cheeks flinched at the sight of Arabella and her eyes crinkled apologetically. 'I–I never actually *saw* her shoot her,' she said.

'But you saw her kneeling over Marie's body with a gun in her hand, yes?' said Jacques.

'Yes. Yes I did, sir. We were in the Cloud Factory, and this woman, Lady Arabella, she led the attack. "Destroy the machines!" she said, and we did. And in the middle of it, while we were swinging our axes and firing our guns at the cloud-making machines, I caught a glimpse of her kneeling, as you said, sir, kneeling over your sister, with a gun in her hand. But I never saw her shoot her. You inferred that yourself, sir. For all I know, your sister was already dying or dead when Lady Arabella found her. She might have been attempting to revive her.'

'With a gun!?'

'We were all carrying guns, sir, and axes and iron bars. It was a revolution. You know, like the one you lot had in 1789. We were trying to overthrow the Taranites. The Cloud Factory was our Bastille. I bet you Frenchies had weapons when you stormed the Bastille, sir.'

Jacques turned away from her in exasperation. Isaac started to say something, but Jacques flung up a hand to quiet him. His red-rimmed eyes burned into Arabella. 'Why did you kill my sister?' he demanded.

'She killed herself,' she replied as calmly as she could. 'If I could have stopped her, I would have. But…'

CALL OF THE PHOENIX

It was hard to know how to continue. She had liked Marie Daguerre and Marie had liked her – but the girl had nursed a fanatical hatred of the English, which had led her to side with the sky pirates. In fact, Marie had been on the point of killing Arabella and Ben, and had only been thwarted by the arrival of the rioters. Even so, Arabella spoke the truth when she said she wished she could have stopped Marie killing herself.

Isaac put his hand on Jacques' shoulder. 'I'm sorry for your loss, Jacques,' he said, 'but we have other business to attend to now. You must come with us to see the marshal.'

Jacques kept his eyes on Arabella. 'I'm going nowhere until I've heard what this woman has to say.'

Isaac shrugged. 'Very well, then. But we must go. Follow on when you're ready. Just make sure these women don't escape. If any of them tries anything, kill them. I'll lock the cell door. Henri will be outside. Knock when you're ready to leave and he will let you out.' He turned to Fabien and Gérard. 'You two come with me.'

Fabien followed Isaac out of the cell, and Henri transferred himself to a stool just outside the door. Gérard chewed his lip savagely for a while, his face eaten through with bitterness. Then he loped after the others. The door slammed shut and the key squeaked as it was twisted home.

'Wait a minute, what about me?' said Sally, turning on Jacques. 'First I get locked up with a bunch of Frenchies because the authorities thought I'd been infected by their ideas while I was on Taranis. Now here I am being locked up again – in the Tower of London of all places! What's an English girl got to do to walk free in her own blooming country?'

Jacques rubbed his forehead distractedly. His lips were moving, his chest heaving. He seemed close to a breakdown. 'I will let you go, don't worry,' he muttered. 'I just… just need to hear this story.' He turned to Arabella. 'Please, tell me what happened.'

'Your sister befriended me,' said Arabella gently. 'She nursed my wounds, and she fixed up Miles after one of the pirates smashed him to pieces. She was a good and capable person. I really liked her. I think we could have been friends – except that she loathed my country, and when she saw that the Taranites were being defeated and the English fleet would get through, it must have seemed like the end of the world to her. She believed the French fleet would be destroyed, and she couldn't bear it. So she turned the gun on herself. That is what happened.'

It wasn't quite all that had happened – but it was as much as he needed to hear.

Jacques didn't say anything for a while. His hand was pressed hard against his face, his chest trembling, and Arabella noticed that he was sobbing. 'She was the only family… I had left.'

Arabella put a hesitant hand on his shoulder, and was glad when he didn't brush it away. 'Marie told me about Allenson,' she said. 'About how he killed your parents in front of her...' As she was saying this, a memory arose of Jacques on his iron horse shooting Allenson and sparing her. 'You killed him, though, didn't you? You avenged your mother and father.'

Jacques nodded, his eyes full of tears. Speech seemed beyond him.

She felt a tremor inside as she looked into his pain-ravaged face. There was something else in his demeanour beyond the misery; she'd glimpsed it before – a strength or nobility. She recalled their snatched conversation on board *Titan*. Perhaps Jacques could be their ally now – help them escape. 'Did you mean it before,' she asked, 'when you said Napoleon must be stopped?'

His lips shook as he spoke. 'I am not like Marie,' he said. 'I do not hate the English – I hate this war. I see every day what it does to people. The wrong people thrive. Scum like Gérard Mesnier, psychopaths like Fabien Leloup, dumb followers like Henri Bilot. Such people do very well in war. Even good men, like Isaac Dreyfus, are obliged to do evil in wartime. My sister was good, as you say, but the war twisted her mind. She loved Napoleon. He could do no wrong in her eyes. I... realised long ago that Napoleon is bad for France. This war is bad for France. Yes, he must be stopped.'

'That's fantastic!' cried Cassie joyfully, looking as if she was about to applaud this speech. Then her eye flickered towards the door, and her voice dropped to a whisper. 'So, will you help us?'

Jacques ground his teeth. 'All that prevented me from helping you before was Marie – the hope that she was alive, and the fear that she would hate me for ever.' His lips were dry and white, his eyes stony. 'The marshal said he had it on good authority that she was alive. He wanted my loyalty for this mission and he won it with that lie. He knew all along that she... that Marie...' His eyes widened with horror, as the realisation struck him once again that she was dead. Then he calmed himself. 'Tell me what I can do.'

'First, perhaps you can tell us about the Phoenix,' said Beatrice.

He shook himself as if emerging from a nightmare. 'What?'

'The Phoenix,' she repeated.

'It is a bird, is it not? A mythical bird that dies and is then reborn from its ashes.'

'We know that,' said Cassie. 'But it means something else as well. Something specific to this invasion.'

Arabella clarified: 'While I was on *Titan*, I heard Napoleon talking about it, saying that very soon the Phoenix would be within his grasp.'

Jacques frowned. 'Now you mention it, I heard the emperor say something similar this morning. It was when we landed in Hyde Park. We were in the hatchway of *Titan*, watching the soldier-automata attacking your forces. He said… Now, what was it? Ah, yes. He said: "If all goes to plan, I shall have the Phoenix in my hands by the end of this day." And then he said: "Once I have the Phoenix, the war will be as good as won." I have no idea what he meant.'

Cassie checked the window and was forced to squint as a shaft of peachy-gold late afternoon light lanced through it. 'The day is nearly ending,' she said. 'Whatever the Phoenix is, he may already have it…'

'We must get out of here,' said Arabella.

'Finally, someone's talking sense,' said Sally.

Cassie smiled at Jacques. 'You'll help us, won't you?' she said.

CHAPTER THIRTY-FOUR

THE
PHOENIX

Henri yawned and adjusted his fancy red-and-black hat. 'Quiet Jacques', they used to call him. The lad never said much, just quietly got on with the job. Now, after today's showing, perhaps they ought to call him 'Crazy Jacques'. Henri was just getting comfortable, with his stool tipped back and his back wedged into a little alcove in the passageway, when he heard a loud pounding on the door.

'I'm ready to leave,' Crazy Jacques' voice shouted from the other side of the thick oak.

'All right, all right,' said Henri with another yawn and stretch. 'Opening up.' He turned the key in the lock and pushed open the door.

A fist came flying out and smashed him in the nose.

Henri heard shattering bone and tasted blood. He began grappling frantically with the woman who came charging at him – the same strong one who'd attacked him in Granville. He felt himself being pushed backwards to the end of the passage, and then he was falling into empty space. *Bang! Bang! Bang!* went his head and shoulders as they bounced down the steps. Everything faded, leaving only pain and confusion as he felt himself twisting and tumbling downwards.

'Catch him!' cried Jacques.

Cassie flung out her hand and caught hold of Henri's boot before he disappeared down the stairwell. She and Jacques pulled him up and laid him out on the floor of the passage. He was mumbling to himself. His nose was a broken, bleeding mess. Cassie pressed hard on a point in the carotid artery in his neck until Henri's lips stopped moving and his body slumped into unconsciousness.

'What did you just do?' gawped Sally.

'Blood choke,' said Beatrice. 'Stops the blood supply to the brain for long enough to induce temporary unconsciousness.'

Jacques stared at Cassie. 'You seem so sweet and gentle,' he muttered.

'Thank you, monsieur,' laughed Cassie.

'We'd better go,' said Beatrice.

They ran down the steps to a path that led to Tower Green. Arabella went first, retracing the route she'd been forced along earlier. From their rear came a sudden heavy tramp of footsteps. They shrank into the shadows of a descending stairway as a patrol of French guards passed behind them along the ramparts of the castle's inner wall.

Arabella was about to step through the door at the bottom of the stairway when Beatrice stopped her with a hiss. She was crouched at the top of the stairs, gazing north. The others reclimbed the steps to see what she was looking at. Fifty yards away, riding through a parade ground to the right of Tower Green, was a group of mounted figures. Four centaurs flanked six humans: Napoleon, Guizot, Isaac, Gérard, Fabien – and Diana.

Cassie pressed her hand to her mouth. Arabella knew how she must feel. Even though she had been told about Diana's treachery, it must still be shocking to see her in such company. They waited until the party had disappeared behind the giant edifice of the White Tower – the four-turreted fortress that lay at the heart of the Tower of London – before daring to speak.

'Was that... The one in the bicorne hat – was that really...?' Sally couldn't quite bring herself to say his name.

'*Oui*,' said Jacques in mock awe. 'Our great emperor!'

'We should follow them,' whispered Beatrice.

'You must be joking,' said Sally.

'Yes, we should,' said Cassie.

Sally looked at them in terror, then turned to Arabella. 'Ma'am, please talk some sense into them for heaven's sake. We'll be killed if we go anywhere near them. I mean, have you seen those metal things with guns instead of hands? We'll be slaughtered.'

Arabella felt torn. Beatrice and Cassie were right, of course – it was their duty to investigate what Napoleon was up to. But she was also desperate to get out of here and find Miles. It pained her to think of him lying broken-headed in the road at the mercy of any passing French troops. Yet she knew what Miles would want her to do.

'I'm sorry, Sally,' she sighed. 'We have to do this.'

Sally turned to Jacques for support. 'Sir, you must see that this plan is ludicrous.'

Jacques knitted his brow. 'I agreed to help you ladies escape,' he said. 'But this is... something else –'

'Finally, the voice of reason,' smiled Sally.

'Nevertheless,' continued Jacques. 'I want to go with you.'

'No!' cried Sally.

'No,' said Arabella in a softer voice.

'It's all right,' Jacques assured Arabella. 'I hate Napoleon as much as you do. I would like to help.'

'It's not that...' Arabella began.

'What, then?' blazed Jacques. 'You don't trust me? Or do you think I'm not good enough?'

'Neither of those,' said Arabella quickly. 'It's only that I need a favour.'

Jacques stared at her, puzzled. 'What favour?'

'My automaton, Miles – I left him lying in the street near Billingsgate Market, west of here. I need you to find him and bring him to me?'

'Your automaton?'

'It… He's rather important to me.'

Jacques bowed his head. 'Then I will do my best to help.'

'Thank you! We can meet you at the Middle Tower in half an hour.' She glanced at Sally. 'And you can help Sally escape from here at the same time.'

'Very well.'

Sally trembled with relief.

From a holster beneath his cape, Jacques drew a long-barrelled pistol. 'Take this,' he said to Arabella, 'and take care.'

Arabella hesitated a moment, then took the weapon and wedged it inside her belt.

When Sally and Jacques had departed, the Sisters edged north, skirting the eastern border of Tower Green with its grim scaffold, until they came to the southwestern corner of the parade ground. A large barrack block and storehouse bounded the northern edge of the cobbled expanse, and the White Tower lay to the south. Napoleon and his entourage had reached the northeastern corner and were disappearing round the far side of the barrack block. The Sisters followed, keeping out of sight in the shadows of the barrack-block wall.

When they reached the corner, they stopped, clustering around so they could see what Napoleon and his group were up to. The Sisters were just in time to witness them climbing a short flight of stone steps leading to the entrance of a tower. Beatrice gasped when she saw this, prompting stares from the other two. It was unusual for her to express surprise about anything.

'What is it?' prompted Arabella.

'The Martin Tower,' said Beatrice, somewhat unhelpfully.

'Yes? And?'

'I've just realised what the Phoenix is. Stupid of me not to have worked it out earlier.'

'Well?'

Beatrice looked at Arabella. 'You were right that Napoleon is after the Crown Jewels,' she said. 'That's where they're stored – in the Martin Tower. But he's not after crowns, sceptres, orbs or any other regalia. He's after a jewel – the biggest jewel of them all.'

'The Phoenix,' murmured Cassie. 'Of course.'

Arabella had heard of the Phoenix – everyone had. But the world of diamonds and jewellery had never particularly interested her, so her knowledge of it was sketchy. She hadn't even realised that the Phoenix was part of the Crown Jewels.

'The largest cut diamond in the world,' Beatrice told them. 'Pear-shaped, with seventy-six facets, and set within the Royal Sceptre.'

'You know a lot about it,' said Cassie, impressed.

Beatrice nodded, her eyes unusually bright. 'In my younger, criminal days, I used to dream about stealing it.'

Isaac placed Gérard, Fabien and the centaurs on guard duty at the entrances of the tower. Then he, Napoleon, Guizot and Diana entered the Martin Tower.

'Perhaps you'll get a chance to fulfil your dream,' said Cassie, 'by stealing the diamond back from Napoleon.'

'Perhaps,' said Beatrice.

'I just don't understand it,' said Arabella. 'All this effort to steal a diamond…'

There was a muffled explosion inside the tower. Ten minutes later, the robber-emperor and his companions re-emerged. Napoleon stood on the ramparts and held out his hand, palm upwards. In the twilight, something gleamed there.

CHAPTER THIRTY-FIVE

THE WEAK SHIELD

Beatrice, mesmerised by the sight of the Phoenix in Napoleon's hand, delayed almost too long. The centaurs suddenly jolted to life and started back towards the parade ground, followed by the Equestrians, with Napoleon, Diana and Guizot at the rear.

'Come on!' hissed Cassie, pulling Beatrice out of sight. The three of them began running as fast as they could alongside the barrack block, where the shadows were deepest. They could hear the clatter and hiss of the centaurs and the iron horses crossing the cobbles behind them, and Arabella prayed they wouldn't be seen.

And then… *disaster*!

They were passing a row of ceremonial field guns

placed on a strip of lawn at the front of the building when Beatrice suddenly let out a squeal and tumbled to the ground. Horrified, Arabella glanced back to see the girl sprawled on the grass clutching her leg, her face a rictus of agony. She must have knocked it hard against one of the guns.

An ominous silence descended on the parade ground as Napoleon, his guards and companions all stopped riding and turned towards the source of the sound. Cassie dragged Beatrice further into the shadows and the three of them tried to conceal themselves behind one of the artillery pieces.

Iron hooves clip-clopped closer.

'Who goes there?' barked a voice. It sounded like Isaac.

'Surrender, or we start shooting,' uttered another with the nasal tones of Gérard.

There were sounds of people dismounting.

Arabella began crawling very slowly forward, her cheek pressed against the grass. A gun clicked.

BANG!

Brickwork detonated above her head.

'Don't move,' grated Fabien. 'Stand up.'

She lay extremely still.

Footsteps approached. A hand closed around her collar and pulled her upright, almost choking her.

She heard Guizot, a few yards behind her, exclaim: 'Why, it's Lady Arabella.' There was a smile in his voice. 'So nice of you to drop by again... Kill her.'

'My pleasure,' Gérard breathed into her hair – for it was he who had her in his grip. She could feel him fumbling for the gun in his chest holster while maintaining his tight hold on her with his other hand.

Gérard's mistake was to assume she was still disarmed. If he'd dragged her out of the shadows, he would have seen the long-barrelled pistol dangling from her belt. It was easy enough, cloaked as she was in darkness, for Arabella to pivot the gun from vertical to horizontal, and fire.

The bullet passed right through Gérard, flying out of his back and lodging itself in Guizot's foot.

Gérard screamed.

Guizot screamed.

Fabien fired, but in the darkness he missed Arabella and hit the howling Gérard in the head, killing him instantly. Fabien fired again. She felt a blow to her shoulder. It didn't hurt, but it made her stagger. She began to run. Before Fabien could fire a third time, he received a flying fist to the point of his jaw from Cassie. He slumped to the ground, dazed.

'After them!' screamed Guizot, who had fallen from his horse and was clutching his blood-soaked boot. 'Kill them!'

Isaac remained at the emperor's side, his personal bodyguard, while the four centaurs galloped forward and began firing blindly into the shadows, shattering windows and peppering the stout walls of the barrack block with bullet holes.

Cassie had Beatrice by the elbow and was pulling the hobbling girl along as they fled in the wake of Arabella. When they reached Tower Green, the three girls spun left and raced across the lawn. They were in the open now, bullets whining through the air around them like deadly insects. They took shelter behind the four-foot-high scaffold. It was a simple wooden structure made up of a platform resting on four timber posts supported by diagonal cross-braces.

Centaur hoofbeats thundered towards them. Arabella searched for an escape route. Tower Green was enclosed on three sides, with a chapel to the north and terraced housing to the west and south. There was no way out. The only exit through the Tower's inner wall was by the portcullised entrance beneath the Bloody Tower, which was seventy-five yards to the southeast across open ground. She could hear Beatrice's hard breathing close to her shoulder and knew she was in pain and probably couldn't run fast.

'You were hit, Bella,' wheezed Cassie. 'Are you all right?'

Arabella glanced at her shoulder but saw no blood there, just a red mark. 'Fine,' she said. *The bullet must have missed, or... First the shot to my forehead, and now this. Have I somehow become shielded?*

Sounds of hissing, bubbling steam from the far side of the scaffold told her the centaurs were close. As hoofbeats approached them from both sides, the Sisters clambered under the platform. They crouched there, watching the turf getting pummelled with bullet holes. Soon the centaurs began firing through the cross-braces, forcing the Sisters further back. The metal centaurs were not designed to stoop or crouch, so were restricted to firing from a high angle.

Suddenly, the ground in front of them erupted in a huge explosion. For a split second, Arabella saw its flame blooming like a hollowed-out red hemisphere, shaping itself around the contours of the nearest centaur's invisible shield. The centaur didn't even tremble. The Sisters, however, were thrown backwards by the force of the blast, their clothes and faces spattered with mud. They stared, blinking, at the crater in the lawn.

'What's going on?' Cassie cried. 'Is this a rescue?'

'I don't know,' said Arabella, peering out from beneath the platform to try and see who had fired the shell. What she saw made her turn pale. She grabbed Cassie's and Beatrice's hands.

'They're coming,' she whispered.

'Who?'

'Centaurs,' Arabella replied. 'Dozens of them – from the towers, from all sides.'

In the waning light, they were hard to see individually – it was like a creeping blackness that consumed all in its path. From north, south and west, the stampede converged on the scaffold at the centre of Tower Green. The Sisters flattened themselves to the ground as bullets clattered into the scaffold timbers and whipped at their hair. Cassie cried out and grabbed her upper arm; blood flowed between her fingers. The rising storm of hoofbeats and gunfire shook the earth and blotted out all other sounds.

Suddenly, Arabella knew what she had to do. Without saying a word to the other two, she crawled out from beneath the scaffold and stood up in full view of the approaching hordes.

'Bella!' yelled Cassie. 'No!'

Arabella began walking slowly away from them, towards the parade ground. The air around her crackled and whined with gunfire. A bullet whacked into her hip, jolting her sideways, but she carried on walking. Another slammed into her thigh. She lurched slightly, but didn't lose her balance. Then three hit her almost simultaneously – on her arm, her back and a stinging one to her cheek. It shook her. She nearly lost her balance, but kept on walking.

As the centaurs found their mark, the trickle became a deluge. She felt like a boxer being pummelled from all sides. Her body was jerked one way then the other. She wanted to hurl herself to the ground to take cover from this rain of pain, but, to the growing concern of the people on the parade ground, she continued on her course towards them.

'*Mon Dieu!*' shrieked Guizot, hopping around on his one good foot, his face the colour of a beetroot. 'She has the shield! She must have the shield! But how?'

If she had the shield, it was a weak version of it,

because every bullet that landed hurt her – even more so now they were landing on already bruised parts of her body. Yet, strangely, it was getting easier. The pain mattered less and less. And her skin did not break. She was glad she was drawing the fire from Cassie and Beatrice. Cassie had bled from a bullet wound, which meant she wasn't shielded.

Why do I have the shield and not Cassie?

Her feet left the turf and began treading the cobbles. Isaac moved protectively in front of Napoleon, and this gave Arabella an idea. It might be the only way she could save her friends' lives. She began to move more urgently, heading straight for the emperor.

Isaac, a desperate fervour distorting his face, took aim at her with his gun and fired. Her head flew back as the bullet struck the top of her nose. But by now she felt as though she were made of India rubber – a walking doll, impervious, unstoppable. She kept on coming. Isaac began backing away, pulling the emperor with him, emptying his gun chamber into her. When she was close enough to touch, he pulled his gun arm back and struck at her head with its butt. She felt it as nothing more than a gust of wind.

Ignoring Isaac, Arabella raised her gun to the head of the most powerful man on earth and said: 'Tell them to stop firing at me and my friends, or I will kill you.'

CHAPTER THIRTY-SIX

THE VERY EMINENT HOSTAGE

As she contemplated her captive, Arabella suddenly found it hard to remember how to breathe. She was standing in the presence of history. Not a man but a spirit, an idea – a nation – in human form.

Napoleon gave her an appraising, hooded-eyed stare, his brown eyes opaque, fearless. Forcing herself to become calm, she drew back the hammer with a click. He didn't flinch. *Would she have to go through with this?* Her name would echo through the ages if she did – but something about the man's pigheaded fearlessness stayed her finger.

It was Guizot who broke.

He screamed an order, and the centaurs, who had been advancing on her from behind, suddenly stopped, causing a juddering ripple through the gleaming black ranks. The guns ceased firing.

Silence.

And into the silence floated the comforting sound of puttering engines. Two steambikes rounded the corner of the White Tower and drew up near Napoleon, Arabella and Isaac. One of them was being ridden by a masked rider; the other, by Miles.

'Good evening, my lady,' said the automaton. Due to his compact size, Miles had to lean forward and spread his arms wide to reach the handlebars. 'I do hope I find you in reasonable fettle,' he ventured.

'I'm fine, thank you, Miles,' said Arabella, even though her body felt like a furnace of pain. The warmth that filled her at the sight of him more than compensated for all the pummelling she'd received. 'How are you?' she asked him.

'A few bumps, but otherwise I do believe I am in reasonable working order.'

She glanced briefly at the young man, who had a cloth covering most of his face. She was fairly sure it was Jacques. 'Thank you for returning, monsieur,' she said. 'Your timing… these bikes. It's perfect.'

'You will not get away with this!' Guizot screamed at Arabella. 'I will hunt you down!'

Arabella ignored him and continued to address herself to the young man, while keeping her eyes and her gun on the emperor. 'Monsieur,' she said, 'my friends are under the scaffold behind me. Please could you signal to them to come here.' The rider raised a hand and beckoned to them.

A moment later, Beatrice and Cassie arrived. Beatrice was limping. Cassie, looking pale with shock and blood loss, had one hand clamped to her wounded arm.

Arabella wondered how exactly she would be able to get everyone away from the Tower without getting them all shot and killed. The obvious thing to do would be to take Napoleon hostage, but how could she do that while riding a steambike?

The masked rider was a step ahead of her in this respect. Turning to Napoleon, he said: 'Excellency, do you know how to ride a steam-powered motorcycle?'

Napoleon looked at him and shook his head.

'Well, it's very simple…'

The few minutes that followed seemed utterly surreal to Arabella as Guizot, Isaac and the entire army of centaurs were forced to watch the rider give the emperor a tour of his two-wheeled vehicle. He pointed out the ignition, firetube boiler, twin-cylinder engine, cooling fan, boiler feed, fuel feed, radiator and air pump. While Arabella kept her gun pointing at the emperor's neck, the rider mimed how to ride the machine. Napoleon nodded thoughtfully throughout the lesson.

Once he'd pronounced himself enlightened in the basics, the diminutive despot climbed aboard the bike and started it up. His tutor got on behind him, keeping his own shotgun aimed at the back of Napoleon's head. The bike then shot forward a few feet, sending the emperor's famous bicorne hat flying. The vehicle proceeded to move in jerks until Napoleon managed to master the sensitivity of throttle and brake.

The masked rider then beckoned to Beatrice, who limped forward and climbed on behind him – the steambike's seat was easily long enough to accommodate three. Meanwhile, Miles shifted backwards on his seat, making room for Arabella and Cassie on the other steambike.

The rider turned to Guizot and uttered a warning: 'If any of your goons shoots at either bike while we are leaving the Tower, the emperor dies.'

Guizot narrowed his eyes and snarled. 'I will get you. I will make it my personal mission to kill each and every one of you.'

The rider whispered something to Napoleon, then leaned back. 'Proceed at your own pace, Excellency,' he said.

The emperor turned in a wide arc around the parade ground and then headed clockwise around the White Tower. Arabella took up position a few yards to the rear. They rode past Guizot, Diana and the downed Equestrians, past the Martin Tower and south through the Inner Ward. To their left flashed the Constable Tower, the Broad Arrow Tower and the Salt Tower. Arabella waited tensely for the shooting to begin. But not a shot was fired as the small convoy turned left through two arched gateways and proceeded out onto the castle wharf.

An evening breeze had roughed up the dark, metallic surface of the river. Broken-masted ships cast long shadows in the waning light. To their left lay Tower Bridge, one of its famous towers crushed as if stamped on by a careless giant. Twisted suspension cables dangled, and the river swirled about a new islet of shattered brown stone and black tile.

Now what? Arabella wondered. *Are we going to take the emperor hostage – or kill him?*

Something was approaching them at a gallop. A shadow swept past Arabella – Isaac on his iron horse, his cape flying out behind him. He leapt from the saddle at the bike in front. The engine screamed as it toppled, spilling the passengers.

As the emperor landed in an untidy sprawl, something shiny flew from his pocket and rolled across the cobbles.

'The Phoenix!' cried Beatrice, and she began to crawl towards it.

Arabella accelerated, hoping to run Isaac down before he could reach the diamond. When he saw her approach he raised his gun and aimed it at Cassie. Arabella had to swerve to prevent her friend being shot, and her rear wheel went into a skid.

Just as Beatrice was about to grab the diamond, Isaac snatched it up. The masked rider set his bike back on its wheels and called to Beatrice: 'Forget it! Let's go!'

Reluctantly, she climbed aboard. Seeing them surge away, Isaac turned his gun on them. His bullet struck a wheel, and the rider lost control. Arabella could only watch as the front wheel collided with a mooring post and the rear end pitched high in the air, sending rider and passenger flying.

Beatrice was catapulted straight over the wharfside into the Thames. As for the rider, he hit the ground in a twisting roll with such force that he almost joined her there. Just as he was rolling over the edge, he grasped hold of some cobblestones and clung on. He hung there helplessly as Isaac took careful aim at his head.

'I wouldn't,' Arabella said to him. She was pointing a shotgun, taken from a holster attached to her bike, at Isaac.

Isaac looked at her and grimaced behind his domino mask. Behind him, the rider took the opportunity to haul himself back up. Then Isaac's face unexpectedly broke into a smile. He'd noticed something going on behind Arabella. She turned briefly to see what was so amusing. On the ramparts of the Outer Wall and on Wakefield and St Thomas's towers, French soldiers were gathering at the battlements and aiming their guns at her. Meanwhile, more centaurs were mustering at either end of the wharfside. They were once again surrounded. As for Napoleon, whose presence as their hostage had thus far kept them alive, he was heading back through the castle gates.

'It's over,' Isaac said to her. 'Give up.'

'Into the river,' Cassie yelled in Arabella's ear.

'What?' Arabella thought she'd misheard.

'Just do it!'

'OK! Here goes!'

CHAPTER THIRTY-SEVEN

THE MASKED RIDER

Bullets had already begun pinging around them as Arabella aimed the prow of the bike at Old Father Thames and ripped open the throttle. The bike's rear wheel screeched as they zoomed forward and hurtled over the edge. A second later, they splashed down into the cold, dark, foul-smelling river. Cassie leaned forward and flipped a switch on the bike's polished walnut dashboard. As Arabella felt her boots sink into the freezing wet murk, there came a loud *PFFFFSSSSSSSSS* of compressed air being released, and a large black canvas raft began to inflate all around the bike. Arabella felt herself rising, and almost immediately the prow surged above the foaming surface. Cassie leaned back behind Miles and pulled a cord, firing up an outboard engine at the rear of the newly transformed bike-boat. There was a gush of power from the rear of the craft and soon they were speeding along the river, raising a huge arching trail of white spray. Glancing behind, Arabella was relieved to see that the other bike had undergone an identical metamorphosis and was now bouncing along in their wake. At the helm was the masked mystery boy, and behind him sat a soaking-wet Beatrice, freshly retrieved from the river.

On the wharfside, Isaac watched them go, his mouth a black circle of astonishment. Bullets continued to spatter the water around them, but at a diminishing rate as they moved out of range of the French guns.

'I didn't have time to tell you about this feature!' Cassie yelled at Arabella above the roar. 'Good old British engineering. Why stop at a bike when you can have a boat as well?'

'It's fantastic!' cried Arabella. The wind was blowing hair into her face and she was shaking from exhilaration at their incredible escape.

The bike's handlebars were connected to a rudder at the rear of the vehicle. She set a course around the new islet created by the wreckage of one half of Tower Bridge. After passing beneath what remained of the bridge, close to the southern bank, she continued west, towards Hades.

'That was amazing what you did back there!' shouted Cassie. 'How come you suddenly have the shield?'

'I have no idea!'

They had travelled almost two miles upstream and were approaching the Strand Bridge (the same one that Arabella had nearly collided with in *Prince* some hours earlier) when something mysterious appeared in the bike-boats' path. Bubbles began to fountain out of the dark river, followed by a reptilian-looking snout with protruding eyes. Its dripping copper scales glimmered in the evening mist.

Arabella pulled up alongside as a hatchway opened in the top of the monster's head, just behind its eyes. The head of a young man appeared.

'Ahoy there!' he called.

'Good evening, Corporal Powers!' replied Arabella. She gathered the rope he threw to her and clambered onto *Kraken*'s deck.

Within a quarter of an hour both boat-bikes had been deflated and stowed in watertight compartments beneath the conning tower, and their occupants were drying themselves off inside the submarine. Corporal Tim Powers was at the wheel, steering *Kraken* through the river's grey-green depths towards what he described as an under-river entrance to Hades.

Once they'd changed into dry clothing, his passengers gathered around the big circular table. Beatrice got to work bandaging Cassie's arm. Arabella winced as she sat down – for now that the excitement of the escape was wearing off, she was beginning to feel, more than ever, all her many bruises.

'Thank you for rescuing Miles, monsieur,' she said to the mysterious rider, who for some reason still insisted on wearing his mask.

'You are very welcome, mademoiselle. And I must thank you for saving my life on the castle wharf. That horseman would have killed me if you hadn't intervened.'

'That horseman?' frowned Arabella. 'But surely you knew it was your colleague, Isaac Dreyfus.'

'Aw, hell, was it really?' The clipped French accent dissolved into a slow Texian drawl, as Ben Forrester removed his mask.

'Mr Forrester!' cried Arabella.

'Agent Z!' exclaimed Cassie. 'I thought you were back at the Lab with the professor, trying to create braydenite.'

'You mean benite,' said Ben.

'Where is Monsieur Daguerre?' asked Arabella.

'I found him with Miles, waiting for you at the Middle Tower entrance,' replied Ben.

'Monsieur Jacques was most solicitous, my lady,' interjected Miles. 'He discovered me in a somewhat discombobulated state near Billingsgate Market. I'm afraid that when I fell from the bike, one of the movable pinions that connect the figure wheels to the ingress axis in my brain suffered slight damage.'

'In other words?'

'I lost my memory. But Monsieur Jacques fixed me up and I remember everything now. Then Mr

Forrester arrived on one of the steambikes, towing a second one behind him…'

'I assured Monsieur Jacques I'd take care of things,' said Ben '– and make sure Miles got reunited with his mistress. He didn't exactly look happy about it, but I persuaded him it was for the best. Not long after Jacques left us, Miles and I heard gunfire inside the Tower. The rest of it you know.'

'And what exactly were you doing at the Tower of London, sir?' asked Arabella.

'I was…' He seemed unusually lost for words. 'I was worried about, uh…'

'About what?' Arabella pressed him.

Cassie laughed. 'He was worried about *you*, silly!'

Ben and Arabella frowned at Cassie until it was her turn to blush. 'Well, it's obvious, isn't it?' she said. 'First he shows up on Taranis, out of the blue, and helps you defeat the sky pirates. Then, a few days later, he crashes into *Titan* and rescues you from there – oh yes, Emmeline told me all about that little escapade. And now this. It's quite obvious, Bella dear, that Mr Forrester is completely –'

'– incapable of letting me manage my affairs by myself,' finished Arabella, fixing Ben with the same glare she'd just directed at Cassie. 'It's true, Mr Forrester. You are starting to make a habit of showing up at these, er… critical moments. Are you following me by any chance?'

'I was concerned about the *mission*,' said Ben,

folding his arms defensively. 'Not just about you, but about Cassie and Beatrice, not to mention my little metal amigo here. I didn't appreciate the way your boss Major Stuart sent you off into that vipers' nest without any back-up. And I was proved right, wasn't I? You had about a thousand guns trained on you with no evidence that I could see of an exit strategy. In fact your prospects looked about as bright as my old man's when he was holed up at the Alamo surrounded by the entire Mexican army. And you know what happened to *him*!'

Arabella fought to keep her temper under control. 'I had a couple of advantages not enjoyed by your late father,' she said through tight lips. 'For one thing, my gun was pointing at Napoleon's head.'

Ben looked up. 'Oh yeah, I was going to ask about that. How exactly did you manage to get so close to him?'

'She has the shield,' said Beatrice.

'Up to a point,' grimaced Arabella. 'I felt every one of those bullets.'

'You mean those bruises on you, they're… bullet wounds?' gasped Ben.

Arabella nodded. 'That was my other advantage.'

'Woah!' Ben leaned back. 'I'm impressed. But how?'

'I have no idea – and it doesn't really matter. However I came by this power, the fact is that we had the situation completely under control before you arrived. Cassie, Beatrice and I could have marched out of that *vipers' nest*, as you call it, any time we wanted, taking Napoleon as hostage. We didn't need your help, Mr Forrester, however much it pleases you to think we did. And from what I gather from Miles, it appears that I owe my thanks for his rescue to Monsieur Daguerre, not to you. All *you* managed to do was to expose my automaton to needless danger by bringing him into the enemy stronghold.'

'Bella,' said Cassie gently. 'Don't you think you're being a little, well, uncharitable? I'm sure Mr Forrester meant well. He heard gunfire, and naturally he… well, he wanted to help.'

Ben said nothing. His hands were twisting in his lap and his jaw muscles were working as if wrestling with a lump of ten-day-old gristle. Eventually, he turned to Arabella and said: 'You, ma'am, are quite insufferable! Mark my words, this is the very last time I will ever lift a finger to help you… Miles, if I ever so much as talk to your mistress again, you have permission to shoot me.' With that, he stood up, strode to the front of the vessel and deposited himself in the seat next to Corporal Powers.

Arabella stared at her hands and tried to will them to stop trembling. In the silence that followed around the table she overheard Ben asking the corporal aggressive questions about the workings of the submarine.

Clearly, she decided, *he feels the need to absorb himself in technical matters as an antidote to someone as insufferable as me.*

'Are you all right, Bella?' asked Cassie.

'Of course I am!' snapped Arabella. Then, in more reasonable tones, she continued: 'I didn't mean to upset him, but he has to learn that I am not some helpless female. If I hadn't been blunt with him, he'd have persisted in trying to rescue me from one thing or another, making it quite impossible to do my job.'

The *Kraken*'s gas lamps penetrated the murky waters and shone against the black pilings of the Thames embankment. Everyone watched as a door beneath the river began to slide open. It was a big circular door, hidden within the ancient timbers.

'A lot of women wouldn't mind being rescued by Agent Z,' commented Cassie.

'Well, I am not "a lot of women".'

'He saved your life on *Titan*,' pointed out Beatrice.

Arabella glared at her. 'It's my life to save or sacrifice as I please,' she said. 'Anyway, perhaps he didn't.'

'What do you mean?' asked Cassie.

'If I'm shielded now, perhaps I was shielded then, too, and just didn't realise it. I might not have needed Mr Forrester's rocket, after all.'

'Maybe not,' sighed Cassie.

Kraken advanced through the open door into an underwater airlock. Its occupants waited as the water level gradually fell. Soon a dock would appear and they could leave the craft and enter Hades.

'Anyhow,' said Cassie, as they waited, 'I think you've made your feelings abundantly clear. From the way Mr Forrester was talking just now, I doubt you're ever going to be bothered by him again.'

'Good,' said Arabella, and she tried her best to feel cheered by this thought.

PART IV

22–23 JULY 1845

CHAPTER THIRTY-EIGHT

THE
DEBRIEF

'Explain to me once again exactly how you managed to avoid getting killed,' Emmeline asked Arabella the following morning.

'I think I've acquired a weak form of the Aetheric Shield,' replied Arabella.

'Do you have any idea how that might have happened?'

'None at all,' Arabella said, squirming in her chair. Her bruises did not make sitting comfortable. At least she'd had a decent night's sleep – sheer exhaustion had seen to that. The following morning, after breakfast, Emmeline had called her, Cassie, Beatrice and Miles to a conference room off an anonymous corridor in the subterranean labyrinth of Hades so they could be debriefed.

'*I* have a theory,' said Miles.

Arabella glanced in some surprise at her logical friend, dwarfed by the capacious leather armchair he was seated in.

'Fire away,' said Emmeline.

'It's possible that my lady may have been exposed to the ASG on board *Titan*... She was in the section of the ship containing the army of soldier-automata during a brief moment when the device transmitted a beam of aetheric energy. It was probably long enough to give her a minor dose.'

Emmeline turned to Arabella for confirmation of this.

'It's true,' Arabella nodded excitedly. 'I remember seeing this strange golden light spreading outwards from the ASG and coating the centaurs. It didn't occur to me then, but I think Miles is right: it must have coated me as well.'

'Well, it was a lucky break,' said Emmeline. She turned to the others. 'You all did extremely well in getting away from the Tower in one piece, and the intelligence you gathered might just help us work out Napoleon's purpose.'

'Ma'am,' said Arabella. 'One of the Equestrians, Isaac, told me that other British cities were also under attack. Is that true?'

Emmeline shook her head. 'He was lying,' she said. 'London is the only city the French have attacked so far, which I admit is puzzling. Still more puzzling is the nature of the attack. There has been no attempt to take over aetherwave broadcasting facilities, military bases or government offices – the usual targets for any invading force. Apart from the hundreds of tons of incendiary bombs dropped on the city, the only concerted attacks have been on our banks and on the Tower of London, an ancient fortress of no strategic value. And from what you say, Napoleon's entire purpose in taking the Tower was to steal a diamond from the Crown Jewels. Can that really be all he was after?'

'It's the Phoenix Diamond,' said Beatrice, 'the largest cut diamond in the world.'

'So what?' Emmeline shrugged. 'It's still just a stone. I'm sure the French have their own impressive collection in the Louvre.'

Beatrice nodded. 'They have the Regent Diamond, and the Sancy Diamond, and the Emerald of Saint-Louis, and the Ruspoli sapphire of Queen Marie Antoinette, and the –'

'Yes, yes, Beatrice, we get the picture!' said Emmeline, drawing an exasperated breath. 'The point is, why go to all this trouble to steal one diamond?'

'It's 540 carats,' said Beatrice. 'To compare, the Regent Diamond is 410 carats, the Sancy just 55.'

'I'm sorry, Bea, but what does that mean?' asked Cassie.

'Carat weight is a measure of the diamond's mass,' Beatrice explained. 'The larger the diamond, the higher the carat weight, and the more valuable it is.'

'OK, so it's big and valuable,' said Emmeline. 'But Napoleon isn't exactly short of cash, is he? Might it have some sentimental value to him? What's its history?'

'It was cut from a 900-carat diamond excavated in Andhra Pradesh, India, in the early eighteenth century,' said Beatrice. 'At first it was owned by the Nawabs of Bengal. Then, in 1757, it was acquired by the British East India Company after their victory at the Battle of Plassey. The diamond was presented to King George III in 1765 at a time when he was gravely ill. It acquired its name because soon after the king was given it, he made a miraculous recovery.'

'Like the mythical Phoenix, he rose again,' smiled Cassie.

'Was it ever owned by the French?' asked Emmeline.

'No,' said Beatrice. 'The French never had any claim on the diamond.'

'How strange!' said Emmeline. 'Is there anything else you can tell me about it – anything unusual?'

'The cut is extraordinarily good,' said Beatrice, 'balancing brilliance, fire and scintillation to create what experts call a superb light performance.'

'I have no idea what that means,' said Cassie, 'but it sounds lovely!'

'And it's also got a very unusual fluorescence,' Beatrice added.

'Meaning?' prompted Emmeline.

'It glows green under strong sunlight. Most diamonds have no fluorescence. About a third glow blue. A really tiny number glow yellow, orange, pink or red. As far as I know, the Phoenix is the only diamond that glows green.'

'And there was I thinking they just sparkled,' grinned Cassie.

'It's a remarkable jewel, not just for its size,' said Beatrice. With some bitterness, she added: 'And I was just three feet away from getting it back.'

'Well,' sighed Emmeline. 'That's the way it goes sometimes. Thank you, Beatrice. I'm seconding you to our Field Ops team who will need briefing on the diamond before attempting to steal it back. You may even wish to take part in that raid yourself.'

The girl's eyes widened. 'I would like that, ma'am. Thank you.'

When Beatrice had departed, Emmeline addressed the others: 'The bad news is that this invasion wasn't simply the most expensive diamond heist in history. Having stolen the jewel, Napoleon seems in no hurry to depart. In fact, more French airships landed during the night. They've taken enough gold from our banks to keep *Titan* and its centaurs shielded for weeks, possibly months, and I don't want to imagine the damage they might do to London in that time. They might start to shield their other airships, too, which will pose problems for the Royal Air Fleet, when it finally gets here.'

'When is our Air Fleet due, ma'am?' asked Cassie.

'It will be four days, at least, before we can muster ships and crews from our coastal bases in sufficient numbers to take on the French. Until then, we must regard London as an occupied city, and ourselves as resistance fighters. The French are determined to root us out. They know we exist somewhere underground, they just don't yet know where. Already, their troops are scouring the Underground Railway network. It's only a matter of time before they find us. I doubt we'll last out before the Air Fleet arrives, which means we'll have to launch our own counterattack, if we want to survive.'

'How are we going to do that?' asked Arabella.

'There have been some developments,' Emmeline smiled. 'I think it's time for a return visit to the Lab.'

CHAPTER THIRTY-NINE

THE BRAYDENITE BOMB

'Behold, braydenite,' said Professor Brayden Storm, holding up a small blue crystal. Arabella thought the blue rather beautiful: it was the deep and mysterious colour of ocean waves.

The professor narrowed his eyes at Ben, who was standing next to him, as if daring the American to contradict him on the name. But Ben, who seemed to be concentrating on something else entirely, said nothing.

Arabella followed the direction of Ben's gaze, but could see nothing in the corner of the Lab he was staring at except an empty mouse cage. He was frowning, his lips pressed firmly together. *He's avoiding me*, she realised. *He still thinks I'm insufferable.*

'My assistant and I', said the professor, 'have spent the past twenty-four hours searching for this substance – or at least *I* have. *He* spent a good part of it gallivanting around the Tower of London like some knight errant.' Again he turned to Ben, who now seemed absorbed by a patch of linoleum-covered floor.

'Can it penetrate *Titan*'s shield?' asked Emmeline.

'Indeed it can,' said the professor. 'The crystal may look small, but we calculate it will be powerful enough to pierce the aetheric envelope surrounding the mother ship. However, we've struck a problem…'

Emmeline frowned. 'You told me you'd cracked it, Professor. Those were your very words!'

Professor Storm bowed his head a little sheepishly. 'Yes, well, perhaps I was a little premature in my declaration of success. We've subsequently noticed a certain… effect of the shield.'

'And what is that?'

The professor sighed. 'Braydenite can break through it, but if we combine it with a large explosive missile, the shield quickly "wakes up" to the threat and activates itself.'

'So you're saying the door opens and then quickly slams shut again,' said Cassie.

'Precisely!' said the professor.

'So how were you able to destroy that centaur?' asked Arabella.

'That took very little explosive,' said the professor. 'By the time the shield woke up to the danger, it was too late. But to destroy something the size of *Titan*, we'll need our braydenite-tipped missile to carry a much larger incendiary charge.'

'I'm not sure we would,' said Arabella. '*Titan* has a room packed with high explosives. It won't take much to set that lot off.'

'I'm afraid those explosives are no longer aboard,' said Emmeline. 'According to our scouts, they were used to blow open the city's bank vaults to steal all the gold.' She sighed. 'I suppose we're back to square one.'

'Not quite,' said Cassie, trying her best to brighten the mood. 'At least we can attack the centaurs now.'

Emmeline nodded. 'Good point, Cassie. Professor, how long would it take you to tip a few thousand shells and bullets with braydenite?'

'Well, uh…' The professor frowned.

'You can have all the labour you need,' said Emmeline. 'We'll drag in volunteers from the Underground Railway shelters if necessary.'

'The thing is, you see…' Professor Storm spluttered.

'Use all the braydenite you have, and we'll set up a team of chemists to create more.'

The professor stared sadly at the little crystal. 'We didn't anticipate…' he began.

'Didn't anticipate what, Professor?'

He looked up. 'This is all we have,' he said.

'That?' scowled Emmeline, pointing at the crystal.

'It took us a day to grow a crystal this size,' he said.

'We'd need weeks to manufacture braydenite in the quantities you're talking about.'

'We don't have weeks,' said Emmeline quietly.

A funereal silence filled the Lab. A tap dripped in a sink somewhere.

We're finished, thought Arabella.

'There is something else we could try,' said Ben, suddenly raising his head. Everyone turned to him expectantly.

'This *braydenite*' – he grimaced as he pronounced the word – 'it's the absolute antithesis of aetheric energy.'

'What do you mean?'

'I mean it's like putting a bunch of Texians in a saloon bar with a bunch of Mexicans.'

'We still don't follow you,' said Emmeline.

'He means that they would annihilate each other,' said Professor Storm with gathering excitement.

'Exactly!' Ben nodded. 'We won't need any explosives. We only need that crystal. If we could fire it into a powerful source of aetheric energy – into the ASG on *Titan*, for example – it would…'

'…create an explosion big enough to destroy the entire mother ship!' finished the professor with a triumphant grin.

'*And* destroy the shields of every centaur at the same time,' said Cassie.

The two men nodded enthusiastically.

'How would we fire it into the ASG?' asked Emmeline.

'A long-range rocket ought to do it,' said the professor. 'A non-explosive rocket, so the shield wouldn't pick it up as a threat. All we need to know is where it is within *Titan*.'

'It was in a large hall, close to the armoury,' said Arabella.

'So in the rear part of the gondola,' said Ben. 'Professor, have you got the plan of *Titan* I sent you?'

'Of course, dear boy.'

A moment later they were all standing around a table with a detailed plan of *Titan*'s five decks unfurled before them on a large sheet of paper. 'Now, where exactly was it in the hall?' the professor asked Arabella.

She pointed to a location at the opposite end of the room to where she had come in.

'Bang in the middle, directly opposite the hatchway,' laughed the professor. 'Perfect!' He drew a straight line across the plan with his finger to show the projected flight of the braydenite-tipped rocket.

'Excellent!' said Emmeline. 'Professor, how soon can you – ?'

'Hold on,' interrupted Arabella. 'How high is this hatch?'

'About half the height of the gondola,' said the professor.

'Then it's not going to work,' said Arabella. 'The ASG is on a high platform. The hall itself is the height of the entire gondola and the ASG is more than halfway to the ceiling. A rocket fired through the hatch would hit the platform and miss the ASG.'

The professor slumped into a chair. His cliff of hair seemed to droop. He grabbed a doughnut from a nearby box and began to chomp it disconsolately. 'So near,' he groaned, 'and yet so far.'

'I could carry it aboard *Titan*, then throw it into the ASG myself,' suggested Arabella.

As she said this, she saw Ben's face fall.

'How?' asked Emmeline. 'Our scouts say there are at least ten centaur guards at every entrance. What's more, they've taken complete control of Hyde Park, with patrols guarding the perimeter. The entire area is utterly impenetrable.'

'There must be a way,' Arabella insisted. 'It wouldn't be the first time I've managed to sneak aboard that ship.'

'It would be a one-way trip, my dear,' said Professor Storm gravely. 'There would be no time to escape after you toss the braydenite into the ASG. We're talking instant vaporisation.'

Arabella nodded. 'I know.'

Her voice sounded firm and strong – no one could have guessed how much she was shaking inside.

She felt Cassie's hand take hold of hers and heard her suppress a sob.

'I can't ask you to do this,' said Emmeline. 'It must be entirely voluntary.'

Arabella bit her lip. 'It's all right. I volunteer.'

What was driving her to do this? Was she really saying these things?

There was a movement to her right, a scrape of furniture. She glanced up in time to see Ben leaving the room, the door swinging closed behind him. Through its circular window, she observed him walking quickly down the long corridor that led to the aerial steam carriages and the underground runway. The dark cloud hanging over his head was almost visible.

Without a word to anyone, she took off after him. Again, she couldn't explain why – she just knew she had to do this.

It was low tide on the Thames. A small beach of grey sand had formed at the base of the embankment. It looked like any other section of riverbank. The spotters in the French airships above could not possibly know that behind those dull black wooden pilings lay the concealed exit ramp of an underground runway, and beyond that: Hades.

Arabella found Ben on the beach, tossing stones into the water. She jumped down to join him.

'Do you mind if I sit here?' she asked. Ben didn't reply, so she sat down on a wooden post sticking out of the sand, the rotten foundations of an ancient jetty.

'Have I done something to upset you?' Arabella eventually asked.

Ben stopped in mid-throw and turned to her, one eyebrow raised. 'Do I look upset?' he said, pulling back his arm and then releasing a stone. It arced thirty or forty feet before disappearing with a splash into the grey-green waters.

'Why did you walk out of the Lab just now?' she asked.

'Maybe because I don't like to witness someone like you throwing their life away,' said Ben, hunting for another stone.

'Someone like me?' she asked. It was her turn to raise an eyebrow.

Ben pursed his lips. He continued searching the beach, but she could tell he was thinking about how to respond.

When he didn't, she began to goad him: 'Someone *like* me? Or me?'

Again, silence. He selected a perfectly round, flat stone and began wiping sand from its surface.

Arabella persisted: 'Was Cassie right to see a pattern in your behaviour, Mr Forrester? First Taranis, then *Titan*, then the Tower.' She laughed. 'Fancy that! They all begin with *T*. What place will you try to rescue me from next, I wonder? The Taj Mahal? Timbuktu? Texas, perhaps?' Her smile faded. 'No, I shall probably never go to any of those places.'

'You're a damn fine agent,' Ben said quietly through gritted teeth. 'You're only eighteen. Why are you so determined to kill yourself?'

'Why are you so determined to stop me?'

'Answer my question first… and then I'll tell you.'

'Promise?'

'I promise.'

Arabella shrugged and began pulling at a loose thread on the sleeve of her flying jacket. 'It's not that complicated,' she said. 'I don't have any family – apart from Emmeline. I have two friends, Cassie and Miles. I love them both dearly, but I love my country more.' She turned her face to the sky. 'I've never wanted to live for the sake of living, Mr Forrester. I want to live meaningfully. If I can help my country by dying for it, that's a way of giving my life meaning.'

'Have you ever given any thought to other ways?'

'Other ways?'

'Of giving your life meaning.'

'Such as?'

'I dunno. Climbing a mountain? Finding the source of the Nile? Helping the poor? Some way that doesn't end in certain death, at least.'

She shook her head. 'This is the life I've chosen. This is what I do. It's what I've always wanted to do – ever since I was a child. My father… he gave his life for this country.'

Was that just a story she told herself?

She ran her fingers over the soft leather jacket – *his* jacket.

I hate this war, Bella, he used to tell her. *I hate this war, but I will never stop loving my country.*

She would go to her death believing in him.

'I imagine my father sometimes,' she said, 'watching over me from somewhere up there in the clouds. I have this need to make him proud of me. Perhaps, if you want to dig really deep, that's the real reason I'm doing this...' She looked at Ben. 'So now I've answered your question. It's your turn to answer mine.'

He contemplated the smooth, disc-shaped stone.

'You chose your life,' he said. 'I chose mine. Choices, as you know, involve sacrifice. Your sacrifice was the chance of a long life. Mine was... companionship. I work alone. I live alone. Because my work is so secret, and so dangerous, I can't afford to have friends. But...'

He fell silent.

'But what?' prompted Arabella.

'But, if friendship were ever an option, I'd... Well, I'd want to be friends with someone like you.'

'Someone like me?' she laughed, even as her heart began beating faster.

'*You*,' he said.

She looked down so he wouldn't see the blush forming in her cheeks. 'Thank you, Mr Forrester. Do I take it that I am not so very insufferable, then?'

Ben groaned at the memory. 'I apologise for that,' he said. 'When I'm angered I sometimes say things I... No, you're not insufferable.'

'It's quite all right,' said Arabella. 'I probably am a little. I think I was harsh on you, and ungrateful. Cassie thought so. I suppose I'm just not used to gallantry.

I don't know how to behave when a man decides to come to my aid. I tend to think I can do everything myself – I've always thought that – and perhaps I ought to realise that it's permissible, sometimes, to accept help from another person. Actually, I'm...' She stopped herself, realising she was babbling. Looking up at him, she said more slowly: 'I'm honoured that you can imagine being friends with me. I would have liked that too, had it been possible. Perhaps if our lives had been different, if our choices had been... But what's the point of speculating?' She raised her eyes once more to the sky – the view she always sought out whenever she felt troubled or uncertain. 'Today will most probably be my last day.'

Her voice wobbled as she said it. She could feel a sob in her chest. This was the right decision, so why couldn't she feel its rightness in her heart? Why did she feel so sad? And what had prompted her to chase after Ben just now? Was it because, deep down, she had hoped he might talk her out of it? Part of her sensed that just a few words from him right now could change everything. If he told her, for example, that he loved her, it would cause an earthquake inside her, and who could tell what sort of Arabella might emerge from it?

But Ben did not reply.

He was a prisoner, as she was. They were both prisoners of the choices they had made.

Instead, he faced the river, leaned back and hurled

the disc-shaped stone with as much anger and venom as he could muster. He threw it in a different way to the previous one, with a much flatter trajectory, using his forefinger to impart spin before releasing it. As a result it flew low across the river, whirling like a discus as it went. Its flat underside grazed the river surface in a series of little bounces; Arabella counted six or seven before it finally sank.

'Perhaps not,' said Ben as he stared at the place where the stone was no longer. He turned to her, and his mouth began curling into a grin. 'Perhaps this doesn't have to be your last day!'

'What do you mean?' she asked.

'Come with me!' he cried, running up the steps to the embankment and throwing open a disguised hatchway in the cobbles. 'I've got a plan.'

CHAPTER FORTY

THE AUDACIOUS PLAN

'A bouncing bomb,' said Ben to the group gathered around the table back in the Lab.

'A what?' said Emmeline.

'A who?' said Cassie.

'A bouncing bomb,' murmured an awe-struck Professor Storm.

On the table was a map of Hyde Park, which Emmeline had procured at Ben's request from the Field Ops department. Ben pointed to the eastern shore of the long, narrow Serpentine lake. '*Titan*,' he said, 'landed here, right in front of nearly a thousand yards of flat, open water. A bomb dropped onto that lake from the right height and at the right speed, angle and spin, could –'

'Wait a minute,' said Emmeline. 'Am I hearing you

correctly? Are you seriously proposing that we bounce a bomb on the surface of the lake?'

'Not *bounce* it, *skim* it,' said Ben. 'Like a flat, round stone on a river. Only "skimming bomb" doesn't sound nearly so good.'

'I agree,' nodded the professor. 'It lacks alliteration.'

Ben took up a fountain pen and drew a crude airship on the map to show the position of *Titan*. He marked the approximate location of the ASG inside it with a cross. He then drew a straight line from the Serpentine Bridge, at the bend in the lake, all the way to the flagship.

'Lady Arabella says that the ASG is positioned higher than the top of the open hatch,' Ben explained. 'So a conventional rocket attack, travelling in a straight line like this through the hatch, won't work. But a bouncing bomb won't travel in a straight line...'

Now Ben covered his earlier straight line with a series of curved lines to represent a bomb hopping across the lake. 'The final bounce,' he said, drawing the final bounce, 'will take our braydenite bomb on an upward trajectory through the hatch, allowing it to leap up high enough to strike the ASG. The nib of Ben's pen struck the cross and he scribbled an explosion.

'Ingenious,' breathed the professor.

The others, though, were full of doubts and questions.

'It seems a pretty far-fetched idea to me,' remarked Emmeline.

'How will you make the bomb bounce?' asked Cassie.

'And how will you make it bounce in the right place so it flies upwards through the hatch?' asked Arabella.

'Details, details,' said the professor. 'I can already see how it would work in theory.'

'In *theory*,' said Emmeline dubiously. 'May I remind you that French battalions will very soon be beating down our door. What we need right now are practical propositions, not theories.'

As if to underline her point, a dull thump reverberated through the Lab at that moment, causing a thin cloud of plaster dust to descend from the ceiling.

'With your permission, major,' said the professor, 'we can get to work on it right away – see if we can turn young Mr Forrester's theory into something workable.'

Emmeline looked at him for a long moment, trying to decide.

'My offer to take the braydenite into *Titan* myself still stands, ma'am,' said Arabella.

'I know it does, Arabella,' said Emmeline. 'But I can't allow it – not while other options might exist.' She turned to Ben and the professor. 'You have forty-eight hours, boys. If you can't make it work by then, we may be forced to go back to Arabella's idea.'

'Forty-eight hours!' spluttered the professor. 'But this is completely untried technology...'

'We'll be lucky if we even get *that* amount of time,'

Emmeline informed him bluntly. 'Hades will not remain undetected for much longer. If I were you, I'd get going right away.'

Work on the bouncing bomb began immediately, with other Lab work suspended so that all available brains and resources could be devoted to this one project. Furniture and equipment were shifted aside and a long, narrow, water-filled tank was constructed in the middle of the room to represent the Serpentine. A spring-loaded release mechanism was placed at one end of the tank, and very soon it was spitting out spinning, bouncing prototypes of the bomb. At the other end of the tank, modelmakers built a crude version of the *Titan*, with a miniature replica of the ASG placed inside it in the approximate position of the real one. Everything was carefully built to precisely 1:100 scale: the tank, for example, was 9.5 yards long, and *Titan*, 3 yards. This would make it easier to scale everything up when it came to planning the actual operation.

Within a few hours, Ben had worked out that a spinning barrel was far more stable and accurate, as well as easier to launch from an air carriage, than a spinning disc. Barrels of different sizes and weights were tried from different heights, with varying success. It was the professor, a keen golfer, who realised that applying backspin to the barrel greatly improved the height of the bounces. Gradually, during the course of the day, the optimum values were calculated and then scaled up:

ALTITUDE OF AIR CARRIAGE:	60 feet
AIRSPEED:	130 miles per hour
DISTANCE FROM TARGET:	394 yards
BACKSPIN:	500 rpm
LENGTH OF BOMB:	60 inches
DIAMETER:	40 inches
WEIGHT:	2,250 pounds
ANGLE OF ENTRY:	10 degrees
NUMBER OF BOUNCES:	5

The climax of the research occurred in the late afternoon. Miles had gently pointed out that the braydenite, if it arrived enclosed in a barrel, might not have the intended effect of destroying the ASG. Indeed, it might not even get through *Titan*'s shield. So a new test was devised: the first live test involving braydenite and an Aetheric Shield Generator. The model of *Titan* was replaced with Professor Storm's miniature ASG at one end of the tank, while at the other a tiny sliver of braydenite was inserted within a scale model of the barrel and placed in the release mechanism.

The professor ordered the Lab to be cleared of all personnel so that the experiment could commence. Everyone took shelter three rooms and two thick concrete walls away. This would be the first time a piece of pure braydenite would come into contact with an aetheric energy source, and no one could be sure quite how big the bang might turn out to be – even at 1:100 scale.

When all the interconnecting doors had been sealed and everyone was ready, a lab assistant pressed a button on an aetherwave transmitter, activating the hydraulic motor inside the release mechanism. The motor drove a belt that imparted backspin to the barrel. It would take exactly 54 seconds for the spin velocity to reach 500 rpm, at which point the mechanism would automatically open and the bomb would be released. In his rich, booming voice the professor counted off the seconds. At 54, he paused and everyone held their breath.

A second later they heard a dull, powdery sort of thud, which sounded to Arabella like a sandbag bursting. The professor led the way as everyone charged back to the Lab. Warm water washed out of the Lab door as it was opened: the entire room was flooded to a depth of at least an inch. A soot-black stain covered almost the entire wall behind where the ASG had stood, and the section of the long metal tank nearest to that end had been ripped and twisted as if made of nothing stronger than cardboard. Water spilling from the broken tank had caused the flood. As for the ASG, literally nothing remained.

The delighted researchers let out a cheer.

'Does that answer your question, Miles?' beamed the professor. He turned to Emmeline. 'With your permission, major, I think it's time we scaled this up to see if it'll work in real-life conditions. We'll modify an air carriage and get it out under cover of darkness to a reservoir or something – outside London, of course. Then we'll do a dummy run.'

He never heard Emmeline's reply, because her words were lost in a loud explosion from another part of Hades.

Seconds later, they heard shouts and screams from further along the corridor, coming from the direction of Charing Cross railway station. Arabella ran to see what was going on. Turning a corner, she saw British soldiers retreating – several of them wounded. 'Get back!' one of them shouted when he saw her. 'The Frenchies have broken through from the station side.'

Another explosion shook the ground, throwing Arabella off her feet. Dust and plaster coated her as she scrambled back towards the Lab.

'They've broken in!' she cried to Emmeline. 'Hades has been breached!'

CHAPTER FORTY-ONE

THE BEST AVIATOR IN THE WORLD

This news was greeted with stunned silence. Emmeline was the first to react. 'We have no choice,' she said. 'We must launch the attack today.'

'Impossible,' objected the professor. 'We need to modify the air carriage, build the bomb, train the aviator, run tests… It can't be done.'

'It *must* be done,' insisted Emmeline. 'We'll hold off the French for as long as we can, while you get to work doing what you need to do. But the attack must take place this afternoon or we're all doomed. Arabella, Cassie, come with me…' With that, Emmeline took off down the corridor.

Cassie ran after her, but Arabella hung back. 'Who did you have in mind to fly the air carriage, gentlemen?'

she asked Ben and the professor.

Professor Storm turned to Ben. 'Who do *you* think would be suitable, young man?'

'For a mission like this one, I'd say we'll need the best damn aviator in the world.' He smiled at Arabella. 'Can't think who that might be.'

Arabella glared at him, then stomped away.

She glanced back once more before rounding the corner. Ben had gone back inside the Lab. The professor was still standing in the corridor staring morosely at the puddle collecting around his feet. 'We'd better get started, I suppose,' he muttered. 'Does anyone, by any chance, have a mop?'

Arabella spent much of the next three hours lying in the junction of two corridors, gun poking round the corner, ready to shoot any French soldiers that came within sight. Hades had been designed for exactly this kind of defence. Its maze of twisting, turning corridors confused attacking forces and provided plentiful locations from which defenders could hide and shoot. The iron-reinforced concrete walls and ceilings were not pretty, but they were sturdy enough to withstand heavy shelling. This was fortunate, because now that Hades had been found, the above-ground shelling was constant and intense. The base shivered with every bombardment, and yet more dust fell, coating Arabella and everything else in a greyish-white blanket. In other parts of the base, she frequently heard the rattle of volley-guns, as well as shouted orders and running footsteps, but the action had yet to reach her sector. Somewhere else in Hades, Cassie would be guarding her own corridor, as would Emmeline and Beatrice. It was impossible to know how they were faring or how the battle was going in general. The most that could be said was that they hadn't yet lost.

As the time dragged on, Arabella grew increasingly bored, tense and frustrated with the lack of news. So she was greatly relieved when she finally received an aethercell message from Emmeline telling her to return to the Lab immediately.

'Good luck, Arabella,' said her aunt.

'Thank you.'

When she reached the Lab, she was told to proceed straight to the underground runway.

Ben, the professor and Miles were gathered around *Comanche Prince*, along with the chief engineer.

'Aha! Our aviatrix is here!' cried the professor when he saw her. 'This mission will need a flyer of rare talent, and we believe you are that woman.'

Arabella glanced at Ben. 'Well, I *am* the best aviator in the world, so it would seem.'

'The best we could find on short notice,' said Ben. His eyes twinkled, but his attempt at humour seemed forced. There was a gauntness to his expression that contrasted with his earlier optimism. The planning was over; the mission was upon them, and it was all happening a lot sooner than any of them would have wished.

'My lady,' said Miles, 'you will have to make your approach at an altitude of just 60 feet – below the height of many trees. You will have to fly at precisely 230 miles per hour in a perfectly straight line. The slightest wobble could mean the difference between a hit and a miss. I've run some calculations and your chances of success are –'

'Hush, Miles!' she said. 'I don't want to know. I'm sure my chances are minuscule and that's fine. I don't care.'

Miles chugged and churned and smoked. 'As long as I remain operational, I will never understand humans,' he said.

'It's true, you probably won't, Miles,' remarked the professor. 'And that is why, in the inevitable battle between humans and automata, we humans will ultimately triumph – the crucial difference being that your species will fight logically, whereas we never know when we're beat.'

The engineer pointed out the modifications that had been made to *Comanche Prince* to allow him to carry the braydenite bomb together with its spin and release mechanisms. The steam condenser had been moved closer to the tail to make room for a new chamber beneath the fuselage. The bomb was held in place by a pair of callipers that would swing away from either end to release it. Spin would be imparted by a belt driven by a Glanville–Wallis hydraulic motor mounted forward of the bomb's starboard side.

'We've done all we can from a mechanical point of view,' the professor said to Arabella. 'The rest is up to you. Your flying will need to be flawless. You'll need to make sure that *Titan*'s hatch is directly in front of your propeller, that your wings are perfectly level and that you're the correct distance and altitude from the target before releasing the bomb.'

'How will I know when I'm at the correct distance and altitude?' Arabella asked.

'There's an island in the lake,' said the professor. 'It's only 60 yards long and doesn't even have a name, but as your port wing passes over its eastern shore, that will be the moment to release the bomb.'

'Split-second timing, then.'

'Indeed! As for altitude, take a look at this.' The professor got down on his knees and pointed at something in the belly of the fuselage. Arabella followed suit and saw that a viewing window had been inserted in *Prince*'s floor. A pair of carbon-arc spotlights had been placed on either side of it. 'When the spotlights converge on the surface of the water, you'll be at exactly the right height,' he said.

'So this has become a night mission,' observed Arabella.

'Perhaps you should check the time, my dear lady,' said the professor. 'The sun went down over an hour ago.'

Arabella checked her chronometer. It was true – time really had moved on!

'And if something goes wrong?'

'Then abort the release and circle back for another attempt. Remember, we only have one go at this. As I said, it's got to be flawless.'

Arabella climbed up onto the wing and searched the cockpit for a newly installed button or lever. She couldn't see one. 'How do I actually, er, release the bomb?' she asked.

'Don't worry, that'll be my job,' said Ben.

'*Your* job? What do you mean?'

'I'll be joining you on this one, ma'am,' he smiled. 'Hope you don't mind?'

'We thought it better if you concentrate on the flying,' said the professor. 'There's a lever by the passenger seat that Master Forrester will use to open the callipers and release the bomb when the time comes.'

'I'm sure I can manage to pull a lever!' snapped Arabella, who was uncomfortable with the idea of Ben accompanying her.

'There's a little more to it than that,' said Ben.

She glared at him. 'Something you think I am incapable of?'

'I have no idea what you're capable of, ma'am', replied Ben smoothly. 'But we can't take any chances. Even though there's no actual explosive in this bomb, and even though it worked in that little test we did, there's still a possibility that it'll activate the shield, so I'm going to have to do what I did when I crashed my air carriage into *Titan*. You know: clear my mind of all violent thoughts and radiate nothing but positive, friendly vibrations as I pull that lever.'

Arabella donned her gloves and leather flying hat. 'Well, Mr Forrester,' she said stiffly. 'I suppose we'd better get started.'

Ben leapt up to join her on the wing, and for a moment they stood very close to each other. He smelled faintly, and pleasantly, of engines. Arabella was uneasily reminded of a moment a few days ago on Taranis when they'd been equally close. As the cloud surrounding the floating city had parted, they'd embraced. But she couldn't think about that now. Her mind had to be fully on the current mission.

Ben pulled back the canopy. 'After you, ma'am.'

She ignored his proffered hand and climbed into the cockpit by herself.

'One more thing,' said the professor, once they were both strapped into their seats. 'The explosion, if you can make it happen, could be monstrous, so you need to put as much distance as you possibly can between yourselves and *Titan* after dropping the bomb.'

Arabella flashed him a thumbs up and ignited her engines. She slid the canopy closed and *Prince* began easing forward. Gaslight beacons flew by at an accelerating rate as they gathered speed along the underground runway. Arabella could feel Ben's presence behind her as she left the ground and floated up into the night. It was almost a tangible thing: something like warm leather – tough, yet tender – that she longed to nestle against. She closed her eyes, banishing those thoughts, at least for now. The eyes that opened a few seconds later were steely and focused.

She flew low, just above the shattered wasteland of Pall Mall and Piccadilly, out of range of the gunners on the *Dessalines* and *Poignards* that haunted the ragged black clouds above. Hyde Park was just over a mile away, and in no time she could see its trees and lawns, pale green like a shallow sea beneath the glow of its gas mantles. Sprawled arrogantly across its southeastern corner was the immense silver bulk of *Titan*. There were centaur patrols all around it, as well as along the park's walkways and perimeter. For now, at least, Hyde Park was a little patch of France. Emmeline was right: approaching *Titan* on the ground would have been next to impossible. Arabella's weak shield might have protected her to some extent, but that was probably fading by now.

As she flew over the park just above treetop height, she attracted stares from the centaurs. A few raised their gun-arms and let off some rounds, all well off target. There didn't seem to be much urgency in their reactions; they clearly didn't view her as a threat.

'Switching on the spinner now,' said Ben, and she heard the hydraulic motor start up. It would take

54 seconds to get the bomb's rotation up to speed, so she circled the park to eat up some time. On her second circuit she closed in on her target, steering *Prince* on a westerly path just north of the Serpentine before wheeling south. She felt calm and confident and her breathing was steady as she flew above the western end of the lake, known as the Long Water. Glancing down through the viewing window by her feet, she saw two bright circles dancing across its oil-black ripples. They were projected by the spotlights beneath her fuselage. The circles were close to each other, but not yet intersecting. She nudged the control stick gently forward and *Prince* descended a few yards. Now the circles converged: they were exactly 60 feet above the surface.

She checked her speed – 124 mph – and opened the throttle slightly. The bridge flashed beneath them. Now they were above the Serpentine itself. Beyond that was *Titan*. The hatch of its golden gondola stood open and inviting. With minute adjustments of her control stick and rudder pedal, she altered her alignment so that her propeller boss was pointing into the dead heart of the gondola's entrance, as if she planned to actually land inside the ship. She could see some figures gathered there – officers on horseback – and wondered what they must be thinking. They had no idea what was coming!

The speed gauge was now hovering around 130 mph and the island was coming up fast on the left.

Everything was in place. She prepared to give Ben the word. But as she opened her mouth to speak, a bizarre thing happened. A black cloak, or something like it, flapped across her cockpit window, briefly blocking her view.

A bird? No, too big!

Her port wing jolted, as if the object had glanced off it.

'Abort!' she cried. 'What in God's name was that?'

And then, right in front of her, she saw what had struck her, and her eyes widened with shock.

Arabella banked to avoid a collision. 'Did you see that?' she gasped above the scream of *Prince*'s engines. 'Did you *actually* see that?'

'I believe it was a man on a horse,' said Ben.

CHAPTER FORTY-TWO

THE FLYING HORSE

They hadn't dreamed it. As Arabella circled back they saw the man again, flying alongside them. He wore a domino mask, a tricorn hat and a black cloak that billowed out behind him. And he was riding a horse through the air – an *iron* horse with enormous iron wings that rose and fell in powerful sweeps. He looked like one of the Equestrians – a flying Equestrian! The wings emerged from the horse's shoulders. As they rose, she glimpsed beneath them a complex mechanism of pumping pistons and straining springs, and a hollow, iron-latticed body – the horse was partly empty, she guessed, to make it light enough for flight.

The horseman turned his face to them, and Arabella recognised the cold, colourless eyes behind the mask, and the dull blond hair poking out beneath the hat. It was Fabien, the scariest of them all. His lips spread into a thin smile as he caught her gaze, and she saw a flash of his gold tooth. Then he pulled a long pistol from within his jacket and took aim through the cockpit window. Arabella jammed the control stick right, tipping her wings. She heard two bangs and a crack. A section of her canopy glass spidered. Fabien was now above her. She could see the hooves of his horse treading air. She reduced her speed, planning to position herself behind him so she could blast him with her guns. But then something heavy jolted her starboard wing, causing a juddering ripple through the craft. She turned to see what had caused it and was horrified to see that Fabien had leapt from his horse and landed on her wing. *Was the man utterly mad?*

He was sprawled flat on his stomach, arms outstretched, clutching the edges of the wing with each hand. His pistol was still clamped beneath his right palm. His hat had disappeared, but his manic grin had not, and he was inching his way steadily towards her. She banked as steeply as she could, so that the wing was sloping almost vertically, but he continued to cling there, and the crazed intensity of his stare told her that he wouldn't be easily shaken off.

What could she do?

At that moment, Ben decided to act. He reached forward, unhitched a clasp and slid open the canopy.

Air blasted in, crashing at her senses, flattening all thought.

'No!' she cried as she saw what he was doing. She reached towards him, but Ben brushed away her hand. Levering himself out of his seat, he forced his way through the raging air onto the wing. He staggered, fell to his knees, and nearly slid right off, but managed to grab the wing's edge and steady himself. He turned to face Fabien, who was just over a yard away. The Frenchman was slowly dragging his gun into aiming position. Ben had manoeuvred himself so he was seated with his back against the canopy. He kicked out at Fabien's hand, dislodging the gun, which went tumbling into the darkness. Fabien's face tightened into a snarl. He grabbed at Ben's ankle and tried to yank him from his perch. But Ben kicked out with his other leg, catching Fabien on the side of the head. Fabien lost his grip and slid right off the wing.

Arabella hoped with all her heart that he had fallen to his death. But then, as in a nightmare, one of his hands reappeared on the wing's edge, followed by the other, thin fingers grasping at the rivets. Fabien's head rose into view. Flecks of blood were flying from his mouth into the rushing wind. His feet must have found purchase on *Prince*'s smaller, lower wing. The forward momentum of the air carriage was pinning his body in place, so he no longer needed to cling on with his hands. Before Ben could kick out again, Fabien reached out and grabbed him by the collar, pulling him away from the canopy so that the two were nose to nose. They wrestled like this, Ben with his hands around Fabien's throat, Fabien trying to haul Ben off the edge of the wing. In this struggle, Fabien had the upper hand because his feet were securely planted on the lower wing and his body was held fast by the press of air against his back. Ben, meanwhile, was sliding around on the smooth metal surface like a baby seal on a frozen sea.

Arabella watched helplessly from the cockpit. If she could have thrown *Prince* into reverse, she would have, as it would have sent Fabien flying – but that was an aerobatic impossibility. Instead she was forced into the role of impotent spectator as Fabien began repeatedly bashing Ben's face with his fist. Ben grappled desperately with Fabien, but could neither defend himself nor fight back against this onslaught. Arabella tried waggling her wings to destabilise Fabien, but he seemed to have superhuman powers of balance.

While this was happening, she caught sight of an iron horse beneath her. At first she thought it was Fabien's, still beating its way across the sky. But then she saw that the horse had a rider – another Equestrian. She prayed it was her friend, Jacques.

With a final shove, Fabien pushed his dazed adversary off the back of the wing. A cry tore through Arabella's throat as she watched Ben fall. She slammed the control stick forward, putting *Prince* into a dive. As the air carriage plummeted, she caught sight of Ben. His fall had been broken by the second horse flying beneath. He was slumped across its head and shoulders. Her heart started beating again.

Arabella pulled out of the dive just as *Prince*'s undercarriage began clattering through the topmost branches of the trees along Rotten Row, on the south side of the park. Rising steeply, she was aware of Fabien edging closer to her along the wing. She reached for the canopy and started to close it, but he thrust his hand against its edge and forced it open again. He levered his body forward until he was almost on top of her. Arabella pushed at him, trying to eject him from her cockpit. But Fabien was unstoppable. He pressed his hand viciously into her face, blinding her to the view through the window. She could scarcely breathe for the stink of grease and metal on his palm. She felt the weight of his upper body falling across hers as he leaned further in, and then his left hand closed around her right, and the control stick was driven forward, tipping *Prince* into another shrieking dive.

Arabella bit hard into the flesh of Fabien's right hand until she could taste blood. His fingers parted in agony, but didn't release her. Between his fingers she could see the gas flares on the ground spiralling closer. *He was going to kill them both!*

Then, from out of nowhere, an iron hoof came down on Fabien's skull. He slumped, unconscious. His right hand fell from her face; his left ceased its pressure on the control stick. She immediately guided *Prince* out of his twisting dive, then pushed Fabien out of the cockpit and closed the canopy. His inert body bounced off the wing and disappeared. Arabella gritted her teeth, forcing herself to stay in control. *Fabien was gone. He was really gone!*

Flying parallel on her port side was the other Equestrian she'd glimpsed, with Ben still draped across his iron horse. He turned his head and raised a hand in greeting. It was Jacques! Her heart flooded with relief. He'd rescued Ben, and had brought his horse's hoof down on Fabien's head. She owed him for this, and hoped she would get a chance to thank him later. Before that, she had a rather important job to do – this time without Ben to help her.

Arabella quickly rediscovered her bearings. She was above Kensington Palace on the western side of the park. She made a wide circle to the north, restarting the hydraulic motor, which had stalled at some point during the tussle with Fabien. Below, in the park, the centaurs had by now decided that she was a threat. They were projecting their search beams and raising their weaponised arms towards her, but she remained high enough to evade their gunfire – at least for the moment. It would be a different story when she came in low for her final run-in above the lake. She'd just have to hope their bullets wouldn't damage her engine or knock her off course at the crucial moment.

By the time Arabella descended towards the Long Water, the bomb was spinning at its correct rotation speed. The viewing window showed the circles gradually converging on the lake surface. She took a deep breath, trying to recover that earlier state of calm. But the task seemed beyond her. After the incident with Fabien, her nerves were like discordant, jangling bells. She wished Ben were still with her to release the lever. How could she possibly fly the plane and…?

Stay calm, Arabella. Clear your mind of all negative thoughts.

She tried to rise above herself – to leave all that tension and anger behind. She tried not to think of the war at all, and forget that she was British and they were French. For the trees and birds and squirrels of this park, the war meant nothing: an unpleasant vibration, a bad smell. And in a hundred years' time it would be history, something for schoolchildren to read about. Young women like her would be taking holidays in France. What she was doing today was the first step towards making that happen. She was starting the process of ending the war. This was an act of love…

As Arabella passed over the Serpentine Bridge, she accelerated to 130 mph. The circles beneath her converged, and she aligned her propeller boss with *Titan*'s hatchway. She had become *Prince* and he had become her. She could move him with more subtlety and grace than she could her own limbs. Vaguely she was aware of bullets flying at her, scraping and puncturing her surface, but she kept her wings rock steady. The little island was coming up on her port side. She reached behind for the lever and released it just as the island's stony, tree-lined shore hurtled by.

Prince suddenly seemed lighter, and the buzzing noise of the hydraulic motor slackened. From far below came a faint thudding splash, and through the viewing window she glimpsed a small flare of white foam. Vaguely, she made out the dark shape of the barrel as it flew upwards on its first bounce, and then down again. Arabella couldn't resist following it in its leaping, plunging journey towards *Titan*, despite the professor's final warning to get as far away as possible once she'd released the bomb. After all this, she had to be absolutely sure it would reach its target. By the fourth bounce she would know. Or maybe by the fifth…

CHAPTER FORTY-THREE

THE CRACK IN THE WORLD

Jacques flew east across the park just above the tree line, tracking Lady Arabella's air carriage as it sped across the long, narrow lake towards *Titan*. He couldn't hope to catch her – *Pégase* was fast, but not that fast. He wondered what she was playing at. Did she plan to crash her craft into the flagship, somehow breaking through the shield like that other aviator had done – the one who'd rescued her from *Titan* on the way over here?

He glanced down at the figure of the young man draped across *Pégase*'s neck. He was the American from yesterday, the one he'd met outside the Tower of London, who'd persuaded him to hand over Miles so he could reunite the little automaton with his mistress.

The man seemed to shadow Arabella. Could *he* have been the mysterious aviator?

Jacques watched as Arabella arrowed ever closer to *Titan*'s gaping maw. Had something dropped from her craft? He thought so, but it was too dark to be sure. Her wings, her trajectory, were perfectly steady, despite the flaming guns of the centaurs on the lake shore. He made out silhouettes of soldiers gathering in the hatchway entrance, guns raised.

The American was stirring. He was murmuring something. It sounded like her name. Jacques hardly noticed. His attention was fixed on the tiny air carriage speeding towards *Titan*. At the last second, just as it seemed she was about to fly right into it, she veered steeply upwards. As she did so, Jacques saw a barrel-shaped object skid off the lake surface and fly up through the hatchway, punching through the line of soldiers as it went.

A self-protective instinct told Jacques that he, too, should get himself clear. Something was about to happen – something big. He reared upwards, urging *Pégase* higher with all the force his arms and legs could impart. As he climbed, he felt a deep shudder in the atmosphere, as if a giant had suddenly been woken from sleep. Looking down, he glimpsed *Titan* through a shiny, gauzy bubble. Her Aetheric Shield, in its awesome entirety, had become visible – but only for a second. The silver-purple surface of the bubble immediately wrinkled, ruptured from within by an enormous, swelling blackness.

And then the entire world seemed to crack open.

The next thing Jacques knew, he was being hurled skywards on a blistering hot, dry wave. His head pulsated with a deep and agonising groan that sounded like the breaking of the bones of the Earth.

For long seconds he had no idea where he was, or whether *Pégase* or the American were still with him. He was aware only of being flung high into the sky with stunning power and at startling speed, and of a strangely relaxing feeling of surrender to forces vastly greater than himself.

After what seemed a very long time, the forces began to diminish. His upward trajectory slowed until it became more like floating, buoyed on the cooling thermals that had rocketed him high above the park. At last, he began to sink. With gathering momentum, sinking became falling, and falling became plummeting.

He crashed into water. It felt like an explosion, like glass smashing beneath him. He descended, stunned, through a cold, dark, slimy underworld.

Jacques surfaced, choking. Scarcely able to breathe, he coughed up a lungful of foul-tasting lake water. Where was he? The lake in the park? In the ghostly light of the gas mantles it seemed different – bigger than before. And what of *Titan*, the great beast that had crouched by the lakeside so menacingly these past two days? There was no sign of it! No search beams, no centaur squadrons – just a dizzying void where it used to be.

What exactly had Arabella done?

There was a loud splash nearby, followed by another smaller one. An object surfaced, and Jacques recognised the gleaming iron head and dripping wings. *Pégase* had survived his fall! And there was the American, floating face down…

Prince was sent somersaulting upwards, end over end, through the clouds, like a toy being cast away by a huge and furious child. His pilot, overwhelmed by the forces acting on her, soon blacked out and lay slumped in her seat. Only the sound of gunfire from a nearby *Poignard* brought her round.

Dazed and barely conscious, her hands and feet somehow found their familiar positions at the controls. Their efforts achieved little: *Prince* was now tumbling, certainly not flying, and Arabella felt consciousness ebbing from her. It was easiest to subside into oblivion, like a soft bed. She felt it dragging on her eyes, shutting down her brain. Sleep began to take her, as the engines whined and the Earth sucked her closer to its deadly embrace…

With ferocious determination, she forced her eyes to open and her muscles to work. The rudder and flaps began shaping the air around them. The tumble became a dive, and, as she strained the control stick to breaking point, the dive eased very gradually into horizontal flight. Perhaps a dozen yards beneath her was the dark, scudding surface of the lake.

Good old *Prince*! He'd been blasted from both sides by gunfire and nearly ripped apart in the explosion that he and Arabella had unleashed. And yet, mechanically speaking, he hadn't let her down.

Arabella put down in a grassy area to the northeast of the Serpentine. Battered and shaken by her experience, she more or less fell out of the cockpit, slid off the wing and collapsed onto the ground.

In the shadows by the lake she could see the gleam of half a dozen centaurs, gun-arms raised. They were moving towards her, but uncertainly, as if the gears in their heads were receiving conflicting instructions. She began crawling backwards, trying to hide herself behind *Prince*'s wheel. A centaur fired. She heard the bullet clatter through the trees behind her. From her waistband she drew out Jacques' pistol and fired at the head of the closest one. The bullet went straight through the centaur's blank metal face. It stopped, the arm fell limp and, like a marionette whose strings had been cut, it toppled onto its side.

The shield was no more!

Arabella shot off four more rounds. Four more centaurs fell. The next time she pulled the trigger, the hammer clicked on an empty chamber. Two centaurs remained, moving clumsily towards her, gun-arms swaying. She was considering a hasty retreat when she heard more gunfire: just a couple of reports that sounded like the *rat-tat* of a snare drum. Both remaining centaurs abruptly keeled over.

Behind their bodies she saw a dripping, stooping form emerge from the lake. It was a horseman, hunched over the neck of his mount, pistol pointing at the fallen centaurs. He rode towards her, water cascading from vents in the horse's iron flanks and from the brim of his tricorn hat.

The figure became a silhouette as a fireball lit up the lake surface behind him and turned the sky a cloudy orange. Arabella's eyes briefly lifted and she saw armoured gun carriages on the move. The British army was advancing into the park, blasting centaur patrols as it came on. She also noticed that the Serpentine had swelled. Where *Titan* had once reposed there was now a huge, ragged-edged crater into which the lake had poured its contents.

The horseman continued his approach. When she saw he was carrying a passenger – a living passenger – Arabella allowed herself a smile. It was a pale representation of the glorious sunshine she felt inside. She climbed painfully to her feet and went to meet them.

CHAPTER FORTY-FOUR

THE CEREMONY

ollowing the destruction of *Titan*, the French commenced an immediate and full-scale retreat. By dawn, the skies above London were filled with nothing but clouds. Most of the French forces on the ground surrendered without a fight. Those at the Tower of London held out until mid-afternoon, but by the evening of 23 July the Union Jack was once again flying above the White Tower, Horatio Nelson was back atop his column, all centaurs had been deactivated or destroyed, and enemy soldiers incarcerated.

As for Napoleon, he was nowhere to be seen. Most Londoners hoped he'd perished in the explosion that had engulfed *Titan*. But others with a gloomier cast of mind reckoned the little general – known for his luck – had probably escaped in one of the departing craft.

The French invasion had been brief yet devastating. London was a mess, its buildings in ruins, most of its gold reserves vaporised along with *Titan*. Yet its population, as they emerged stiff-backed and grimy from their underground shelters, remained upbeat and determined. The city had survived and would be rebuilt, bigger and better than ever before.

Arabella slept very late the following morning. After all her recent adventures, she needed the rest. She shared a room with Cassie on one of the lower floors of Hades. After lunch, they took a wander through the ruined streets of their city, trying to come to terms with all that had happened and the fact that they were still alive.

'I thought we'd die on Tower Green, just like Anne Boleyn,' laughed Cassie.

'I never believed we'd get out of that ASG chamber in Granville,' said Arabella. 'Every moment since then has felt like a blessing.'

Cassie nodded.

'Is Mr Forrester all right?' she suddenly asked. 'And Monsieur Daguerre?'

'I believe so,' said Arabella. 'Mr Forrester is recuperating in the sick bay, but he seemed in not too bad shape last time I saw him. Monsieur Daguerre was being interrogated by Emmeline when I went to bed.'

'I am most relieved,' said Cassie. 'For you especially.'

'Why for me?'

Cassie smiled. 'I know you harbour feelings for Mr Forrester. As he does for you.'

Arabella coloured. 'I don't know what you mean. We're friends. Not even that. *Would* have been friends, if Mr Forrester allowed himself such things.'

'Oh!' said Cassie. She seemed disappointed. 'You *do* seem as though you could be a lot more than that. You seem... suited.'

'We most definitely are not!' Arabella explained to her. 'We fight ALL the time!'

'Well, you can't fight with him now, not while he's recuperating,' said Cassie softly.

'I wouldn't bet on it.'

'Are you going to see him?'

'I might,' said Arabella with a carelessness she did not exactly feel. In truth, she felt paralysed, wanting to see him, but at the same time thinking she probably ought to keep her distance. What was the point, after all, in showing friendship to a person who had no need of friends?

They sat down on a bench in Whitehall Gardens and watched as two pigeons fought over a scrap of bread. Arabella was reminded of her thoughts just before she dropped the bomb: *For the birds this war means nothing.*

'So, what next for us?' Cassie wondered.

'That all depends.'

'On what?'

'On Napoleon – *if* he's alive.'

'I do hope he isn't,' shuddered Cassie.

Arabella thought of Napoleon being blasted to smithereens in *Titan*. If he was dead, who would be their enemy now? The thought made her feel strangely empty.

But he wasn't dead – she was absolutely sure of it.

Cassie looked unhappy. 'I'm sorry,' she said, 'I just can't help thinking about Diana. I mean, she must have been on board *Titan* as well... What a tragic ending for someone I once thought of as a friend.'

Arabella placed a hand on her shoulder. 'She was never your friend. It was all pretence... Anyway, I'm sure she's still alive, and Napoleon, too.'

'Really?'

Arabella nodded. 'He only came here to steal the Phoenix, and once he had it, I'm sure he went straight back to France, taking Diana and the rest of his cronies with him. This entire invasion was a diversion. I've no doubt he enjoyed laying waste to London and placing himself on top of Nelson's Column – but it was all most definitely a smoke screen. The Phoenix was what he came for. I just wish I knew why.'

Miles was waiting in their room on their return to Hades. The Logical Englishman looked immaculate in white tie and tails.

'Miles, you *do* look dashing,' said Arabella. 'What's the occasion?'

'We are going to the Palace, my lady. The Queen wishes to award you a medal.'

'Oh, my!' said Arabella, butterflies instantly awakening in her stomach. 'Really?'

'How exciting!' cried Cassie. 'I'm so pleased for you, Bella.'

'You're going to get one, too, Cassie,' said Emmeline, entering the room. 'We all are!'

The ceremony took place in the garden, because the palace itself was deemed unsafe due to bomb damage. Nevertheless, it was a splendid occasion. The Sky Sisters dressed in their ceremonial uniforms: long blue skirts and jackets, red sashes and white blouses. They stood side by side as a brass band played and Queen Victoria came out onto the terrace, accompanied by Sir George Jarrett and an attendant carrying a tray of gleaming medals.

As well as the Sisters, Ben and Jacques were also present. Arabella couldn't help peeping at them. It was the first time she'd seen them since the previous night. They both looked very handsome in the top hats and frock coats they had been provided with – though Ben's face bore the marks of its encounter with Fabien's fists, and she noticed he was carrying a walking stick. He kept his eyes to the front. Jacques, however, noticed her looking in his direction, and smiled briefly at her.

Each of the Sisters was called up in turn, and Sir George introduced them to the Queen, who said a few words of congratulations and placed a gold medal on a purple ribbon around their necks.

When it was Arabella's turn to approach, Sir George informed the Queen that it was she who had dropped the bomb that had destroyed *Titan*. Her Majesty looked thoughtfully at her and said: 'Thank you, dear. You did us a great favour. That enormous vessel was visible from our bedroom window. It was most unsightly. We were not amused.'

Dinner was served under the stars, on a long candlelit table covered in white linen. Everyone from the medal ceremony attended, except for Sir George Jarrett who had been called away on some urgent business. Course after course was brought out on silver platters, served by immaculately attired servants.

Arabella found herself seated next to Jacques. She took the opportunity to thank him for his intervention over the Serpentine.

'It was my pleasure, mademoiselle,' he replied.

'How did you come to be there?' she asked.

Jacques dabbed his mouth with his napkin. 'I knew Fabien was determined to kill you after what you did at the Tower. When our soldiers found your underground base, Fabien waited outside in ambush.

He suspected you would try to break out, and when you did, he followed you. I followed him.'

'Is he dead now, do you think?'

'I hope so, but who knows? A tree or water may have broken his fall.'

'I imagine it must be difficult for you, helping us…' ventured Arabella.

Jacques shrugged. 'Not really. After all, I have lost everything. My heart is empty. It beats for no one… But Napoleon did have to be stopped, that much I know.'

'What will you do now?'

'Your boss, Sir George Jarrett, wants me to work for your government as a spy. As far as Guizot knows – assuming Guizot is still alive – I remain a loyal servant of France. I am also the best rider of an iron horse in his service, and he will certainly want me to continue as an Equestrian. So I suppose I could be useful to your country.'

'Will you do it?'

'I don't know. I need to take a break now and think about what I want to do with my life. With Marie gone, everything has changed.' He looked at her. 'And you? What will you do now?'

'I will continue as a Sky Sister,' said Arabella, 'flying missions in the service of my country.'

He smiled bitterly. 'I envy you such clarity of purpose.'

Arabella sipped her soup.

'May I ask you something?' said Jacques.

'Of course.'

He nodded towards Ben, who was deep in conversation with Miles at the other end of the table. 'Why is that American boy always where you are?'

'You're not the first to wonder about that,' smiled Arabella. 'The truth is, I have no idea – and I don't believe he does either.'

She felt a tap on her shoulder and turned. It was Emmeline, looking tense. Arabella felt a quick stab of anxiety. 'We have to get back to Hades,' said her aunt. 'Something's come up.'

CHAPTER FORTY-FIVE

THE BROKEN TABLET

he Sky Sisters, still in their ceremonial outfits, gathered in an anonymous corridor in Hades. A solemn-looking Sir George Jarrett emerged from the conference room and closed the door behind him. After a quick nod towards Emmeline, he turned his ice-blue gaze on Cassie, Beatrice and Arabella.

'I warn you, ladies,' he said, 'you may all get rather a shock when you enter this room. Please don't let your emotions get the better of you. Remain calm. Take your places around the table and listen to what is said. After that, you may ask all the questions you like.'

He opened the door and stood aside for them to enter. Burning with curiosity, Arabella filed in behind the others. She saw Cassie falter as she caught sight of something in there, seemingly unable to continue until Emmeline guided her to her chair. Arabella crossed the threshold and turned to look at what Cassie had seen. The long, polished oak conference table that dominated the room was empty, save for a solitary figure seated at the far end.

A start of surprise shook Arabella, followed quickly by a hot flush of anger. For it was the traitor, Diana Temple, sitting there, an arrogant smile playing across her perfect pink lips. She wore a close-fitting leather jacket with a black silk scarf and black lacy cuffs. Her dark bobbed hair shone, her green eyes sparkled expectantly as she regarded each of them, almost as if waiting for them to applaud.

Arabella felt like walking over and strangling her with her scarf. Her fists clenched. Then she felt Sir George's hand on her arm, steering her to an empty chair.

'May I introduce Agent Y,' said Sir George once they were all seated. 'You know her as Diana Temple, one of your fellow Sky Sisters.'

The inside of Arabella's mouth suddenly felt dry as paper. Her hand shook as she poured some water into a glass and took a sip.

'Agent Y has been working directly for me these past few weeks,' explained Sir George. 'She's been deep under cover – so deep, and so endangered, I couldn't risk telling any of you about it – not even Major Stuart.'

Emmeline reddened. The tense line of her mouth told Arabella how angry she was about having been kept in the dark about this.

As for Arabella, she could no longer stay quiet. She stood up and flung out her finger at Diana. 'That woman stopped me from blowing up *Titan* and killing Napoleon!' she thundered. 'She told Marshal Guizot that I'd laid dynamite. How exactly is that spying for our side?'

Sir George turned to her. His face, split by a long white scar that ran from his cheekbone to the corner of his mouth, did not alter in the slightest, but his tone was harsh: 'Do you not remember me telling you to remain calm and listen, Arabella? Once you've heard everything, there will be a chance to have your say.' He returned his attention to Diana. 'Now I'm going to hand over to Agent Y. She has gathered some information for us, and it's better if you hear it from her directly.' He gave her a quick nod.

Diana glanced at her black-gloved hands and cleared her throat. 'Before I begin, I would like to make one thing clear to *you*, Arabella.' She flashed her eyes at her. 'I am *not* a traitor. I love this country just as much as you do. If I prevented you from destroying *Titan* and killing Napoleon, it is because I can see the bigger picture – a picture you are entirely unaware of. I know, because I have studied these things. I know where the real threats to this country lie, and they did not lie on *Titan*…'

Arabella was aghast. *What was she saying? That Napoleon wasn't a threat? That Guizot wasn't a threat?* It was only Sir George's steely glare that kept her from exploding once more with accusatory questions.

'If Napoleon had died, there would have been a power struggle in France,' said Diana. 'The warmongers in the French government would have fought the pacifists, and the warmongers would almost certainly have won. They're a powerful group, and far more dangerous than Napoleon. Only *he* can keep them in check. That is why it's in our interests to keep him alive, at least for now. Your antics on board *Titan* very nearly wrecked everything. The only positive to come out of it was that it gave me a chance to demonstrate my loyalty to Napoleon, so he would continue to trust me, even though Guizot was determined to kill me.'

'Are you sure Napoleon is alive now?' asked Sir George.

Diana nodded. 'I watched him escape in a departing *Poignard* last night.'

Arabella squeezed the hard edge of the table, needing something solid to cling to in a world that had suddenly gone very soft and lopsided. *Napoleon was the enemy, wasn't he? He'd just flattened London, hadn't he? What was going on?*

Even Emmeline seemed to be struggling to make sense of what Diana was saying. 'So you were acting as some sort of bodyguard for Napoleon, is that it?'

Diana shook her head. 'No, I was there for one reason only: to find out why he wanted the Phoenix.'

Beatrice sat straighter in her seat when she heard mention of the diamond, her ears almost pricking like a cat's.

Diana glanced at Sir George, as if to seek clearance to go on. He nodded.

'As you've probably all worked out, conquest was never Napoleon's real aim,' said Diana. 'That's not to say he didn't lie awake in bed each night dreaming about it. He was hoping as late as yesterday afternoon that our government might surrender. But he knew in his heart of hearts that it wasn't going to happen. His invasion fleet was far too small – even with the Aetheric Shield, he was never going to take the whole country. After half a century of war, France is exhausted. It's running out of men and materiel. A conventional battlefield victory is now beyond him. That's why he decided to steal the Phoenix.'

Diana's soft, slightly husky voice was mesmerising. It lured them on, like something elusive and glittering in the undergrowth. Arabella was as transfixed as anyone – anger still throbbed within her, but it had been eclipsed by an insatiable need to know the truth.

'I know what you're all wondering,' smiled Diana. 'How can a diamond, even one as large and valuable as the Phoenix, help Napoleon fulfil his fading dream? To answer that we must travel back more than forty years, to 1801, and Napoleon's campaign in Egypt.

While his armies were busy fighting the Mamluks and the Ottomans, a team of French archaeologists set out into the desert, searching the tombs for ancient treasures. Among their discoveries was a broken stone tablet covered in mysterious hieroglyphics. It was one of several they found during that expedition, and attracted little notice at the time. The tablet was stuck away in a vault in the Louvre museum for decades, gathering dust – until last year, when someone finally got around to deciphering it, and then all at once it became the most valuable ancient relic of all time. You see, it contained instructions for making a bomb...'

'A bomb?' Cassie couldn't help blurting. 'Are we still referring to the Egyptians here? As in the *ancient* Egyptians?'

'Indeed,' said Diana. 'And the bomb they describe on this tablet is unlike any other seen on Earth. You might call it an aether bomb, because it makes use of aetheric energy. Apparently the Egyptians discovered the Aethersphere thousands of years before we did. They harnessed its energy to build the pyramids. *And* they designed this weapon – this insanely powerful bomb. We've all seen the destruction wrought by thousands of tons of conventional explosives on London. Well, a single aether bomb could do far worse than that: it could, quite literally, flatten this city.'

The silence that followed was sticky with dread.

'Are you saying that Napoleon has the... the technology to build this weapon?' asked Emmeline.

'Almost,' said Diana.

'But what has the Phoenix got to do with all this?' asked Beatrice.

'I thought you of all people might have guessed, Bea,' said Diana. 'He needs the Phoenix to build the aether bomb.'

They all stared at her.

'Why?' asked Arabella.

'Because of its special qualities – well, *one* special quality.'

'Its size?' guessed Cassie.

Diana shook her head.

'Its perfect balance of brilliance, fire and scintillation?' suggested Beatrice.

Again Diana shook her head.

'Then you must be talking about its fluorescence,' said Beatrice.

'Yes!' said Diana. 'That's *exactly* what I'm talking about. Its fluorescence marks it out from every other diamond, and it's that quality that is needed to make the aether bomb. The aether shield needs gold to power it, but the aether bomb needs diamond – to be precise, it needs the particular green fluorescent light emitted by the Phoenix.'

'I'm sorry,' said Beatrice, 'but how can a diamond discovered in the early eighteenth century have been known to the Egyptians?'

'They didn't know about it,' said Diana. 'That's why they never managed to create the bomb themselves...

But they described it. They described the exact diamond, the exact light, they needed. The Phoenix fits that description.'

'And now he has the Phoenix, surely he can build the bomb?' said Emmeline.

'No,' said Diana. 'Not yet. The instructions for building it are incomplete. The tablet, as I said, was broken. It must have formed part of a larger stone. The missing part contains the remainder of the recipe.'

Emmeline closed her eyes and let out a slow breath. 'And the missing part of this tablet is somewhere in Egypt?'

'That is what we must assume,' said Sir George. 'But he won't let this stop him. We should be in no doubt that Napoleon intends to build this aether bomb. He calls his plan – what is it again, Diana?'

'*Opération Ciel de Fer*,' she said.

'Ah yes,' muttered Sir George. '*Ciel de Fer*... Iron Sky.'

He rose to his feet and swivelled his head slowly, meeting the eyes of each Sister in turn. His gaze crossed Arabella's only briefly, but she could feel its intensity.

'Ladies,' he said, 'Napoleon has taken possession of the Phoenix, named for a mythical bird that rises again from the ashes of destruction. Through fire, new life. With the Phoenix he is now capable of building a bomb that will burn his enemies to ashes and allow his empire to rise again. Through fire, new life. That is his dream, and all he needs to fulfil it is a missing piece of stone. He will shortly be returning to Egypt to find it. Your job is to stop him…'

THE END

A selected list of Scribo titles

The prices shown below are correct at the time of going to press. However, The Salariya Book Company reserves the right to show new retail prices on covers, which may differ from those previously advertised.

Gladiator School by Dan Scott
1	Blood Oath	978-1-908177-48-3	£6.99
2	Blood & Fire	978-1-908973-60-3	£6.99
3	Blood & Sand	978-1-909645-16-5	£6.99
4	Blood Vengeance	978-1-909645-62-2	£6.99
5	Blood & Thunder	978-1-910184-20-2	£6.99
6	Blood Justice	978-1-910184-43-1	£6.99

Iron Sky by Alex Woolf
1	Dread Eagle	978-1-909645-00-4	£9.99*
2	Call of the Phoenix	978-1-910184-87-5	£6.99

Aldo Moon by Alex Woolf
1 Aldo Moon and the Ghost at Gravewood Hall
978-1-908177-84-1   £6.99

* Collectors' edition in hardback with fold-out full-colour illustrations.

Visit our website at:

www.salariya.com

All Scribo and Salariya Book Company titles can be ordered from your local bookshop, or by post from:

The Salariya Book Co. Ltd,
25 Marlborough Place
Brighton BN1 1UB

Postage and packing **free** in the United Kingdom